Gobsh

Quadruple Trouble

MW01141380

15.00 USDOL ‖ € 13.00 EURO ‖ £ 11.00 GBP (UK) ‖ $ 20.00 AUD (Oz) ‖ $19.00 CAN ‖ ¥ 1600.00 JPY (japan yen) ‖ 225.00 SAR (S. Africa)

‖ € 13.00 EURO ‖ £ 11.00 GBP (UK) ‖ $ 20.00 AUD (Oz) ‖ $19.00 CAN ‖ ¥ 1600.00 JPY (japan yen) ‖ 225.00 SAR (S. Africa)

This issue is dedicated to the memory of:

Kęstutis Navakas (24 Feb., 1964 – 16 Feb., 2020)
Joan Micklin Silver (24 May, 1935 – 31 Dec., 2020)
Guadalupe Grande Aguirre (30 May, 1965 – 2 Jan., 2021)
David Darling (4 Mar., 1941 – 8 Jan., 2021)
Diana O'Hehir (23 May, 1922 – 19 Jan., 2021)
Walter Bernstein (20 Aug., 1919 – 23 Jan., 2021)
Hal Holbrook (17 Feb., 1925 – 23 Jan., 2021)
Cloris Leachman (30 Apr., 1926 – 27 Jan., 2021)
Cicely Tyson (19 Dec., 1924 – 28 Jan., 2021)
Christopher Plummer (13 Dec., 1929 – 5 Feb., 2021)
S. Clay Wilson (25 July, 1941 – 7 Feb., 2021)
Chick Corea (12 June, 1941 – 9 Feb., 2021)
Larry Flynt (1 Nov., 1942 – 10 Feb., 2021)
Peter Gotti (15 Oct., 1939 – 25 Feb., 2021)
Yaphet Kotto (15 Nov., 1939 – 15 Mar., 2021)
George Segal (13 Feb., 1934 – 23 Mar., 2021)
Larry McMurtry (3 June, 1936 – 25 Mar., 2021)
Bertrand Tavernier (25 Apr., 1941 – 25 Mar., 2021)
Arthur Kopit (10 May, 1937 – 2 Apr., 2021)
Richard Rush (15 Apr., 1929 – 8 Apr., 2021)
Monte Hellman (12 July, 1929 – 20 Apr., 2021)
Olympia Dukakis (20 June, 1931 – 1 May, 2021)
Patrick McGreal (10 May, 1953 – 31 May, 2021)
Vilen Galstyan (12 Feb., 1941 – 4 June, 2021)
Ned Beatty (6 July, 1937 – 13 June, 2021)
Jon Hassell (22 Mar., 1937 – 26 June, 2021)
Louis Joseph Andriessen (6 June, 1939 – 1 July, 2021)
Djivan Gasparyan (12 Oct., 1928 – 6 July, 2021)
Robert John Downey (24 June, 1936 – 7 July, 2021)
Michael Horovitz (OBE) (4 Apr., 1935 – 7 July, 2021)
Angélique Ionatos / Αγγελική Ιονάτου (22 June ,1954 – 7 July 2021)
Chiba Shin'ichi Sonny / 千葉 真一 (22 Jan., 1939 –
19 Aug., 2021)

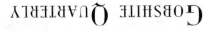

Gobshite Quarterly

Quadruple Trouble / Issue 39 – Winter Spring 2022

©SHANNON WHEELER

Little Beirut, Oregon

The Usual Suspects
STAFF

Editor R. V. BRANHAM

Co-editor M.F. MCAULIFFE

Office Mgr. SOFIA SENSEI SATORI ŠOSTAKOVNA SATYAGRAHA STOLIČNIYA SASHIMI SHITKICKER

Asst. Ed. BRYAN MILLER

Assoc. Editor T. WARBURTON Y BAJO

Contrib. Editors MICHAEL LOHR & DOUGLAS SPANGLE

Field Correspondent MICHAEL LOHR

House Tr. T. WARBURTON Y BAJO & RVB (SP./TO & FR.), MIGUEL CAMINHÃO (PORTUGUESE), チャニング・ドッドソン (JAPANESE). Алекса Сигала & Андрей Сен-Сеньков (RUSSIAN), ANI GJIKA (ALBANIAN), ART TOLIN (TAGALOG), MICHAEL LOHR (SCAND.), & ANA KATANA & DIJANA JACOVAK (CROATIAN) & JOANNA ROSIŃSKA (POLISH) & A COHORT OF LITHUANIAN TRANSLATORS

House Spanish Copyediting LYDA ALVAREZ, BRYAN MILLER, M.F. MCAULIFFE

Cover Illo GRAHAM K. WILLOUGHBY *Design* T. WARBURTON Y BAJO

Cover comix & phfoto illos & franking VAR POSTAL SERVICES.

Photos (except as noted) M. F. MCAULIFFE, T. WARBURTON Y BAJO

Layout T. WARBURTON Y BAJO & R. V. BRANHAM

Prod. Tools INDESIGN, PHOTOSHOP (OCCASIONALLY, WHEN FUNCTIONAL), GIMP

Tech Support SAM WARD

Additional Editorial & Design Assistance DOUGLAS SPANGLE & M.F. MCAULIFFE

Legal PETER SHAVER

Publisher GOBQ LLC/REPROBATE BOOKS

QUADRUPLE TROUBLE FLIPBOOK ISSUES PRINTED ANNUALLY DURING COVID-19.

Post-production printing INGRAM SPARK/LIGHTNING SOURCE

Also distrib. & printed nationally & internationally through INGRAM SPARK/LIGHTNING SOURCE POD SOLD THROUGH INDEPENDENT BOOKSTORES & AVAILABLE THROUGH INGRAM & AMAZON DOT COM & GOBSHITEQUARTERLY DOT COM

P.R. P. H. VAZAK

Gobshite Quarterly: Quadruple Trouble, Nos. 39/40, Winter/Spring & Summer/Fall 2022
ISBN 978-1-64871-489-4

GobQ volunteers: Qualified candidates please send résumé to
GobQ LLC, 338 NE Roth St., Portland, OR 97211, or to gobq at yahoo dot com

o ◯ o

*) as in *pomes penyeach*

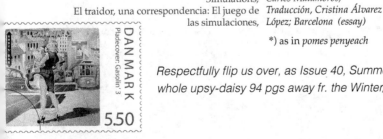

Respectfully flip us over, as Issue 40, Summer/Fall 2022, is a whole upsy-daisy 94 pgs away fr. the Winter/Spr. 2022 issue

Gob Words

Meet 2021, same as 2020:

(1) Suppose that several efficacious COVID-19 vaccines were developed & given at hospitals, stadiums, & pharmacies, world-wide, but the world wide intertube paranoics persuaded a sufficient no. of people not to get vaccinated, a no. sufficient to cut short the world's summer 2021 reopening due to mutant strains arising from the global unvaccinated pool.

(2) Suppose that the Urine Soaked Putin-Sponsored Orange Cockroach, upon losing their Presidential re-election bid held a rally in DC just as Congress was certifying the electoral vote & persuaded a sufficient number of paranoics, already upset by mask mandates & other infringements, to storm the capitol, to stop what they kept labeling as *the steal*. Now, suppose that this   Urine Soaked Putin-Sponsored Orange Cockroach were to be prosecuted, jailed even, for an internationally televised failed insurrection.

& of course, everyone came to their senses, got vaccinated, wore their masks, & the US, Europe, & Asia were able to lift most restrictions. & of course, the Urine Soaked Putin-Sponsored Orange Cockroach graciously conceded the election & the transition of powers, & we were able to turn the page so to speak. Those melting icecaps, cops murdering black people, both crises solved! 2022 is going to be amazing! Am I right? An Observation for 2022, for 2023, & perhaps, beyond, *Gobshite Quarterly*'ll be an annual, & feature more pages. — *rvb*

●○○●

The Usual Suspects
CONTRIBUTORS

Cristina Álvarez Lopez, whose essays have been in *Transit, GobQ, & other pubs.*, returns w/ Sp. tr. of Adrian Martin & Carles Matamoros' *The Traitor, A Correspondence: The Game of Simulations/El traidor, una correspondencia: El juego de las simulaciones*. (Eng./Sp./[& on the flipside, in Isl.)

Μαρουσώ Αθανασίου/Marouso Athanasiou's GobQ debut is a Grk tr. of M. F. McAuliffe's essay *Pictures on a piano/Φωτογραφίες πάνω στο πιάνο/Slike na glasoviru/Fotografie na pianine/Imágenes en un piano/Myndir á píanó* (Eng./Grk./Croat./Polsk/Sp.Isl.)

J. Randall Brett lives in NYC. His work's been in *I-70 Rev., foam:e, & Poetry Breakfast*. He returns to *GobQ* with *Ezrasure/Ezrasure/RistraðurEzradura* (Eng./Croat./Isl./Sp.)

Marius Burokas returns w/ his Lithuanian tr. of Rimas Uzgiris' *The Lesser Light/Mažesnė šviesa/Minna ljósið/La luz menor/Ang mas kaunting liiwanag* and *Binary Star/Dvinarė žvaigždė/Tvöfaldur stjarnaKaksoistähti/Estrella binaria/Buklod bitwin/Binarna zvijezda* (Eng./Lith/Isl/Finn./Polks/Sp./Tagalog)

David Conolly did the Eng. tr. of Eléna Tzatzimaki's pomes *Αν πυροβολούσα το φεγγάρι/If I shot the moon/Si disparara a la luna/Kad bih raznijela mjesec & Μέλμπα Ερνάντες Ροντρίγκες/Melba Hernandez Rodriguez/Melba Hernandez Rodriguez/Melba Hernandez Rodriguez* (Grk./Eng./Sp./Croat.)

Holly Day, who resides in Minneapolis, MN, & whose pomes have been in *Tampa Rev., SLAB, & Gargoyle*, & whose books incl. *Music Theory for Dummies*, makes her debut *GobQ Wednesday's mail/Mail srijede/Miðvikudagspósturinn/Correo del miércoles* (Eng./Croat./Isl./Sp.)

Marija Dejanović, living in Larísa, Greece, runs a small press w/Thanos Gogos. She returns to *GobQ* w/ a pome, *Zvuk/The Sound/O ήχος/See hääl/El Sonido/Hljóðið* (Croat./Eng./Grk./Eston./Sp./Isl.)

Michael Fikaris, based in Melbourne, Vic., Oz., returns w/ *Altered Identity in Public Theatre Transports/ romijenjeni identitet u javno-kazališnom prijevozu/Alteración de la identidad en el teatro de transportes públicos/Veranderde identiteit op het OV theatre/ τροποποιημένη ταυτότητα στο δημόσιο θέατρο των συγκοινωνιών* (Eng., with captions tr. into Croat./Dutch/Grk./Russ./Sp.)

Tanni Haas is a Prof. in CUNY– Brooklyn/Dept. of Comm. Arts, Sciences, & Disorders. Their fiction & pomes have been in *Blue Moon, Cholla Needles, Meat for Tea, & Santa Clara*. Their *GobQ* debut is two feuelletons, *Tug-of-war/Διελκυστίνδα/Fuego de tira/Przeciąganie liny, & Old Friends/Παλιοί φίλοι/Viejos Amigos/Starzy Przyjaciele* (Eng./Grk./Croat./Sp.)

Monika Herceg (Sisak, 1990) won the 2017 Goran Award for Yng. Poets for *Početne koordinate/Initial Coordinates*. She returns w/ *Drugorazredni otac/Second-rate Father/Padre fallido/Annað flokks faðir* (Croat./Eng./Sp./Isl.)

Dijana Jakovac returns w/Croat. tr. of J.R. Brett's pome *Ezrasure/Ezrasure/Ristraður/Ezradura* (Eng./Croat/Isl./Sp.), Ann Farley's *Grandmother Ocean/Baka Ocean/Mędrczyni Ocean/Abuela océano* (Eng./Croat./Polsk./Sp.), Holly Day's *Wednesday's mail/Mail srijede/Miðvikudagspósturinn/Correo del miércoles* (Eng./Croat/Isl./Sp.)

Ana Katana returns to *GobQ* w/Coat. tr. of Petros Skythiotis' pome *ΓΙ' ΑΥΤΟ ΗΤΑΝ ΑΜΕΡΙΚΑΝΟΣ/American/Što te Čini Amerikancem/ Americano/Amerykanin* (Grk./Eng./Croat/Sp./Polsk), & M. F. McAuliffe's essay *Pictures on a piano/Φωτογραφίες πάνω στο πιάνο/Slike na glasoviru/Fotografie na pianine/Imágenes en un piano/Myndir á píanó* (Eng./Grk./Croat./Polsk/Sp.Isl.)

Η Κωνσταντίνα Α. Κοντοπούλου/Constantina A. Kontopoulou (Constance Kont), living in Thessaloniki Θεσσαλονίκη, has published pomes in the UK & US (under the *nom de guerre* Connie Di), as well as two collections & incl. var. Grk. anthols., as well as being honoured in two nat'l Grk. pome competitions; & an equal rights columnist/journalist in a Greek newspaper. They make their *GobQ* debut w/two pomes, *Innuendo/Innuendo/Insinuando/ΥΠΑΙΝΙΓΜΟΣ & Diminuendo/Diminuendo/Disminución/Φθίνουσα* (Germ./Eng./Sp./Grk)

Michael Lohr, quarentining in Ohio, has for this issue done Icelandic tr. for a goodly baker's doz. of works. & a Finnish tr., too.

M.F. McAuliffe, a founding *GobQ* ed., w/ texts in *Overland, In Other Words: Merida, Adelaide Rev., & GobQ*. Her pome cycle *Orpheus* became the libretto for an oratorio by Dindy Vaughan, perf. by La Mama in Melbourne, Vic., Oz. Her most recent coll. is *25 Poems on the Death of Ursula K. LeGuin*. She returns w/ an essay, *Pictures on a piano/Φωτογραφίες πάνω στο πιάνο/Slike na glasoviru/Fotografie na pianine/Imágenes en un piano/Myndir á píanó* (Eng./Grk./Croat./Polsk/Sp.Isl.)

Adrian Martin, Oz-born & Barcelona-based essayist & film scholar returns to *GobQ* with an essay, or rather, a correspondence w/Carles Matamoros, *The Traitor, A Correspondence: The Game of Simulations/El traidor, una correspondencia: El juego de las simulaciones* (Eng./Sp./[& on the flipside, in Isl.])

Carles Matamoros, co-founder of Barcelona's online film journal *Transit*, returns to *GobQ* w/ an essay, or rather, a correspondence w/ Adrian Martin, *The Traitor, A Correspondence: The Game of Simulations/El traidor, una correspondencia: El juego de las simulaciones* (Eng./Sp./[& on the flipside, in Isl.])

Kęstutis Navakas, a celebrated Lithuanian poet appears here w/a pome, *holocenas/holocene/holocen/голоцен/holocen/holoceno* (Lith./Eng./Polsk/Russ.Croat./Sp.) Sadly, he passed away whilst translations were being solicited for publication.

Veronica O'Halloran, a recovering Eng. & media teacher from So. Oz, has been in *Poetry Australia*, & other pubs., & currently resides in the goth city of Adelaide. She makes her *GobQ* debut w/the pome *my arms worse than windmills/Moje ramiona gorsze niż wiatraki/мои руки хуже ветряных мельниц/mis brazos peores que molinos de viento* (Eng./Polsk./Rus./Sp.)

Βασιλεία Οικονόμου/Vasileia Oikonomou, born in Piraeus; her colls. incl. *Εφήμερα ζώα/Ephemeral Animals* (2018). She co-edits *Thraca*, a mag. & small press, w/Thanos Gogos & Marija Dejanović. returns w/ two Greek tr. of Tanni Haas feuilletons, *Tug-of-war/Διελκυστίνδα/Fuego de tira/Przeciąganie liny*, & *Old Friends/Παλιοί φίλοι/Viejos Amigos/Starzy Przyjaciele* (Eng./Grk./Croat./Sp.)

Triin Paja, living outside a tiny Estonian town, returns w/their pome *Seitse Lille/Seven Flowers,/Sedam cvjetova/Siete Flores* (Eston./Eng./Croat./Sp.)

Marjam Parve did the Eston. tr. of Marija Dejanović's pome, *Zvuk/The Sound/O ήχος/See hääl/El Sonido/Hljóðið* (Croat./Eng./Grk./Eston./Sp./Isl.)

Mirza Purić returns w/their Eng. tr. of Monika Herceg's pome, *Drugorazredni otac/Second-rate Father/Padre fallido/Annað flokks faðir* (Croat./Eng./Sp./Isl.)

Josip Razum returns w/*Bluz pod košem/The blues under the hoop/Los blues bajo del aro* (Croat./Eng./Sp.)

Joanna Rosińska's GobQ debut is w/var. Polish tr., incl. M.F. McAuliffe's essay *Pictures on a piano/Φωτογραφίες πάνω στο πιάνο/Slike na glasoviru/Fotografie na pianine/Imágenes en un piano/Myndir á píanó* (Eng./Grk./Croat./Polsk/Sp.Isl.); Kęstutis Navakas' pome *holocenas/holocene/holocen/голоцен/holocen/holoceno* (Lith./Eng./Polsk/Russ.Croat./Sp.); Tanni Haas feuilleons *Tug-of-war/Διελκυστίνδα/Fuego de tira/Przeciąganie liny*, & *Old Friends/Παλιοί φίλοι/Viejos Amigos/Starzy Przyjaciele* (Eng./Grk./Croat./Sp.); Petros Skythiotis'pome *ΓΙ' ΑΥΤΟ ΗΤΑΝ ΑΜΕΡΙΚΑΝΟΣ/American/Što te Čini Amerikancem/Americano/Amerykanin* (Grk./Eng./Croat./Sp./Polsk); Ann Farley's *Grandmother Ocean/Baka Ocean/Mędrczyni Ocean/Abuela océano* (Eng./Croat./Polsk./Sp.); & Veronica O'Halloran's *my arms worse than windmills/Moje ramiona gorsze niż wiatraki/мои руки хуже ветряных мельниц/mis brazos peores que molinos de viento* (Eng./Polsk./Rus./Sp.)

Hana Samaržija did the Eng. tr. of Marija Dejanović's pome, *Zvuk/The Sound/O ήχος/See hääl/El Sonido/Hljóðið* (Croat./Eng./Grk./Eston./Sp./Isl.)

Πέτρος Σκυθιώτης/Petros Skythiotis returns w/ another pome, *ΓΙ' ΑΥΤΟ ΗΤΑΝ ΑΜΕΡΙΚΑΝΟΣ/American/Što te Čini Amerikancem/Americano/Amerykanin* (Grk./Eng./Croat/Sp./Polsk)

Андрей Сен-Сеньков, author of *Anatomical Theatre*, returns w/Russ. tr. of Kęstutis Navakas' pome *holocenas/holocene/holocen/голоцен/holocen/holoceno* (Lith./Eng./Polsk/Russ.Croat./Sp.), as well as providing Russ. captions for Melb. comix artist Michael Fikaris' *Altered Identity in Public Theatre Transports*.

Art Tolen returns w/Tagal. tr. of two Rimas Uzgiris

pomes, *The Lesser Light/Mažesnė šviesa/Minna ljósið/La luz menor/Ang mas kaunting liwanag* (Eng./Lith./Isl./Sp./Tagalog), & *Binary Star/Dvinarė žvaigždė/Tvöfaldur stjarna/Kaksoistähti/Estrella binaria/Buklod bitwin/Binarna zvijezda* (Eng./Lith./Isl./Finn./Sp./Tagalog./Croat.)

Giorgos Tsavdaridis & Maria Tsanakalioti make their *GobQ* debut w/ their Eng. tr. of Petros Skythiotis' pome *ΓΙ' ΑΥΤΟ ΗΤΑΝ ΑΜΕΡΙΚΑΝΟΣ/American/Što te Čini Amerikancem/Americano/Amerykanin* (Grk./Eng./Croat/Sp./Polsk)

Ελένη Τζατζιμάκη/Eleni Tzatzimaki, based in Athens, Greece, is a prof. jazz singer. Eleni's colls. of pomes incl. *Meta tin enilikiosi* (2012), *Se poion anikei mia istoria?/Who does a story belong to?* (2015) & *The Twin Paradox* (2018). Eleni makes her *GobQ* debut w/the pomes *Αν πυροβολούσα το φεγγάρι/If I shot the moon/Si disparara a la luna/Kad bih raznijela mjesec* and *Μέλμπα Ερνάντες Ροντρίγκες/Melba Hernandez Rodriguez/Melba Hernandez Rodriguez/Melba Hernandez Rodriguez* (Grk./Eng./Sp./Croat.)

Rimas Uzgiris, who pandemics in Vilnius, returns w/two pomes, *The Lesser Light/Mažesnė šviesa/Minna ljósið/La luz menor/Ang mas kaunting liwanag* (Eng./Lith./Isl./Sp./Tagalog), & *Binary Star/Dvinarė žvaigždė/Tvöfaldur stjarna/Kaksoistähti/Estrella binaria/Buklod bitwin/Binarna zvijezda* (Eng./Lith./Isl./Finn./Sp./Tagalog./Croat.), as well as his Eng. tr. of a Kęstutis Navakas pome, *holocenas/holocene/holocen/голоцен/holocen/holoceno* (Lith./Eng./Polsk/Russ.Croat./Sp.)

Mitzi Waltz, a Little Beirut refugee, is now firmly ensconsed in Amsterdam. She returns to *GobQ* w/ Dutch captions for M. Fikaris's *Altered Identity in Public Theatre Transports/Veranderde identiteit op het OV theatre* (Eng., w/ Croat./Dutch/Grk./Russ./Sp. captions)

T. Warburton y Bajo y rvb did Span. tr. of a goodly baker's doz. of works in this issue.

Graham Willoughby, whose artwork's adorned our covers since is. 2, returns, this time in glorious black & white!

Τώνια Τζιρίτα Ζαχαράτου did Grk. captions for M. Fikaris's *Altered Identity in Public Theatre Transports/τροποποιημένη ταυτότητα στο δημόσιο θέατρο των συγκοινωνιών* (Eng., w/ Croat./Dutch/Grk./Russ./Sp. captions)

ZVUK

Jutros sam u snu uspjela
    zvučati
kao mehaničko biće. Ton mi je
    svijetlio
u tisuću maternica

koje su letjele iz mojih usta.
    Probudila sam se
i živim u zvučniku,
prozor mi vibrira kamionima

koji prolaze cestom. Tragovi su
    mi savijeni
kao sirene na glavnim
    trgovima.
Protegnula sam se i tražila
    ljude da posvjedoče:
tu sam sunce u obliku konja,
živim u vunenom jajetu.

Povoji su nepropusni svjedoci
    želje
da izletim u žilice
na listovima slobodnog bilja.
    Jutro je

želja da me nema
kao da se glazba nije dogodila.

— *Marija Dejanović*

The Sound

This morning, in my dream, I
    sounded
like a mechanical creature. My tone
    glowed
in the thousand uteruses

dashing from my mouth. I woke up
    and
live in an amplifier,
my window reverberates with the
    trucks

passing down the road. My signs are
    bent
like the sirens on main squares.
I stretched and sought men to bear
    witness:
here I am a horse-shaped sun,
living in a woolen egg.

The bandages, impermeable
    witnesses of my desire
to creep into the veins
on the leaves of free plants. The
    morning is

the desire to disappear,
as if there had been no music.

— *Marija Dejanović*
    (tr. fr. the Croatian, Hana Samaržija)

Ο ήχος

Το πρωί, στο όνειρό μου, ακούστηκα
σαν ένα πλάσμα μηχανικό. Ο τόνος μου
                    έλαμπε
στις χίλιες μήτρες

που εφορμούσαν από το στόμα μου.
            Ξύπνησα και
ζω σε έναν ενισχυτή,
το παράθυρό μου αντηχεί τα διερχόμενα

φορτηγά κάτω στον δρόμο. Τα σημάδια μου
                είναι
λυγισμένα όπως οι σειρήνες στις κεντρικές
            πλατείες.
Τεντώθηκα και αναζήτησα άνδρες για
                μάρτυρες:
Να με λοιπόν ένας ήλιος σε σχήμα αλόγου,
που ζει σε ένα μάλλινο αυγό.

Τα παντζούρια είναι αδιαπέραστοι μάρτυρες
της επιθυμίας μου να διεισδύσω μέσα στις
            φλέβες
στα φύλλα των ελεύθερων φυτών. Το πρωί
            είναι

η επιθυμία της εξαφάνισης,
σαν να μην έχει υπάρξει μουσική.

— *Μάρια Ντεγιάνοβιτς*
  (μετάφραση, Τώνια Τζιρίτα Ζαχαράτου)

See hääl

Täna hommikul unes kõlasin
nagu masinlik olend. Mu tämber
    hõõgus
tuhandes üsas,

mis mu suust tuiskasid. Ärkasin ja
elan võimendis,
mu akendes täriseb vastu veokite

sõit all tänaval. Mu märgid on
    kooldus
nagu keskväljakute sireenid.
Sirutasin end ja otsisin, kes
    tunnistaks:
siin ma olen, hobusekujuline
     päike,
ja elan villast munas.

Plaastrid, läbitungimatud
    tunnistajad mu kihule
imbuda soontesse
vabade taimede lehtedes. Hommik
     on

kihk kaduda,
nagu muusikat poleks olnudki.

– Marija Dejanović
(Inglise keelest tõlkinud Mirjam
Parve)

El sonido

Esta mañana, en mi sueño, sonaba
como una criatura mecánica. Mi
    tono brilló
en los mil úteros

corriendo de mi boca. Me
    despierto y
vivo en un amplificador, mi
ventana reverbera con camiones

pasando por la carretera. Mis
    señales se doblan
como sirenas en las plazas
    mayores.
Me esparcé, luego busqué hombres
    para testificar:
aquí soy un sol en forma de
    caballo,
viviendo en un huevo de lana.

Los vendages son testigos
    impermeables de mi deseo
de arrastrarme por las venas
     frondosas
de plantas libres. La mañana es

el deseo de desaparecer, como
si no hubiera habido música.

— Marija Dejanović
(Traducción, T. Warburton y
Bajo y rvb)

Hljóðið

Í morgun hljómaði ég í draumi
        mínum
eins og vélrænni veru. Tónn minn
        ljómaði
í þúsund legunum

hljót frá munni mínum. Ég vaknaði
        og
búa í magnara,
glugginn minn endurtekur með
        vörubílunum

liggur niður götuna. Merki mín eru
        bogin
eins og sírenurnar á helstu reitum.
Ég rétti og leitaði manna til að bera
        vitni:
hérna er ég hestalaga sól,
býr í ull eggi.

Bindurnar eru órjúfanleg vitni um
        löngun mína
að skríða í æðarnar
á laufum ókeypis plantna.
        Morguninn er

löngunin til að hverfa,
eins og það hefði ekki verið tónlist.

    – Marija Dejanović
     (Þýtt úr Ensku, Michael Lohr)

ΓΙ' ΑΥΤΟ ΗΤΑΝ ΑΜΕΡΙΚΑΝΟΣ

Ήμασταν στην ανάλυση της δεύτερης κούπας
καφέ
του Αλμπέρτο όταν του
είπα πως πείνασα.
Επανέλαβε πως η τροφή είναι κοινωνική
κατασκευή των άθεων,
αλλά εγώ επέμεινα ν'
ανάψει την κουζίνα.

Σηκώθηκε και πάτησε το κουμπί της
τηλεόρασης.

Αμέσως άνοιξε μια υποδοχή κάτω απ' την
οθόνη γεμάτη αστρόσκονη.
Την μάζεψε και την έριξε στον καφέ μου.
Τι με κοιτάς, είπε,
δεν υπάρχει τίποτα θρεπτικότερο.

Γι' αυτό πάτησε ο άνθρωπος στο φεγγάρι.

— *Πέτρος Σκυθιώτης*

AMERICAN

We were analyzing Alberto's second cup of coffee
when I told him
I was hungry.
He repeated that food is a social construct of the
godless,

but I insisted that
he turn on the stove.

He stood up and pushed the television button.

Immediately a tray full of stardust opened under
the screen.
He picked it up and put it in my coffee.
'What are you looking at', he said,
'there's nothing more nourishing.'

This is why man walked on the moon'.

— *Petros Skythiotis*
(tr. fr. the Greek, Giorgos Tsaodaridis, Maria
Tsanakalioti)

ŠTO TE ČNI AMERIKANCEM

Analizirali smo Albertovu
    drugu šalicu kave
    kad sam mu rekao
da sam gladan.
Ponovio je da je hrana društveni
    konstrukt bezbožnika,
no ja sam navalio
da upali štednjak.

Ustao je i pritisnuo gumb na
    televizoru.

Plitica puna zvjezdane prašine
    pojavila se ispod zaslona.
Uzeo ju je i istresao umoju
    kavu.
„Što blejiš tako' reče
    „ne postoji ništa
    hranjivije.

Zbog ovoga je čovjek hodao po
    mjesecu.'

– Petros Skythiotis
(prijevod s engleskoga, Ana Katana)

AMERICANO

Estábamos analizando la segunda
    taza de café de Alberto
    cuando le dije
    que tenía hambre.
repitió que la comida es una
    construcción
    social de los impíos,
aun así, insistí en que
    encendiera la estufa.

Se levantó y presionó el botón de la
    televisión.

Inmediatamente una bandeja llena
de polvo
    se abrió debajo de la pantalla.
Lo recogió y lo puso en mi café.
‹Qué estás mirando›, dijo,
‹No hay nada más nutritivo.

Por eso el hombre caminó sobre la
    luna›.

– Petros Skythiotis
(traducción, T. Warburton y Bajo
    y rrb)

AMERYKANIN

Analizowaliśmy drugą filiżankę kawy
    Alberta
    gdy mu powiedziałam,
    że jestem głodna.
On powtórzył mi, że jedzenie to
    konstrukt
    społeczny
    bezbożnych
    ale ja nalegałam
    by ja włączył kuchenkę.

Wstał i nacisnął guzik w telewizorze.

Natychmiast szuflada pełna pyłu
    gwiezdnego
otworzyła się pod ekranem.
wziął ją i nasypał do mojej kawy.
"No i co się tak patrzysz"
    powiedział
"Nie ma nic bardziej odżywczego.
Dlatego właśnie człowiek spacerował po
    Księżycu."

– Petros Skythiotis
(Tłumaczenie: Joanna Rosińska)

INNUENDO

Ein Traum Ein Traum
Ein Blatt
Gefallen
Unter Einem Baum

    — *Kontopoulou*
      Constantina

INNUENDO

A dream a dream
A leaf
fallen
Under a tree

    — *Kontopoulou Constantina*
      (tr. fr. the Germ., K.
        Constantina)

INSINUANDO

Un sueño un sueño
Una hoja
caída
Debajo un árbol

    — *Kontopoulou Constantina*
      (traducción, T. Warburton
       y Bajo y rvb)

ΥΠΑΙΝΙΓΜΟΣ

Ένα όνειρο, ένα όνειρο
ένα φύλλο
πεσμένο
κάτω από ένα δέντρο

    — Κοντ Κωνσταντς,
      Κοντοπούλου Α.
      Κωνσταντίνα

Diminuendo

Every day
A city falls within
   us
Like a dream
stolen
By a clue

> *— Kontopoulou Constantina*
> *(tr. fr. the Germ., K.*
> *Constantina)*

DIMINUENDO

Jeden Tag
Eine Stadt fällt in uns hinein
Wie ein Traum
Gestohlen
Von einem Hinweis

> *— Kontopoulou Constantina*

Φθίνουσα

Κάθε μέρα
Μια πόλη
   καταστρέφεται εντός
Μας
Σαν όνειρο
Που εκλάπη
Από ένδειξη

> *— Κοντ Κωνσταντ,*
> *Κοντοπούλου Α.*
> *Κωνσταντίνα*

Disminución

Cada día
Una ciudad cae dentro
   de
nosotros
Como un sueño
robado
Por una pista

> *— Kontopoulou*
> *Constantina*
> *(traducción, T. War-*
> *burton y Bajo y rvb)*

my arms worse than windmills
my face flat screens welded to a
    crane
all my mechanisms a heavy visible
    black.

visible,
visible,

– Veronica O'Halloran

мои руки хуже ветряных мельниц
мое лицо с плоскими сетками
    приварено к крану
все мои механизмы тяжелые
    выглядят черными.

обнаженными,
обнаженными,

– Вероника О'Хеллоран
(Перевод, Андрей Сен-Сеньков)

Moje ramiona gorsze niż wiatraki
moja twarz płaskie ekrany przyspawane
    do żurawia
wszystkie moje mechanizmy ciężka
    widoczna czerń.

widoczna,
widoczna,

– Veronica O'Halloran
(Tłumaczenie: Joanna Rosińska)

mis brazos peores que molinos de viento
mi cara, pantallas planas soldadas a una
grúa
todos mis mecanismos desnudoss negros y
pesados.

desnudos,
desnudos,

— *Veronica O'Halloran*
(traducción, T. Warburton y Bajo y rvb)

τα χέρια μου χειρότερα κι από ανεμόμυλους
το πρόσωπό μου επίπεδες οθόνες
συγκολλημένες σ' ένα γερανό
όλοι μου οι μηχανισμοί ένα ασήκωτο
ξεκάθαρο μαύρο.

ξεκάθαρο,
ξεκάθαρο,

— *Βερόνικα Ο'Χάλλοραν*
(μεταφρασμένο, Βασιλεία Οικονόμου)

MICHAEL FIKARIS   μ.κ. φικάρις

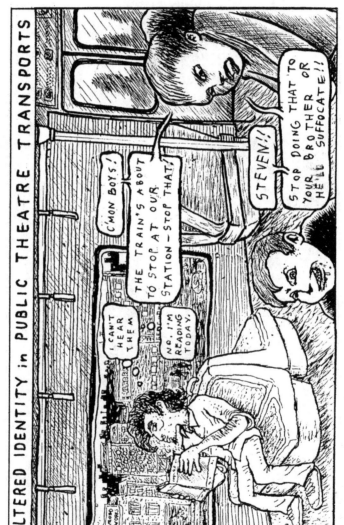

promijenjeni identitet u javno-kazališnom prijevozu: prijavid. marija dejanović

MAJKA (djeci): Haj'mo, dečki!

MAJKA: Vlak će sad stati na našoj stanici – prestani!

PUTNIK (pokušavajući čitati & neprisluški-vati): Ne čujem ih...

MAJKA (djeci): Steven!!

ČITATELJ (pokušavajući neprisluškivati): Ne, danas čitam...

MAJKA (djeci): Prestani to raditi bratu ili će se se ugušiti!

MICHAEL FIKARIS

Alteración de la identidad en el teatro de transportes públicos: traducción, t. warburton y bayo y rvb

MADRE (a los niños): ¡¡Vamos, chicos!!

MADRE [...]: ¡¡El tren está en punto de parar en nuestra estación!! ¡¡Para eso!!

PASAJERO (tratando a leer y no espiar): No puedo oírlos...

MADRE (A los niños): ¡¡Esteban!!

PASAJERO (tratando a leer y no espiar): No, estoy leyendo hoy...

MADRE (A los niños): ¡¡Déja de hacerle eso a tu hermano o se asfixiará!!

(Перевод, Андрей Сеньков)

МАТЬ (детям): Прекратите, мальчики!

МАТЬ [...]: Поезд вот-вот остановится на нашей станции! Прекратите это!

ПАССАЖИР (пытающийся читать и не подслушивать): Я их не слышу...

МАТЬ (детям): Стивен!

ПАССАЖИР (пытающийся не подслушивать): Нет, я сегодня читаю...

МАТЬ (детям): Перестань так поступать со своим братом, иначе он задохнется!!

Veranderde identiteit op het OV theatre: Vertaling, Mitzi Waltz

MOEDER (OP KINDEREN): Hou op, jongens!

MOEDER [...]: Onze station komt eraan, de trein staan op het punt te stoppen! Hou op met dat!

MEDEREIZIGER (PROBEERT TE LEZEN & NIET AF TE LUISTEREN): Ik kan ze niet horen...

MOEDER (OP KINDEREN): Steven!!

MEDEREIZIGER (PROBEERT TE LEZEN & NIET AF TE LUISTEREN): Nee, vandaag lees ik door...

MOEDER (OP KINDEREN): Doe je broer dat niet nog of hij stikt!!

τροποποιημένη ταυτότητα στο δημόσιο θέατρο των συγκοινωνιών: Τώνια Τζιρίτα Ζαχαράτου

ΜΗΤΕΡΑ (στα παιδιά): Ελάτε, αγόρια!

ΜΗΤΕΡΑ [...]:Το τρένο έχει σχεδόν φθάσει στη στάση μας! Σταματήστε πια!

ΕΠΙΒΑΤΗΣ (ΠΡΟΣΠΑΘΩΝΤΑΣ ΝΑ ΔΙΑΒΑΖΕΙ ΚΑΙ ΝΑ ΜΗΝ ΚΡΥΦΑΚΟΥΕΙ): Δεν μπορώ να τους ακούω...

ΜΗΤΕΡΑ (στα παιδιά): Στήβεν!!

ΑΝΑΓΝΩΣΤΗΣ (ΠΡΟΣΠΑΘΩΝΤΑΣ ΝΑ ΜΗΝ ΚΡΥΦΑΚΟΥΕΙ): όχι, σήμερα διαβάζω...

ΜΗΤΕΡΑ (στα παιδιά): Σταμάτα να το κάνεις αυτό στον αδελφό σου αλλιώς θα πνιγεί!!

Pictures On A Piano

M. F. McAuliffe

During the '80s we lived in L.A.

I worked as a clerk in a large majority-minority high school in the South Bay. Sometimes the clerks and secretaries would have a girls' night out – we were all women – we'd go to someone's house for the evening. I can't remember the occasions. Birthdays, perhaps. In these established working class living rooms there were no books; surprisingly often they'd be a piano. On the piano or a shelf, so many times, there would be a framed 5x7 or 8x10 inch black and white photo of a young man sparkling with youth and happiness, looking upwards and to the left, dressed in a cap and the knife-sharp creases of a military uniform. They were the graduation photos, sons in the service.

There were so many, over the years, so identical, so insistent on the knife-sharp clothing they struck me as a code I couldn't understand could see – there, insistent, glimmering just below the surface of the cloth, elusive and in plain sight.

One of the teachers had twin sons; one was in the Army in

Φωτογραφίες πάνω στο πιάνο

M. F. McAuliffe
(Μετάφραση, Μαρουσώ Αθανασίου)

Κατά τη διάρκεια της δεκαετίας του '80 ζούσαμε στο Λος Άντζελες.

Εργαζόμουν ως υπάλληλος σε ένα μειονοτικό λύκειο στο Σάουθ Μπέι. Κάποιες φορές οι υπάλληλοι και οι γραμματείς διοργανώναμε βραδιές μόνο για γυναίκες -ήμασταν όλες γυναίκες-πηγαίναμε στο σπίτι κάποιας για να περάσουμε το βράδυ. Δεν μπορώ να θυμηθώ με τι αφορμή. Γενέθλια, ίσως. Σε αυτά τα εργατικά σαλόνια δεν υπήρχαν βιβλία- παραδόξως συχνά υπήρχε πιάνο. Πάνω στο πιάνο ή σε ένα ράφι, πολλές φορές, υπήρχε μια κορνιζαρισμένη ασπρόμαυρη φωτογραφία 5x7 ή 8x10 ιντσών ενός νεαρού άντρα που έλαμπε από νιάτα και ευτυχία, με το βλέμμα πάνω αριστερά, με καπέλο και τις αιχμηρές γραμμές μιας στρατιωτικής στολής. Ήταν οι φωτογραφίες απόλυσης, οι γιοι που υπηρετούσαν τη θητεία τους.

Ήταν τόσο πολλές, όλα αυτά τα χρόνια, τόσο πανομοιότυπες, τόσο επιβλητικές με τα αιχμηρά ενδύματα που μου φάνταζαν σαν ένας κώδικας που δεν μπορούσα να καταλάβω, που μπορούσα να δω - εκεί αδιάκοπα, να λαμπυρίζει ακριβώς κάτω από την επιφάνεια του υφάσματος, ασύλληπτος και σε κοινή θέα.

Ένας από τους δασκάλους είχε δύο δίδυμους γιους- ο ένας ήταν στον

Slike na glasoviru

M. F. McAuliffe
(prijevod s engleskoga, Ana Katana)

Tijekom osamdesetih živjeli smo u Los Angelesu.

Radila sam u administraciji jedne velike srednje škole u South Bayu koju su pohađali učenici većinskog i manjinskog podrijetla. Katkad bismo se mi službenice i tajnice našle na ženskoj večeri – sve smo bile žene – i otišle kući kod neke od nas. Ne sjećam se prigoda. Možda su to bili rođendani. U dnevnim boravcima situirane radničke klase nije bilo knjiga; no začuđujuće često ugledali biste glasovir. Na glasoviru ili na polici nalazila bi se crno – bijela fotografija veličine 2 x 12 cm, ili 10 x 13 cm, koja prikazuje muškarca koji prši od mladosti i sreće, pogleda uperenog lijevo prema gore, odjevenog u kapu i kirurški oštro izglačane crte na vojnoj odori. Bile su to fotografije nakon mature, fotografije sinova koji služe domovini.

Bilo ih je strašno mnogo, naoko posve istih, uz neizostavne oštro glačane odore koje su mi se činile poput kodeksa koji ne shvaćam – a tu je, nepobitan je, blješti tik ispod površine, skri-

Fotografie na pianinie

M.F. McAuliffe
(Tłumaczenie: Joanna Rosińska)

W latach 80-ych mieszkaliśmy w Los Angeles.

Pracowałam jako urzędniczka w dużej szkole średniej w South Bay, gdzie większość uczniów to grupy mniejszościowe. Czasem urzędniczki i sekretarki – cała żeńska grupa – spotykały się wieczorem w domu którejś z nas. Nie pamiętam z jakiej okazji. Może urodzin. W tych salonach przeciętnej klasy pracującej nie było książek; zaskakująco często natomiast pianino. Na nim, albo na półce, często stało oprawione w ramkę, czarno-białe zdjęcie młodego mężczyzny tryskającego młodością i szczęściem, patrzącego do góry, w lewo, w czapce i starannie wyprasowanym mundurze. Były to zdjęcia z przysięgi. Synowie w służbie wojskowej.

Przez lata widziałam ich tak wiele, wszystkie podobne – odznaczające się odprasowanym starannie mundurem – że kojarzyły mi się z kodem niezrozumiałym, choć wyraźnie widocznym: upartym, migoczącym pod powierzchnią tkaniny. Nieuchwytnym, lecz widzialnym.

Jeden z nauczycieli miał synów bliźniaków, z których jeden służył w piechocie w Niemczech. Pokazał mi kiedyś polaroid, który syn mu przysłał – trzech, czy czterech młodych

Germany. He showed me a Polaroid his son had sent: three or four very young men in fatigues with beer cans and grins, high-fiving below the banner above them on the canteen wall. DOOMSDAY DOGS. An earthquake of fear and unmooring in that photo, in me as I looked at it.

Doomsday: the end of the world: war, chaos, fire, fury, rubble, death; smashed land and landscapes, cities, smashed wheat and insects and trees…

The unit had been formed to function there, couldn't function properly anywhere else. "Doomsday Dogs." The mindbreaking relish in that phrase.

We moved to Portland in 1992.

During the last week of September 2002, for the first anniversary of 9/11/01, the first of the public art projects commissioned by the Portland Institute for Contemporary Art was installed on a downtown vacant lot. Portland artist and sculptor Daniel Duford kiln-fired four huge crouching clay figures on the vacant lot at SW Taylor & 3rd. He called these figures golems. They were inspired by photos of Afghani prisoners at Guantanamo.

On the wall facing 3rd Ave. he painted two more figures, large male nudes with the same physique. They stood with open

στρατό στη Γερμανία. Μου έδειξε μια πολαρόιντ που είχε στείλει ο γιος του: τρεις ή τέσσερις πολύ νεαροί άνδρες με στολές, με κουτάκια μπύρας και γελάκια, που πανηγύριζαν κάτω από το λάβαρο που βρισκόταν στον τοίχο της καντίνας. ΣΚΥΛΙΑ ΤΗΣ ΑΠΟΚΑΛΥΨΗΣ. Ένας κραδασμός τρόμου και απομάγευσης σε εκείνη τη φωτογραφία, σε μένα καθώς την κοίταζα.

Αποκάλυψη: το τέλος του κόσμου: πόλεμος, χάος, φωτιά, μανία, συντρίμμια, θάνατος, διαλυμένη γη και τοπία, πόλεις, τσακισμένο στάρι, έντομα και δέντρα...

Η μονάδα είχε σχηματιστεί για να λειτουργεί εκεί, δεν μπορούσε να λειτουργήσει σωστά πουθενά αλλού. "Σκυλιά της Αποκάλυψης." Η ανατριχιαστική απόλαυση αυτής της φράσης.

Μετακομίσαμε στο Πόρτλαντ το 1992.

Την τελευταία εβδομάδα του Σεπτεμβρίου 2002, για την πρώτη επέτειο της 11ης Σεπτεμβρίου 2001, το πρώτο έργο τέχνης που ανέθεσε το Ινστιτούτο Σύγχρονης Τέχνης του Πόρτλαντ εγκαταστάθηκε σε ένα εγκαταλελειμμένο οικόπεδο στο κέντρο της πόλης. Ο γλύπτης Ντάνιελ Ντούφορντ από το Πόρτλαντ έψησε τέσσερις τεράστιες πήλινες φιγούρες που έσκυβαν στο εγκαταλελειμμένο οικόπεδο της οδού Σάουθ Τέιλορ και 3ης Λεωφόρου. Ονόμασε αυτές τις φιγούρες γκόλεμ. Ήταν εμπνευσμένες από φωτογραφίες Αφγανών κρατουμένων στο Γκουαντάναμο.

Στον τοίχο που έβλεπε την 3η Λεωφόρο ζωγράφισε άλλες δύο φιγούρες, μεγάλα

va se usred bijela dana.

Jedan od nastavnika imao je sinove blizance; jedan je bio u vojsci u Njemačkoj. Pokazao mi je Polaroid fotografiju koju mu je poslao sin: trojica ili četvorica jako mladih muškaraca u radnim odorama, s limenkama piva i velikim osmijesima davala su si „petice" ispod zastave obješene na zidu kantine. Na zastavi je pisalo DOOMSDAY DOGS (Psi Sudnjeg Dana). Potres uslijed straha i gubitka uporišta pod nogama razjapio se u meni dok sam gledala fotografiju.

Sudnji Dan: kraj svijeta: rat, kaos, plamen, bijes, ruševine, smrt; sravnjena zemlja i krajobrazi, gradovi, uništena pšenica i kukci i stabla...

Jedinica je oformljena da opstane tamo, i nigdje drugdje ne može pravilno opstati.

„Psi Sudnjeg Dana." Razarajuće olakšanje unutar te rečenice.

Godine 1992. preselili smo u Portland.

Tijekom posljednjeg tjedna rujna 2002., prve obljetnice Jedanaestog rujna 2001., prvi javni umjetnički projekt pod pokroviteljstvom ustanove Portland Institute for Contemporary Art bio je postavljen na jednom praznom parkiralištu u centru grada. Gradski umjetnik i kipar Daniel Duford u glinenoj je peći ispekao četiri velike čučeće prilike i postavio ih na sjeveroza-

mężczyzn w polowych mundurach z puszkami piwa, uśmiechniętych, przybijających sobie piątkę pod napisem na ścianie stołówki: PSY DNIA SĄDNEGO. Tektoniczne trzęsienie strachu i dryf po utracie stabilizacji na zdjęciu i we mnie gdy na nie patrzyłam...

Sąd Ostateczny: koniec świata, wojna, chaos, ogień, furia, zgliszcza, śmierć, rozbita ziemia i krajobraz, miasta, zbombardowane pola pszeniczne, zniszczone owady, drzewa...

Jednostka ta została utworzona by działać tam – nie mogła funkcjonować nigdzie indziej. Psy Dnia Sądnego – rozkosz rozsadzająca umysł.

Przeprowadziliśmy się do Portland w 1992.

W ostatnim tygodniu września 2002, w pierwszą rocznicę Ataku 11 Września, zainstalowano pierwszy z projektów sztuki miejskiej zamówiony przez Portlandzki Instytut Sztuki Współczesnej. Miejscowy artysta, Daniel Duford zainstalował swe rzeźby z wypalanej gliny na pustym placu pod budowę, na rogu pd. wsch. ulicy Taylor i Trzeciej Alei. Nazwał swe postacie golemami. Rzeźby były zainspirowane zdjęciami więźniów afgańskich w Guantanamo.

Na murze od strony Trzeciej Alei namalował jeszcze dwie takie postacie, wielkie akty męskie o takich samych sylwetkach. Stały, z otwartymi dłońmi patrząc w dal, uosobienie siły bez mocy...

Instalacja miała być prezentowa-

hands, looking outward, representations of strength without power.

The installation was intended to last a month.

Vandals immediately attacked the clay figures. By the fourth night they had all been smashed and psycho-sexually mutilated. Body parts – hands, heads and the penis – were missing.

The fragments were pushed into piles: the lot reclaimed for parking, tyre marks running through charcoal remains from the original firing.

Despite cut flowers and other gifts of grief and respect left by passers-by, the piles of fragments were clearly torsos, thighs, hands. The figures were still simulacra, still also bodies as garbage, identifiable limbs and stone-sized pieces of clay with the shine of wet blood (after the rain), flung by cars or chance next to a single carnation or discarded stalk.

From the street the lot looked like remnants of some sordid private anonymous and unsolvable crime. Standing in it, it felt like a battlefield.

It was a battlefield, the rubble from conflicting claims on public space, conflicting ideas about what to do with (or to) vulnerability, about who should be permitted a place

ανδρικά γυμνά με την ίδια σωματική διάπλαση. Στέκονταν με τα χέρια ανοιχτά, κοιτάζοντας προς τα έξω, αναπαραστάσεις δύναμης χωρίς εξουσία.

Η εγκατάσταση προβλεπόταν να διαρκέσει ένα μήνα.

Βάνδαλοι επιτέθηκαν πολύ γρήγορα στις πήλινες φιγούρες. Μέχρι την τέταρτη νύχτα είχαν όλες σπάσει και ακρωτηριαστεί με τρόπο ψυχοεξουαλικό. Μέρη του σώματος - χέρια, κεφάλια και πέος - έλειπαν.

Τα θραύσματα στοιβάχτηκαν σε σωρούς: το οικόπεδο αξιοποιήθηκε ως χώρος στάθμευσης, με τα σημάδια από τις ρόδες των αυτοκινήτων να διασχίζουν τα απομεινάρια του κάρβουνου από το αρχικό ψήσιμο.

Εκτός από τα λουλούδια και τα άλλα αντικείμενα θλίψης και σεβασμού που άφησαν οι περαστικοί, οι σωροί των θραυσμάτων ήταν εμφανώς σώματα, μηροί και χέρια. Οι φιγούρες εξακολουθούσαν να είναι ομοιώματα, εξακολουθούσαν επίσης να είναι σώματα ως απόβλητα, αναγνωρίσιμα άκρα και κομμάτια πηλού σε μέγεθος πέτρας με τη στιλπνότητα του νωπού αίματος (μετά τη βροχή), που πετάχτηκαν από αυτοκίνητα ή τυχαία δίπλα σε ένα μονάχα γαρύφαλλο ή ένα πεταμένο κοτσάνι.

Από τον δρόμο το οικόπεδο έμοιαζε με τα συντρίμμια κάποιου ειδεχθούς και ανεξιχνίαστου εγκλήματος. Όταν στεκόσουν μέσα σε αυτό, έμοιαζε με πεδίο μάχης.

Ήταν πεδίο μάχης, τα συντρίμμια από αντικρουόμενες διεκδικήσεις του δημόσιου χώρου, αντικρουόμενες ιδέες για το τι πρέπει να γίνει με την ευαλωτότητα (ή στην ευαλωτότητα), για το σε ποιον πρέπει να επιτραπεί να έχει

padno križanje ulica Taylor i Third Avenue. Te je prilike nazvao *golemi*. Nadahnule su ga fotografije afganistanskih zarobljenika u Guantanamu.

Na zidu koji gleda na Third Avenue naslikao je još dvije prilike, velike muške aktove jednake fizionomije. Stajali su otvorenih šaka, gledali pred sebe, prikazujući snagu bez moći.

Instalacija je mjesec dana trebala stajati ondje.

Vandali su odmah napali glinene prilike. Do četvrte noći sve su ih razbili i psihoseksualno unakazili. Dijelovi tijela – šake, glave i penisi – nedostajali su.

Ostatci su smeteni na hrpe; mjesto je ponovo postalo parkiralište, a tragovi kotača prolazili su kroz ugljene ostatke prvog pečenja gline. Usprkos buketima cvijeća i ostalim znakovima tuge i poštovanja koje su prolaznici ostavljali, jasno se vidjelo da su na hrpama ostala prsa, bedra, ruke, još uvijek simulakrumi, tijela kao smeće, raspoznatljivi udovi i komadi gline koji sjaje kao da su mokri od krvi (nakon kiše), koje su auti ili slučajnost raznijeli uz usamljen karanfil ili otrgnutu stabljiku.

Parkiralište je s ulice izgledalo poput poprišta kakvog gadnog, privatnog, nerješivog zločina. Kad staneš unutra, bilo je kao da si na bojištu.

I bilo je bojište. Ruševine nastale nakon sukoba za vlast nad javnim na do końca miesiąca. Wandale natychmiast napadli na gliniane figury. Czwartej nocy wszystkie już były potłuczone i okaleczone psycho-seksualnie. Brakowało im części ciała: rąk, głów i penisów.

Skorupy zmieciono na kupę, plac przeobrażono w parking, opony rozjeżdżały zwęglone pozostałości z wypalania gliny.

Mimo kwiatów i innych darów żalu i szacunku zostawianych przez przechodzących, rozpoznawalne jeszcze tułowie, uda i ręce tworzyły zaledwie stos odłamków.

Postacie – właściwie symulakra, również jako śmiecie wciąż były ciałami, rozpoznawalnymi kończynami i kamykami skorup błyszczącymi morką krwią (po deszczu), rozrzucane przez opony lub przypadek, obok pojedyńczych goździków lub wyrzuconych łodyg.

Od ulicy plac wyglądał jak pozostałość jakiejś brudnej, prywatnej, anonimowej, nierozwiązywalnej zbrodni. Stojąc na nim czuło się jak na polu bitwy.

To było pole bitwy: ruiny sprzecznych roszczeń co do publicznego miejsca, sprzecznych pomysłów co zrobić z bezbronnością, (albo co zrobić bezbronności), kto może zajmować miejsce w uwadze publicznej, co zrobić w sprawie niezgody czy niewygody, jak mamy się zachowywać jako osoby i grupy, różnice między zgrupowaniami a zbirami, różnica między

in the public's attention, what to do with disagreement or discomfort, how to behave as individuals and groups, the difference between bands and bandits, between what happens at night and what happens by day. It was what any moment might break apart and become, the hellscape at the bottom of a hole normality normally covers.

In 2011, on the tenth anniversary of 9/11/01, Daniel and I published an artist's book about the destruction of the golems. Despite documenting the site I knew I didn't fully understand it. Standing there I felt as though I were inside a hologram.

A little while ago a friend sent me her Bookiversary announcement. I realized that it had been ten years since *Golems Waiting Redux* – rare and fragile and out of print now. A few days later I began remembering the graduation photos and the loss of all anchor in the Doomsday Dogs polaroid.

Body parts – hands, heads and the penis – were missing.

There! The secrets in the photos and the vacant lot joined like the halves of a walnut in its shell.

On the left war, revealed as a vast permission, gathering up all the psychoses already swirling through any population and annexing them, nominally controlling and directing them, unleash-

θέση στη δημόσια θέα, τι πρέπει να γίνει με τη διαφωνία ή τη δυσφορία, πώς πρέπει να συμπεριφέρονται τα άτομα και οι ομάδες, για τη διαφορά ανάμεσα σε ομάδες και συμμορίες, ανάμεσα σε ό,τι συμβαίνει τη νύχτα και σε ό,τι συμβαίνει την ημέρα. Ήταν αυτό που κάθε στιγμή μπορεί να διαλυθεί και να γίνει το κολαστήριο στον πάτο μιας τρύπας που κανονικά καλύπτει η κανονικότητα.

Το 2011, στη δέκατη επέτειο της 11ης Σεπτεμβρίου 2001, ο Ντάνιελ και εγώ εκδώσαμε ένα λεύκωμα για την καταστροφή των γκόλεμ. Παρά την τεκμηρίωση της εγκατάστασης ήξερα ότι δεν την είχα κατανοήσει πλήρως. Στεκόμουν εκεί κι ήταν σαν να βρισκόμουν σε ένα ολόγραμμα.

Πριν από λίγο καιρό μια φίλη μου έστειλε την ανακοίνωση για την επέτειο του βιβλίου της. Συνειδητοποίησα ότι είχαν περάσει δέκα χρόνια από το Γκόλεμς Περιμένοντας την Επιστροφή- σπάνιο και θρυλικό και εξαντλημένο πλέον. Λίγες μέρες αργότερα άρχισα να θυμάμαι τις φωτογραφίες της απόλυσης και την απώλεια κάθε σταθεράς από την πολαρόιντ των Σκυλιών της Αποκάλυψης.

Μέρη του σώματος - χέρια, κεφάλια και πέος - έλειπαν.

Ορίστε! Το μυστήριο των φωτογραφιών και το εγκαταλελειμμένο οικόπεδο ενώνονταν σαν τα ημισέληνα καρύδια στο κέλυφός τους.

Στα αριστερά ο πόλεμος, που παρουσιάζεται ως μια τεράστια παραχώρηση, συγκεντρώνει όλες τις ψυχώσεις που ήδη επικρατούν σε κάθε πληθυσμό και τις προσαρτά, τις ελέγχεικαιτιςκατευθύνειονομαστικά,

prostorom, sukoba što činiti s ranjivošću, ili što učiniti ranjivima, tko smije, a tko ne smije primiti pozornost javnosti, kako postupiti s neslaganjem ili nelagodom, kako se ponašati kao pojedinac i kao skupina, razlika između bandi i bandita, između onoga što se događa danju i što se događa noću. Onoga što se svaki trenutak može raspasti i postati nešto drugo. Pakleni krajobraz na dnu jame koju inače pokriva normalnost.

Godine 2011., na desetu obljetnicu Jedanaestog rujna, Daniel i ja objavili smo knjigu jednog umjetnika o uništenju *golema*, usprkos tome što dokumentiramo mjesto koje nismo u potpunosti razumjeli. Dok sam stajala tamo osjećala sam se kao da se nalazim unutar holograma.

Nedavno mi je prijateljica poslala objavu za obljetnicu izdavanja knjige. Shvatila sam da je prošlo deset godina otkad je izišla *Golems Waiting Redux* – rijetko, krhko izdanje koje se više ne tiska. Nekoliko dana kasnije počela sam se prisjećati fotografija s mature i gubitka uporišta zbog fotografije Pasa Sudnjeg Dana.

Dijelovi tijela – glave, šake, penisi – nedostaju.

Eto! Tajne fotografija i praznog parkirališta spojile su se poput polovica orahove jezgre u ljusci.

S lijeve je strane bio rat, okupljajući sve psihoze koje već haraju svim populacijama i pripajaju ih,

tym co dzieje się w nocy a co za dnia. Było to tym, czym jakikolwiek moment stanie się po swym rozpadzie: piekielny krajobraz w głębi dziury, którą zazwyczaj zakrywa.

W 2011, w dziesiątą rocznicę Ataku 11 Września, Daniel i ja wydaliśmy album o zmasakrowaniu golemów. Mimo dokumentowania tego miejsca, wiedziałam, że jednak do końca go nie rozumiem. Stojąc tam wówczas czułam się jak w hologramie.

Jakiś czas temu znajoma przysłała mi zawiadomienie o rocznicy wydania swej książki. Uświadomiłam sobie wtedy, że minęło już dziesięć lat od ukazania się naszych „Golemów Czekających na Zmartwychwstanie", unikatowej, delikatnej publikacji z wyczerpanym nakładem. Parę dni później przypomniałam sobie te fotografie z przysięgi i destabilizację na polaroidzie Psów Dnia Sądnego.

Części ciała: ręce, głowy i penisy...brakujące.

No właśnie! Tajemnice na fotografiach i pustym placu połączyły się jak dwie połowy orzecha włoskiego w skorupie.

Po lewej, wojna ujawniona jako szerokie przyzwolenie, kumulująca wszystkie psychozy krążące w każdym społeczeństwie, złączając je, pozornie nimi kierując – w rzeczywistości dając im wolną rękę. Zbrodniarze wojenni są

ing them. War criminals outnumber their trials.

On the right graduation photos, revealed as false promises. The code of the knife-sharp crease avers that destructive potential is under control, leashed, leashable, commandable, unbetraying and unbetrayed. And always and only released in defence of the good. Q

τις εξαπολύει. Οι εγκληματίες πολέμου είναι περισσότεροι από τις δίκες τους.

Στα δεξιά οι φωτογραφίες απόλυσης, που αποδεικνύονται ψεύτικες υποσχέσεις. Ο κώδικας της αιχμηρής γραμμής που δηλώνει ότι το καθοδηγημένο δυναμικό βρίσκεται υπό έλεγχο, είναι δεμένο με λουρί, μπορεί να δεθεί με λουρί, μπορεί να διαταχθεί, να μην προδίδει και να μην προδίδεται. Και απελευθερώνεται πάντα και μόνο για την υπεράσπιση του καλού. Q

nazivajući to upravljanjem i usmjeravanjem, te driješenjem. Ratnih je zločinaca mnogo više nego suđenja.

S desne strane nalaze se maturalne fotografije, otkrivene kao lažna obećanja. Kodeks oštro izglačanih odora vara nas da je uništavajući potencijal pod kontrolom, obuzdan i upravljiv, poslušan, nije izdajnički i ne potiče na izdaju. A driješit će ga se samo i isključivo u svrhu obrane dobra. *Q*

liczniejsi niż procesy zbrodniarzy wojennych.

Po prawej, zdjęcia z przysięgi, ujawnione jako fałszywe obietnice. Kod odprasowanych starannie mundurów stwierdza, że destrukcyjny potencjał jest pod kontrolą, na wodzy, kontrolowalny, sterowalny, wierny, niezdradzony. I uwalniany zawsze i tylko w obronie dobra. *Q*

Imágenes en un piano

M. F. McAuliffe

(traducción, T. Warburton y Bajo y rvb)

Durante los años 80 vivíamos en L. Á.

Trabajada como oficinista en una enorme escuela secundaria de mayoría minoritaria en South Bay. A veces, los empleados y las secretarias tenían una noche de chicas – todas éramos mujeres – fuimos a la casa de alguien por la noche. No recuerdo las ocasiones. Cumpleaños, tal vez. En estas salas de estar de la clase obrera establecida no había libros; sorprendentemente a menudo había un piano. En el piano, o estante, tantas veces, había una foto enmarcada de 5x7 u 8x10 pulgadas en blanco y negro de un joven que brillaba de juventud y felicidad, mirando hacia arriba y hacia la izquierda, vestido con una gorra y los pliegues afilados de un uniforme militar. Eran fotos de graduación, de hijos que ahora sirven en el ejército.

Había tantos, a lo largo de los años, tan idénticos, tan insistentes en la ropa afilada con cuchillos que me parecieron un código. No podía entenderlo pero podía verlo: allí, insistente, brillando justo debajo de la superficie de la ropa, elusiva y claramente visible.

Uno de los maestros tuvo hijos gemelos; uno en el ejército en Alemania.

Me mostró una Polaroid que su

Myndir á píanó

M. F. McAuliffe

(Þýtt úr Ensku, Michael Lohr)

Á níunda áratugnum bjuggum við í L.A.

Ég vann sem skrifstofumaður í stórum meirihluta-minnihluta menntaskóla í South Bay. Stundum héldu skrifstofumennirnir og ritararnir stelpukvöld – við vorum allar konur – við fórum heim til einhvers um kvöldið. Ég man ekki tilefnin. Afmæli, kannski. Í þessum rótgrónu verkamannastofum voru engar bækur; ótrúlega oft væru þeir píanó. Á píanóinu eða hillu, svo oft, væri innrammað 5x7 eða 8x10 tommu svarthvít mynd af ungum manni glitrandi af æsku og hamingju, horfði upp og til vinstri, klæddur hettu og hnífsörður. skrúfur hermannabúninga. Þeir voru útskriftarmyndirnar, synir í þjónustunni.

Þeir voru svo margir, í gegnum árin, svo eins, svo ákaftir við hnífskvarða fötin að þeir slógu mig sem kóða sem ég gat ekki skilið að ég gæti séð - þarna, áleitinn, glampandi rétt fyrir neðan yfirborð klútsins, fimmti og í látlaus sjón.

Einn kennaranna átti tvíburasyni; einn var í hernum í Þýskalandi. Hann sýndi mér Polaroid sem sonur hans hafði sent: þrír eða fjórir mjög ungir menn í þreytu með bjórdósir og glottandi, háfleygandi fyrir neðan borðann fyrir ofan þá á mötuneytisveggnum. DÓMSDA-

hijo le había enviado: tres o cuatro hombres muy jóvenes con uniformes con latas de cerveza y sonrisas, *damecincos*, debajo de la pancarta en la pared de la cantina. **PERROS APOCALIPSIS**. Un terremoto de miedo y desamarre en esa foto, en mí mientras la miraba.

El fin del mundo: guerra, caos, fuego, furia, escombros, muerte; tierra y paisajes destrozados, ciudades, trigo destrozado e insectos y árboles...

La unidad había sido formada para funcionar allí, no podía funcionar correctamente en ningún otro lugar. «*Perros Apocalipsis*». El deleite alucinante y enculcado en esa frase.

Nos mudamos a Portland en 1992.

Durante la última semana de septiembre de 2002, para el primer aniversario del 9/11/01, el primero de los proyectos de arte público encargados por el Instituto de Arte Contemporáneo de Portland se instaló en un terreno vacío del centro. El artista y escultor de Portland Daniel Duford coció al horno cuatro enormes figuras de arcilla agachándose en el terreno vacante en Sudoeste Taylor y 3ª. Llamó a estas figuras golemos. Se inspiraron en fotos de prisioneros afganos en Guantánamo.

En la pared que da a la 3ª Ave. pintó dos figuras más, grandes desnudos masculinos con el mismo físico. Estaban de pie con las manos abiertas, mirando hacia afuera, representaciones de fuerza sin poder.

La instalación estaba destinada a durar un mes.

Vándalos atacó inmediatamente

GSHUNDAR. Jarðskjálfti ótta og losunar á þeirri mynd, í mér þegar ég horfði á hana.

Dómsdagur: heimsendir: stríð, glundroði, eldur, heift, rústir, dauði; mölbrotið land og landslag, borgir, mölbrotið hveiti og skordýr og tré...

Einingin hafði verið mynduð til að starfa þar, gat ekki virkað almennilega annars staðar. „Dómsdagshundar". Hin hugljúfa yndi í þessari setningu.

Við fluttum til Portland árið 1992.

Síðustu vikuna í september 2002, á fyrsta afmælisdegi 9/11/01, var fyrsta opinbera myndlistarverkefnið á vegum Portland Stofnunin Fyrir Samtímalist sett upp á lausri lóð í miðbænum. Portland listamaður og myndhöggvari Daniel Duford ofnaði fjórar risastórar krjúpandi leirfígúrur á lausu lóðinni í SW Taylor & 3rd. Hann kallaði þessar tölur golems. Þeir voru innblásnir af myndum af afgönskum föngum í Guantanamo.

Á vegginn sem snýr að 3rd Ave., málaði hann tvær fígúrur til viðbótar, stórar karlkyns nektarmyndir með sömu líkamsbyggingu. Þeir stóðu með opnum höndum, horfðu út á við, framsetningar af styrk án krafts.

Uppsetningin átti að standa í mánuð.

Vandals réðust strax á leirfígúrurnar. Fjórða nótt höfðu

a las figuras de arcilla. A la cuarta noche todos habían sido aplastados y psicosexualmente mutilados. Faltaban partes del cuerpo (manos, cabezas y pene).

Los fragmentos fueron empujados a pilas: el lote reclamado para estacionamiento, marcas de neumáticos coriendo a través depósitos de carbón del fuego original.

A pesar de las flores cortadas y otros regalos de dolor y respeto que los transeúntes habían dejado, los fragmentos apilados eran claramente torsos, muslos, manos. Las figuras eran todavía simulacros, también cuerpos como basura, también extremidades identificables y pedazos de arcilla del tamaño de piedra con el brillo de sangre mojada (después de la lluvia), arrojadas por los coches o el azar junto a un solo clavel o tallo desechado.

Desde la calle el terreno parecía restos de un sórdido crimen privado anónimo e irresoluble. De pie en él, se sentía como un campo de batalla.

Fue un campo de batalla, los escombros de demandes contradictorias sobre el espacio público, de ideas contradictorias sobre qué hacer con (o para) la vulnerabilidad, sobre a quién se le debería permitir un lugar en la atención del público, qué hacer con el desacuerdo o la incomodidad, cómo comportarse como individuos y grupos, sobre la diferencia entre bandas y bandidos, entre lo que sucede por la noche y lo que sucede por el día. Era lo que y en que cualquier momento podría

þau öll verið mölbrotin og limlest kynferðislega. Líkamshluta - hendur, höfuð og getnaðarlim – vantaði.

Brotunum var ýtt í hrúga: lóðin endurheimt fyrir bílastæði, dekkjamerki liggja í gegnum viðarleifar frá upphaflegu brennslunni.

Þrátt fyrir afskorin blóm og aðrar sorgar- og virðingargjafir sem vegfarendur skildu eftir voru brotahaugarnir greinilega búkur, læri, hendur. Fígúrurnar voru enn simulacra, enn líka líkamar sem rusl, auðþekkjanlegir útlimir og steinstórir leirbútar með skína blauts blóðs (eftir rigninguna), hent af bílum eða tilviljun við hlið einni nelliku eða hentum stöngli.

Frá götunni leit lóðin út eins og leifar af einhverjum svívirðilegum nafnlausum og óleysanlegum glæp. Þar sem hann stóð í honum leið það eins og vígvöllur.

Þetta var vígvöllur, rústurnar frá misvísandi fullyrðingum um opinbert rými, misvísandi hugmyndir um hvað gera ætti við (eða við) varnarleysi, um hver ætti að fá sæti í athygli almennings, hvað ætti að gera við ágreining eða vanlíðan, hvernig á að haga sér sem einstaklingar og hópar, munurinn á hljómsveitum og ræningjum, á því sem gerist á nóttunni og því sem gerist á daginn. Það var það sem hvert augnablik gæti brotnað í sundur og orðið, helvítismyndin á botni holu sem eðlilegt er að hylur venjulega.

Árið 2011, á tíu ára afmæli

romperse y convertirse – el paisaje infernal en el fondo de un agujero que normalmente cubre la normalidad.

En 2011, en el décimo aniversario del 9/11/01, Daniel y yo publicamos un libro de artista sobre la destrucción de los golemos. A pesar de documentar el sitio, sabía que no lo entendía completamente. De pie allí me sentí como si estuviera dentro de un holograma.

Hace poco tiempo una amiga me envió su anuncio de *Bookiversary*. Me di cuenta de que habían pasado diez años desde *Golems Waiting Redux*, raro y frágil, y ahora sin imprimir. Unos días más tarde comencé a recordar las fotos de graduación y la pérdida de todo el ancla en la polaroid de los *Perros Apocalipsis*.

Faltaban partes del cuerpo (manos, cabezas y pene).

¡Hay! Los secretos en las fotos y el terreno vacante se unieron como las mitades de una nuez en su concha.

En la izquierda hay la guerra, revelada como un vasto permiso, reuniendo todas las psicosis que ya se arremolinan a través de cualquier población, anexándolas, controlándolas y dirigiéndolas nominalmente, desencadenándolas. Los criminales de guerra superan en número a sus juicios.

A la derecha están las fotos de graduación, reveladas como promesas falsas. El código del pliegue afilado del cuchillo afirma que el potencial destructivo está bajo control, atado, que se puede tenerlo a raya, mandarlo; que está sin traición y nunca está traicionado. Y que siempre y sólo está liberado en defensa de lo bueno. *Q*

9/11/01, gáfum við Daníel út listamannabók um eyðingu gólanna. Þrátt fyrir að skrásetja síðuna vissi ég að ég skildi hana ekki að fullu. Þar sem ég stóð þarna leið mér eins og ég væri inni í heilmynd.

Fyrir stuttu síðan sendi vinur mér bókaafmælistilkynningu sína. Ég áttaði mig á því að það voru tíu ár síðan Golems Waiting Redux - sjaldgæft og viðkvæmt og úr prentun núna. Nokkrum dögum síðar fór ég að muna eftir útskriftarmyndunum og tapi á öllu akkeri í *Doomsday Dogs* polaroid.

Líkamshluta - hendur, höfuð og getnaðarlim — vantaði.

Þarna! Leyndarmálin á myndunum og lausa lóðin sameinuðust eins og helmingar valhnetu í skelinni.

Vinstra stríðið, opinberað sem víðtækt leyfi, safna saman öllum geðrofunum sem þegar þyrlast í gegnum hvaða íbúa sem er og innlima þá, að nafninu til stjórnandi og stýra þeim, sleppa þeim úr læðingi. Stríðsglæpamenn eru fleiri en réttarhöld þeirra.

Á réttum útskriftarmyndum, opinberaðar sem svikin loforð. Kóðinn fyrir hnífbeittu hvolfinu segir að eyðilegging-armöguleikar séu undir stjórn, taumlausir, lausir, stjórnanlegir, ósviknir og ósviknir. Og alltaf og aðeins sleppt til varnar hins góða. *Q*

Drugorazredni otac

Londonska magla je koncept o kojem ne znam ništa
iako sam uvijek mislila da ću putovati
Zaprimati svijet u dlačice,
depilirati ga i puštati šume, New York, Brač,
      Niagarine slapove niz odvode
Da ću samouvjereno kao predizborna kampanja
      secirati autoceste
i savijati ih u cijev svoje nerastezljive rodnice

Ali ovih dana osjećam se kao magla strogog
      britanskog naglaska
i težim kao cijela Zemlja koju nisam prisno upoznala
Biljke se boje rascvasti kraj mene
jer ću im nepovratno zaraziti zavodljivost
Stabla se boje pljunuti pupove iz vršaka
da im ne pojedem kisele zametke

Mjesecima plešem na oštrici nedjelje mada bih je
      trebala poslužiti
obitelji uz svoje marinirane oči i batake
Istina je da sam usamljena i u čekaonicama posvajam
svakog uglađenog djeda i njegovu staračku kožu

Jadna Persefona, ništa ne pomaže provjetriti komore
      srčanog mišića
Niti tješenje izmišljenim košticama nara kojima se
      igram gurajući ih u pupak
kao da su svaka mali Pluton, ničije mjesto u
      vakuumu
Nebo oguljeno do plave preskakuje u aorti kao da će
      ponovno potopiti planet
Znaš, sanjam nekad da šetamo parkom
Držiš me za ruku poput izvrsnog oca
Tako si pažljiv kad te sanjam

Šest mjeseci si, Zeuse
Šest mjeseci puštao
da me skidaju i siluju
u bestežinskom mraku

    — *Monika Herceg*

Second-rate Father

London fog is a concept I know nothing about
although I've always thought I would travel
Admit the world into my hairs,
shave it off and flush the shavings, New York, Brač and Niagara
       Falls down the drain
That I would dissect motorways, as cocky as an election
     campaign,
bend them into the tube of my inflexible vulva

But these days I feel like fog with a stern British accent
And I weigh as much as all that soil I never came to love
Plants are reluctant to bloom near me
lest I infect their seductiveness
Trees are chary of spitting out shoots
lest I eat their acrid foetuses

For months I've been dancing on Sunday's edge though I should
serve it to my family with drumsticks and my marinated eyes
The truth is I'm lonely and in waiting rooms I adopt
every courteous granddad and his old man skin

Poor Persephone, airing your heart chambers avails nothing
As does soothing yourself with imaginary pomegranate pips I
     playfully push into my navel
As if each were a little Pluto, a no-man's land in the vacuum
A sky stripped down to the blue skips in the aorta as if to re-flood
      the planet
You know, I sometimes dream of us walking in the park
You hold my hand like an excellent father
You're so considerate when I dream of you

For six months, Zeus
For six months you
let them strip me and rape me
in the weightless dark

   — Monika Herceg
    (Tr. fr. the Croatian, Mirza Purić)

Padre fallido

la niebla de Londres es un concepto del que no sé nada
aunque siempre he pensado habría viajar
admito el mundo en mis pelos,
afeitarlo y limpiar las virutas, Nueva York y Brač y las
      Cataratas del Niágara por el desagüe
que diseccionaría las autopistas, tan arrogantes como una
      campaña electoral,
dóblelos en el tubo de mi vulva inflexible

Pero en estos días me siento como niebla con un acento
      británico severo
y peso tanto como todo la tierra que nunca lluegé a amar
Las plantas tienen miedo a florecer cerca de mí
no sea que infecte su seductor
Los árboles tienen cuidado con escupir brotes
no sea que coma sus fetos acres

durante meses he estado bailando al borde del domingo,
      aunque debería
servirlo a mi familia con patas de pollo y mis ojos marinados
la verdad es que estoy solo, y en las salas de espera adopto
a cada abuelo amable y a su piel anciano

Pobre Perséfone, ventilando sus cámaras del corazón no sirve
      nada
como lo hace calmarse con pipas imaginarias de granada que
   caprichosamente empuje en mi ombligo
como si cada una fuera un pequeño plutón, tierra de nadie en
      el vacío
un cielo despojado a los saltos azules en la aorta como si
      volviera a inundar el planeta
usted sabe, a veces tengo sueños de nosotros andando en el
      parque
que sostiene mi mano como un padre excelente
eres tan considerado cuando sueño de usted

durante seis meses, Zeus
durante seis meses
les deja quitarme, vióleme
en la oscuridad sin peso

    — *Monika Herceg*
     (traducción, T. Warburton y Bajo y rvb)

Annað flokks faðir

Þoka í London er hugtak sem ég veit ekkert um
þó ég hafi alltaf haldið að ég myndi ferðast
Leyfðu heiminum í hárið á mér,
raka það af og skola spónana, New York, Brač og Niagara-
        fossarnir niður í holræsi
Að ég myndi kryfja hraðbrautir, eins krítandi og kosningabaráttu,
beygðu þá í slönguna á ósveigjanlegu dauðanum

En þessa dagana líður mér eins og þoka með ströngum breskum
        hreim
Og ég vega eins mikið og allur jarðvegurinn sem ég hef aldrei
        bundist við
Plöntur eru tregar til að blómstra nálægt mér
svo að ég smiti ekki tælandi þeirra
Tré eru táknræn við að spýta út skýtum
svo að ég borði ekki skarpa fóstur þeirra

Ég hef dansað mánuðum saman á sunnudagskantinum þó ég ætti
        að gera það
þjóna því fyrir fjölskyldu mína með trommustikum og
        marineruðum augum
Sannleikurinn er að ég er einmana og í biðstofum tileinka ég mér
sérhver kurteis afi og gamli maðurinn hans

Aumingja Persefóna, að láta í hjartahólf þín gagnast engu
Eins og að róa sjálfan sig með ímynduðum granatepliöddum ýti
        ég leikandi inn í nafla minn
Eins og hver og einn væri lítill Plútó, enginn staður í tómarúminu
Himinn sviptur niður í bláa skipið í ósæðinni eins og til að flæða
        jörðina aftur
Veistu, mig dreymir stundum um að við göngum í garðinn
Þú heldur í hönd mína eins og framúrskarandi faðir
Þú ert svo yfirvegaður þegar mig dreymir um þig

Í sex mánuði, Seifur
Í sex mánuði þú
láttu þá rífa mig og nauðga mér
í þyngdarlausu myrkri

    — *Monika Herceg*
      (*Þýtt úr Ensku, Michael Lohr*)

holocenas	holocene

holocenas

akių užuolaidos rašo man mergina. taip.
kiemo alyvos šakelė uždengia
man mano
pasaulį kontūrai ima meluoti ir
vidinis
kolumbas dar kartą atranda ne tą
indiją.
mes per daug visko matėm ir akių
užuolaidos nepajėgė to pridengti
mūsų
akys įsižiebė dar holoceno epochoje kuri
tęsiasi ligi šių dienų. kiek keista
gyventi
holoceno epochoje tačiau šioje
dienoje
išbūti yra dar keisčiau. akių
užuolaidos
rašo man mergina nepagalvo-
dama kad
jos ir ją uždengs ji liks kitame holoceno
epochos debesy praslinkusiam
prieš
vienuolika tūkstančių metų.
nupiešiu
jai mamutą ant urvo sienos. juk
esu per
vieną kūną nuo mirties. arba per
du.

— *Kęstutis Navakas*

holocene

the curtains of my eyes write a
woman. indeed.
the branch of lilac in my yard covers my
world whose contours begin to lie
and an inner
columbus discovers the wrong in-
dia again.
we saw too much of everything
and the curtains
of our eyes couldn't cover it and
our eyes
flamed up in the holocene era
which
continues to this day. it is strange
to live in
the holocene era but to remain in
this day
is even more strange. the curtains
of my eyes
write a woman for me and fail to
consider that
they will cover her as well and
she will be
in another cloud of the holocene
that slunk by
eleven thousand years ago. i'll
draw
her a mammoth on the cave wall.
after all
i'm just one body away from
death. maybe two.

— *Kęstutis Navakas*
(Tr. fr. the Lithuanian, Rimas
Uzgiris)

Holocen

zasłony moich oczu malują kobietę. Istotnie.
gałąź bzu na podwórku zasłania
mój
świat którego kontury zaczynają
kłamać a wewnętrzny
kolumb ponownie odkrywa nie-
prawdziwe indie.
widzieliśmy zbyt wiele wszyst-
kiego a zasłony
naszych oczu nie mogły tego zakryć i nasze oczy
zaogniły się w erze holocenu
która
trwa do dziś. to dziwne żyć
w erze holocenu lecz trwać w
dniu dzisiejszym
jest nawet dziwniej. zasłony moich oczu
malują kobietę dla mnie a ja nie
biore pod uwage że
one także ją zasłonią i będzie
w innej chmurze holocenu która
przemknęła obok
jedenaście tysięcy lat temu. nary-
suję
dla niej mamuta na ścianie jaski-
ni. w końcu
dzieli mnie tylko jedno ciało od
śmierci. może dwa.

– *Kęstutis Navakas*
(Tłumaczenie: Joanna
Rosińska)

голоцен

завесы моих глаз пишут
женщину. именно.
ветвь сирени во дворе накрывает
мой
мир контуры которого начинают
расплываться и внутренний
колумб снова открывает не ту
индию.
мы видели слишком много и
завесы
наших глаз не могли этого
скрыть и наши глаза
вспыхнули в эпоху голоцена
продолжающуюся по сей день.
странно жить в
эпоху голоцена но оставаться в
нашем времени
еще более странно. завесы моих
глаз
пишут за меня женщину и не
учитывают
что накроет и ее и она окажется
в другом облаке голоцена
проскользнувшим мимо
одиннадцать тысяч лет назад. я
нарисую
ей мамонта на стене пещеры. в
конце концов,
я всего в одном теле от смерти.
может быть, в двух.

– *Кястутис Навакас*
(перевел на русский Андрей
Сен-Сеньков)

holocen

zastori mojih očiju ispisuju ženu.
doista.
grana jorgovana u mojem dvorištu
pokriva moj
svijet čiji obrisi započinju laž i
unutarnji
kolumbo nanovo otkriva pogrešnu
indiju.
previše toga smo vidjeli i zastori
naših očiju
nisu to mogli prekriti i oči su nam
planule u holocenu koji dandanas
traje.
Čudno je živjeti u holocenu no
ostati u današnjici još je čudnije.
Zastori mojih očiju ispisuju mi ženu
no zaboravljaju
da će pokriti i nju da će i ona
nestati
u još jednom oblaku holocena koji
nam se prikrao prije jedanaest
tisućljeća. Nacrtat ću joj
mamuta na zidu špilje. Na kraju
krajeva, samo me jedno tijelo dijeli
od smrti. Možda dva.

– *Kęstutis Navakas*
(prijevod s engleskoga, Ana
Katana)

holoceno

las cortinas de mis ojos escriben una
                            mujer. en efecto.
la rama lila en mi patio cubre mi mundo
cuyos contornos comienzan a mentir y un
columbus interior descubre de nuevo la
                    India equivocada.
Miramos demasiado de todo y las
                    cortinas
de nuestros ojos no podían cubrirlo y
                    nuestros ojos
se encendieron en la era del holoceno que
continúa hasta hoy. es extraño vivir en
la era del holoceno, pero permanecer en
                    este día
es aún más extraño. las cortinas de mis
                ojos
escribir a una mujer para mí y no llega a
            considerar que
la cubrirán también y ella será en
otra nube del holoceno que se escabulló
hace once mil años. La dibujaré a ella un
                mamut
en la pared de la cueva. después de todo
sólo estoy a un cuerpo de la muerte. tal
                vez dos.

— *Kęstutis Navakas*
(Traduccion, T. Warburton y Bajo y
rvb)

The Lesser Light

I'm tied down tight in Vilnius
and the sky is drizzling again.
Thunder trundles closer and
I'm sitting here in the corridor
of my copacetic flat where
the lamp has gone out in the hall
because I've been so stock still
as wild wind caroms through
the slushing, shushing spruce out-
    side
while a jetplane groans to ground
and the earth circumnavigates a
    star
like some mad Magellan repeat-
    edly
at unimaginable speed – the star
    itself
flung into a vast, fast-expanding
whatness out to where? Yet, here
my fingers, eyes and heart make
but tiny flickers like the whispers
of the little boy's breath on my
    neck.

– Rimas Uzgiris

Mažesnė šviesa

Esu ilgam susaistytas su Vil-
    nium,
o iš dangaus vėl dulkia.
Griaustinis sudunda arčiau, o
    aš
sėdžiu čia, savo jaukaus buto
koridoriuje ir prieškambaryje
užgęsta lempa – nejudu
    sustingęs,
kol pašėlęs vėjas siaučia
    varvančiose
šniokščiančiose eglėse už lango
kol dejuoja leisdamasis
    lėktuvas
ir žemė skrieja aplink žvaigždę
beprotišku greičiu, vėl ir vėl
it pamišęs Magelanas – pati
žvaigždė išsviesta į
    neaprėpiamą
kažikur, į vis platėjantį kažką.
    Bet čia
mano pirštai, akys ir širdis
    virpa
vos girdimai it mažo berniuko
kvėpavimas ant mano kaklo.

– Rimas Uzgiris
(iš anglų kalbos vertė
Marius Burokas)

Minna ljósið

Ég er bundinn þétt í Vilníus
og himinn driðar aftur.
Þrumur þrumast nær og
Ég sit hérna á ganginum
af copacetic íbúðinni minni þar
lampinn hefur slokknað í forsto-
                                    funni
af því að ég hef verið svo mikið
                        lager ennþá
eins og villtur vindur hleypur í
                                    gegn
kraumurinn, kjaftagranið fyrir
                                    utan
meðan þotuflugvél stynur til
                                    jarðar
og jörðin snýst um stjörnu
eins og einhver vitlaus Magellan
                                    ítrekað
á ólýsanlegum hraða – sjálfri stjör-
                                    nunni
hent í víðáttumikla, ört stækkandi
hvað út í hvert? Samt, hérna
fingur mínir, augu og hjarta gera
en pínulítill blikkar eins og hvíslið
andardráttar litla drengsins á hál-
                        sinum á mér.

– *Rimas Uzgiris*
(Þýtt úr Ensku, Michael Lohr)

Mniejsze światło

Jestem uwiązany w Wilnie na
                                    dobre
i niebo znowu siąpi.
Grzmot toczy się zbliżając
a ja siedzę w korytarzu
mego niezłego mieszkanka
żarówka wypalona w holu
bo ja zastygłem w bezruchu
gdy szalony wiatr przebija się
                                    przez
mokry, ośnieżony świerk na
                                    dworze
gdy odrzutowiec monotonnie
                        warkocze lądując
a Ziemia okrąża gwiazdę
jak jakiś oszalały Magellan,
                                    ponownie
z niewyobrażalną prędkością, a
                        sama gwiazda
wystrzelona w głęboką prze-
                                    strzeń,
jak jakiś szybko rosnący byt
pędzi, ale dokąd? Zaś tu
moje palce, oczy i serce
ledwie migoczą jak szept
                                    oddechu
małego chłopca na mojej szyi.

– *Rimas Uzgiris*
(Tłumaczenie: Joanna Rosiń-
ska)

La luz menor

Estoy atado en Vilna
y el cielo llovizna de nuevo.
Truena rueda más cerca y
me siento aquí en el pasillo
de mi apartamento copacético donde
la lámpara se ha apagado en la sala
porque he estado tan complamente quieto
mientras carambolas de viento salvaje a
        través del
árbol de abeto que sacudida y sacidida
        fuera
y un avión se estremece a la tierra
y la tierra circunnavega una estrella
en como uno Magallanes loco repetidam-
        ente
con velocidad inimaginable: la estrella
        misma
se envolvió en un vasto, rápido-
        expandiéndose,
¿entrese hasta dónde? Sin embargo, aquí
mis dedos, ojos y corazón hacen
solo pequeños destellos como los susurros
del aliento del niño en mi cuello.

    – Rimas Uzgiris
      (Traducción, T. Warburton y Bajo y rvb)

Ang mas kaunting liwanag

Abala ako sa Vilnius
at ang langit ay umaambon na
naman Ang kulog ay gumugulong palapit
Nakaupo ako dito sa pasilyo ng aking
maayos na apartamento kung saan ang ilaw
 sa bulwagan ay napundi dahil sa hindi
ko pagkilos habang ang malakas na
hangin ay bumabangga sa humahampas na
basang puno sa labas habang
ang isang eroplano ay humahalinghing
sa lupa at ang mundo ay naglalayag ng
        pagka bilis
katulad ng isang baliw na Magellan – ang
        bituin
ay pumukol sa isang malawak, mabilis na
lumalawak na ano patungo saan?
                Gayunman, dito
ang mga daliri ko, mata at puso ay
kumuti-kutitap na waring bulong ng
        paghinga
ng isang maliit na batang lalake sa aking
        leeg.

    – *Rimas Uzgiris*
     (halaw, Art Tolen)

Dvinarė žvaigždė

man labai patiko naktys, kai dar visai mažiukas
jis ropštės – ar veikiau mėgino ropštis – iš lovelės,
kad galėtų būt su tėčiu jo didžiulėj lovoj.

mama su naujagime miegojo mergaičių kambary,
ant patiesto čiužinio, susirišusi su ta
maža budria burnyte, vis žįstančia ir žįstančia

priklaupęs pakeldavau jį iš lovelės, paguldydavau
        šalia,
nė viena naktis su jokia moterimi neprilygo šiam
        jausmui:
abu skriejom vienoj orbitoje, nesusiliesdami, ir visa-
        dos kartu,

kol naujagimė paaugo, žmona pakilo iš savo guolio
ir man teko pirkti namą su atskirais kambariais.

    – Rimas Uzgiris
      (iš anglų kalbos vertė Marius Burokas)

Binary Star

i loved those nights when not yet two
he would climb – or try – from crib to be
with daddy in his king-size bed.

mommy slept with baby in the girls'
    room,
attached across the floor on a mattress to
the wakeful mouth, suckling sucking
    more…

and i would kneel and lift him in with
    me,
no night with any woman could
    compare:
we two in orbit, never touching, always
    one

until the baby grew, my wife rose off the
    ground,
and i had to buy a house with separate
    rooms.

    – Rimas Uzgiris

Tvöfaldur stjarna

ég elskaði þessar nætur þegar ekki enn tvær
hann myndi klifra – eða reyna – frá barnarúmi til að
                        vera
með pabba í king-size rúminu sínu.

mamma svaf með barninu í stelpuherberginu,
fest yfir gólfið á dýnu til
vakandi munninn, sogandi sog meira ...

og ég myndi krjúpa og lyfta honum inn með mér,
engin nótt með neinni konu gæti borið saman:
við tveir á braut, aldrei snert, alltaf einn

þangað til barnið óx, reis kona mín af jörðu,
og ég þurfti að kaupa hús með aðskildum
                        herbergjum.

> *– Rimas Uzgiris*
> *(Þýtt úr Ensku, Michael Lohr)*

Kaksoistähti

rakastin niitä yötä, kun en vielä kahta
hän kiipesi – tai yritti – sängystä
isän kanssa king-size-vuoteessa.

äiti nukkui vauvan kanssa tyttöjen huoneessa,
kiinnitetty lattian poikki patjalla
hereillä oleva suu, imee enemmän imee ...

ja polvistuin ja nosin hänet kanssani,
mikään yö kenenkään naisen kanssa ei voinut verrata:
me kaksi kiertoradalla, koskematta koskaan, aina yksi

kunnes vauva kasvoi, vaimoni nousi maasta,
ja minun piti ostaa talo, jossa oli erilliset huoneet.

> *– Rimas Uzgiris*
> *(Käännetty Englant tekijän, Michael Lohr)*

Estrella binaria

Me encantó esas noches cuando aún no tenía dos
que subiría – o intentaría – de cuna para ser
con papá en su cama extralargo.

mamá dormía con el bebé en el cuarto de las niñas,
junto al suelo sobre un colchón para
la boca despierta, chupando más, más...

y yo lo arrodillaría y lo levantaría conmigo,
ninguna noche con ninguna mujer podía comparar:
nosotros dos en órbita, nunca tocando, siempre uno

hasta que el bebé creciera, mi esposa se levantó del
                    suelo,
y tuve que comprar una casa con cuartos distinctos.

– *Rimas Uzgiris*
  (Traducción, T. Warburton y Bajo y rvb)

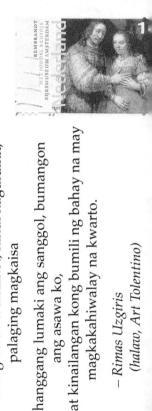

Buklod Bitwin

Noon hindi pa sya dalawa, kinagigiliwan ko
        ang
mga gabing tumatakas sya o nagtatangkang
        tumakas sa kanyang
        kuna upang tumabi
sa kanyang ama sa Malaki nyang kama.

Natulog ang ina sa isang kutson na kasama
        ang
sanggol sa kuwarto ng mga babae nakadikit
        sa isang
gising na bibig, sumisipsip sumususo at
        higit pa....

at luluhod ako at kakargahin ko siya,
hindi hihigit dito kahit anong gabing kapi-
        ling ko ang isang babae;
kaming dalawa umiikot, hindi nagdidikit,
        palaging magkaisa

hanggang lumaki ang sanggol, bumangon
        ang asawa ko,
at kinailangan kong bumili ng bahay na may
        magkakahiwalay na kwarto.

– *Rimas Uzgiris*
  (halaw, Art Tolentino)

Binarna zvijezda

obožavao sam one noći kad se on
ni dvije godine star – penjao – ili
       pokušavao
popeti iz krevetića u tatin veliki krevet.

mama je tad spavala s bebom u sobi za
       djevojčice,
na madracu, privčršćena za vječito budna
ustašca, koja samo sišu i sišu...

tad bih kleknuo i podigao ga k sebi,
nijedna noć uz ženu nije vrijedna uspo-
       redbe:
nas dvojica u vrtnji, ne dodirujemo se, a
           kao jedan smo

dok beba nije porasla, moja se gospođa
       digla s poda
a ja sam morao kupiti kuću sa zasebnim
       spavaćim sobama.

– Rimas Uzgiris
(prijevod s engleskoga, Ana Katana)

Wednesday's
Mail

Suddenly, I know what is in the package. It's
another piece of child, sent to drive me crazy. The
    package
is just the right size to hold either
a bunch of little bits
or one big piece, a torso, perhaps,
a well-cushioned head.
I gently pick the package up and put it
in the spare bedroom with the rest of the packages
the tiny finger-sized boxes
the still-sealed shoeboxes concealing bare, uncalloused
    feet.

The rest of the mail sits waiting to be sorted through
I flip through pizza coupons, form invitations
to local beheadings, a flyer advertising the opening
of a new Baptist church in my neighborhood.
At the very bottom of the stack is a large manila
    envelope,
thick with paperwork. I open it, curiously, not
recognizing the handwriting, watch in confusion
as photographs of people I don't know
pour out onto the floor.

    – Holly Day

LIETUVA 1,35

Mail
srijede

Odjednom, znam što je u paketu. To je
još jedno dijete, poslano da me izludi.
     Paket
je upravo odgovarajuće veličine za držanje ili
gomile sitnih komadića
ili jednog velikog komada, torza, možda,
okrugle glave.
Nježno uzmem paket i stavim ga
u gostinjsku sobu s ostatkom paketa
malene kutije veličine prstiju
još uvijek zatvorene kutije za cipele koje skrivaju bosa,
     nežuljevita stopala.

Ostatak pošte sjedi čekajući da se sortira
prelistavam kupone za pizzu, oblikujem pozivnice
lokalnim dekapitacijama, letak kojim se oglašava
     otvaranje nove baptističke
          crkve u mojem susjedstvu.
Na samom dnu hrpe je velika manila
     omotnica,
debela s papirologijom. Otvorim je, znatiželjno,
ne prepoznajući rukopis, gledajući zbunjeno
kako se fotografije ljudi koje ne poznajem
prosipaju po podu.

    – Holly Day
    (prijevod na hrvatski, Dijana Jakovac)

Miðvikudagspósturinn

Allt í einu veit ég hvað er í pakkanum. Það er
annað stykki barn, sent til að brjála mig.
    Pakkinn
er bara rétt stærð til að hafa annað hvort
fullt af litlum bitum
eða eitt stórt stykki, búkur,
vel púðuð höfuð.
Ég tek pakkann varlega upp og legg
í varaherberginu með afganginum af
                pökkunum
pínulitlu fingurstærðu kassana
enn innsigluðu skókassana sem leyna berum,
           ósönnuðum fótum.

Restin af póstinum situr og bíður þess að
           verða flokkaður í gegnum
Ég fletti í gegnum pizzukuponur, fæ boð
til hálsmeðferðar á staðnum, flugmaður sem
           auglýsir opnunina
af nýrri baptistakirkju í hverfinu mínu.
Neðst í staflinum er stórt umslag Manila,
þykkt með pappírsvinnu. Ég opna það,
           forvitinn, ekki
kannast við rithöndina, horfðu í rugl
sem ljósmyndir af fólki sem ég þekki ekki
hella út á gólfið.

      — Holly Day
       (Þýtt úr Ensku, Michael Lohr)

Correo del miércoles

De repente, sé lo que hay en el paquete. Es
otro pedazo de niño, enviado para volverme insano.
        El paquete
es del tamaño adecuado para sostener
un montón de pedacitos diminutos
o una pieza grande, un torso, tal vez,
una cabeza bien acolchada.
Suavemente recojo el paquete y lo pongo
en el dormitorio de repuesto con el resto de los
                          paquetes
las pequeñas cajas del tamaño de un dedo
las cajas de zapatos aún selladas que ocultan los pies
        desnudos y sin callosidades.

El resto del correo está a la espera de ser ordenado
hojeo cupones de pizza, formulario invitaciones a
decapitaciones locales, un folleto anunciando la
        apertura
de una nueva iglesia bautista en mi vecindario.
En la parte inferior de la pila hay un gran sobre de
        manila,
grueso con documentación. Lo abro, curiosamente,
sin reconocer la escritura, ver con confusión
mientras fotografías de personas que no conozco
se vierten en el suelo.

    – Holly Day
    (Traducción, T. Warburton y Bajo y rvb)

Tug-of-War: It's winter, there isn't much one can do in the playground during recess, my friends and I are playing tug-of-war.

I'm strong, they're not. I'm on one side, they're on the other. I can pull so hard that they fall but I don't.

We're not using a rope, we're using the scarf my grandmother knitted for me and that I'm supposed to wear around my neck when it's cold outside.

The scarf is getting stretched as we battle. My mother will be furious and punish me when I get home but what choice do I have if I want to have friends to play with?

— *Tanni Haas*

Διελκυστίνδα: Είναι χειμώνας, δεν υπάρχουν και πολλά να κάνει κανείς στην παιδική χαρά κατά τη διάρκεια της ύφεσης, οι φίλοι μου και εγώ παίζουμε διελκυστίνδα.

Είμαι δυνατός, αυτοί δεν είναι. Εγώ είμαι από τη μια πλευρά, αυτοί από την άλλη. Μπορώ να τραβήξω τόσο δυνατά ώστε να πέσουν, αλλά δεν το κάνω.

Δεν χρησιμοποιούμε σχοινί, αλλά το κασκόλ που έπλεξε η γιαγιά μου για μένα και που υποτίθεται θα φοράω στο λαιμό μου όταν κάνει κρύο έξω.

Το κασκόλ τεντώνεται καθώς παλεύουμε. Η μητέρα μου θα γίνει έξαλλη και θα με τιμωρήσει όταν γυρίσω σπίτι, αλλά τι επιλογή έχω αν θέλω να έχω φίλους να παίξω.

— *Τάνι Χάας*
(μεταφρασμένο, Κοντοπούλου Α. Κωνσταντίνα)

Fuego de tira: Es invierno, no hay mucho que hacer en el patio de recreo durante el recreo, así que mis amigos y yo jugamos al fuego de tira.

Soy fuerte, ellos no lo son. Yo estoy de un lado, ellos del otro. Puedo tirar tan fuerte que se caen pero no me caigo.

No usamos cuerda, usamos la bufanda que mi abuela tejió para mí y que se supone que debo envolver alrededor de mi cuello si hace frío afuera.

La bufanda se estira mientras luchamos. Mi mamá será lívida y me castigará cuando llegue a casa, ¿pero qué opción tengo si quiero tener amogos con los que jugar?

— *Tanni Haas*
(Traducción, T. Warburton y Bajo y rvb)

Przeciąganie liny: Jest zima i nie ma nic do roboty na podwóru szkolnym na przerwie. Moi koledzy i ja bawimy się w przeciąganie liny.

Ja jestem silny a oni nie. Ja ciągnę z jednej strony, oni z drugiej. Mogę pociągnąć tak mocno, że się poprzewracają, ale tak nie robię.

Właściwie to nie ciągniemy liny, ale szalik który babcia mi zrobiła. Miałem go nosić na szyi jak jest zimno.

Szalik rozciąga się gdy się mocujemy. Mama będzie wściekła i będzie kara jak wrócę, ale co robić jak chce mieć kolegów do zabawy?

— *Tanni Haas*
(Tłumaczenie: Joanna Rosińska)

Παλιοί φίλοι Όταν συναντηθείς με έναν παλιό φίλο, γείρε πίσω στην καρέκλα σου και άσε τον φίλο σου να αρχίσει την κουβέντα. Καθώς ο φίλος σου σκύβει προς τα εμπρός στην καρέκλα του, άκουσε προσεκτικά όλες τις λέξεις που απελευθερώνει. Οι λέξεις, θα έρθουν για σένα. Κάποιες αργά, κάποιες γρήγορα, όμως κάποιες με ακριβώς τη σωστή ταχύτητα για να σε βγάλουν από τη σύγχυση και να σε επιστρέψουν στην βεβαιότητα της νιότης.

– *Τάννι Χάας*
(μεταφρασμένο, Βασιλεία Οικονόμου)

Old Friends When you get together with an old friend, lean back in your chair and wait for your friend to do the talking. As your friend leans forward in his chair, listen carefully to all the words that he releases. The words, they will be coming for you. Some slowly, some fast, but some at just the right speed to lift you out of your confusion and into the certainty of youth.

— *Tanni Haas*

523 SE Morrison St
Portland, OR 97214

503-236-2665

Viejos amigos: Cuando te reúnas con un viejo amigo, inclínese detrás en su silla y espere a que su amigo hable. Mientras tu amigo se inclina hacia adelante en su silla, escucha atentamente todas las palabras que él libera. Las palabras, vendrán por ti. Algunos lentamente, algunos rápidos, pero algunos a la velocidad justa para sacarte de tu confusión y entrar en la certeza de la juventud.

— *Tanni Haas*
(Traducción, T. Warburton y Bajo y rvb)

Starzy Przyjaciele: Gdy spotkasz się ze starym przyjacielem, rozsiądź się w fotelu i poczekaj aż on zainicjuje rozmowę. Gdy przyjaciel w swym fotelu pochyli się ku tobie, słuchaj uważnie wszystkich płynących słów. Bo słowa popłyną dla ciebie. Niektóre powoli, inne szybko, lecz będa też takie, płynące w tempie stosownym by unieść cię ponad zdezorientowanie, wprost do młodzieńczej pewności.

— *Tanni Haas*
(Tłumaczenie: Joanna Rosińska)

---

wear a mask!

Nosite maske!

Kanna maski!

Maskenpflicht!

Vera með grímu!

Dėvėk kaukę!

носи маску!

ino se enferme, use una máscara!

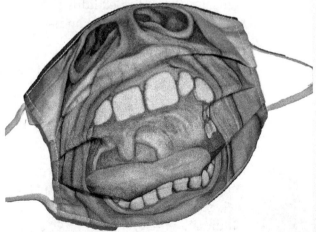

Seitse Lille

1.

kehas kumab väikene kivi. peale surma
  jääb alles vaid kivi, ent me ei leia
  seda ealgi üles.

2.

kreegipuuõied langevad suurematele
  asjadele, rabarberilehtedele,
  karjamaa putukate küüsis kulunud
  mantlile. leina juuksed katavad mu
  õlgu.

asetan su silmadele lilli.

kas näed maailma mis ei ole lill?

3.

kui hakkad metsas surema, võid
  kuulda metskitse südamelööke.

4.

elavad neelavad valgust ja leinajad
  neelavad vett.

oled nüüd jumalakartmatu ja kõrbetuul
  ja ma alustan su hääle kildude
  korjamist randadelt, kus kõndisid.

5.

kuulen sind lainete mühinas, pleekinud
  merekarpides ja soolatud alades.
  heli on lubjastunud valgus. sinu
  käed, majakas mu peas.

öö, pimestatud vares, laskub mu
  keha oksa peale. unetuse põhjavesi
  voogab. soolatud alades magavad
  meie sündimata lapsed. meie
  sündimata linnad.

Seven Flowers

1.

there is a small, luminous stone within the
    body. when you die, only the stone
    remains, though we will never find it.

2.

petals fall from a damson tree over larger
    things, the rhubarb leaves, the field's
    insect-thinned coat. the hair of grief is
    spreading over my shoulders.

I place flowers over your eyes.

do you see a world that is not flower?

3.

if you begin to die in a forest, you may
    hear the heartbeat of deer.

4.

the living swallow light and the grieving
    swallow water.

now you are debacle and sirocco, so I will
    begin to collect the fragments of your
    voice from the shores you walked.

5.

I hear you in the ocean noise, in
    discolored shells and sheets of salt. a
    sound is calcified light. your hands, a
    lighthouse in my head.

night, the blinded crow, lands on the
    branch of me. the groundwater of
    insomnia expands. sheets of salt are
    where our unborn children sleep. our
    unborn cities.

6.

enamasti leitakse jõest alumiiniumpurke, kuid kord leidis
mees Seine'i jõest terve Gaeli laeva. jõest võib leida
juuksed, terve keha, aastatuhandeid vana. midagi sinust
jääb korjamiseks alles. keegi punub su hõbekangast
juukseid. keegi näeb, et su suu on tüümian, sidrunite uni.
keegi hoiab su kätt hävinud sillal.

7.

täna olid valguse käed julmad, nagu käed mis nõeluvad
kinni madude suud.

on keel, mida suudavad kõneleda vaid nemad, kellel on keel
suust välja lõigatud. iga koit kuulen nende laulu. Iga koit
saab sellest sinu hääl.

valgus, vili mis mädaneb ja tumeneb me kehade vahel.

  – Triin Paja

Sedam cvjetova

1.

u tijelu je maleni, svjetleći kamen.
      kada umreš, samo kamen ostaje, ali
      teško da ćemo ga pronaći.

2.

latice padaju sa stabla Damsona preko većih stvari,
      lišće rabarbare, poljski prekrivač proriječen
          kukcima.
      kosa tug

stavljam cvijeće preko tvojih očiju.

vidite li svijet koji nije cvijet?

3.

ako počnete umirati u šumi, možda ćete čuti
otkucaje srca jelena.

6.

mostly, one finds aluminum cans in a river, but once, a man found
   an entire Gallic ship in the Seine. one may find hair in a bog, a
   whole body, thousands of years old. something of you can still
   be collected. someone will braid your hair of samite. someone
   will recognize your mouth as thyme, as the sleep of lemon
   blossoms. someone will hold your hand on a devastated bridge.

7.

today the hands of light became heartless, like hands that stitch up
   the mouths of snakes.

there is a language only those with their tongues cut out may utter.
   each dawn, I hear their singing. each dawn, it becomes your
   voice.

light, the fruit that rots and blackens between my body and yours.

   – Triin Paja

Siete Flores

1.

hay una pequeña y luminosa piedra dentro del cerpo.
   cuando mueres, sólo la piedra permanece, aunque nunca la
   encontramos.

2.

pétalos caen de una ciruela damascena sobre cosas más
   grandes, las hojas del ruibarbo, el pelaje del campo
   adelgazado por insectos. el pelo de pena se extiende sobre
   mis hombros.

Yo coloqué flores sobre tus ojos.

¿ves un mundo que no es la flor?

3.

si usted comienza a morir en un bosque, puede oír el latido
   del corazón de los ciervos.

4.

živući gutaju svjetlost i tugujući gutaju
    vodu.

sada si nepogoda i jugo, pa ću početi skupljati
    fragmente vašeg glasa s obala
    kojima ste hodali.

5.

Čujem vas u buci oceana, u izblijedjelim školjkama
    i plahtama soli. zvuk je kalcificirana svjetlost.
    tvoje ruke, svjetionik u mojoj glavi.

noć, zaslijepljena vrana, sliјеće na moju granu.
    podzemna voda nesanice se širi. plahte su
    soli gdje naša nerođena djeca spavaju.
    naši nerođeni gradovi.

6.

uglavnom se u rijeci nađu aluminijske limenke, ali jednom je čovjek
    pronašao čitavu galiju u
Seni. može se naći kosa u močvari, cijelo tijelo,
tisućama godina staro. nešto od vas može se još uvijek prikupiti.
    netko će vam isplesti kosu od brokata. netko će vam prepoznati
    usta kao timijan, kao što san limuna cvjeta.
netko će vas držati za ruku na razorenom
    mostu.

7.

danas su ruke svjetlosti postale bešćutne,
poput ruku koje šivaju usta zmija.

postoji jezik koji mogu izgovoriti samo oni
kojima su jezici izvađeni. svake zore, čujem njihovo pjevanje. svake
    zore, postaje tvoj glas.

svjetlo, plod koji trune i crni između
mog tijela i tvoga.

    – Triin Paja
    (prijevod na hrvatski, Dijana Jakovac)

4.

los que viven beben luz, los que lloran con dolor beben
agua.

ahora eres el fracaso y sirocco, así que comienzo a
recoger sus fragmentos de voz de las costas que antes
caminaste.

5.

te oigo en el ruido del océano, en conchas descoloridas y
hojas de sal. suenan como luz calcificada. tus manos, un
faro en mi cabeza.

la noche, el cuervo cegado, cae sobre mi rama. el agua
subterránea del insomnio se se amplía. las hojas de
sal son donde nuestros niños no nacidos duermen.
nuestras ciudades aún no nacidas.

6.

En su mayoría, se encuentran latas de aluminio en el
río, pero una vez, un hombre encontró un barco galo
entero en el río Sena. uno puede encontrar el pelo en
un pantano, un cuerpo entero, de miles de años de
edad. algo de usted todavía puede ser recogido. alguien
trenzará su pelo de samita. alguien reconocerá su boca
como el tomillo, como los sueños de las flores de limón.
alguien sostendrá su mano en un puente devastado.

7.

hoy las manos de la luz se volvieron sin corazón, como
las manos que cosen las bocas de serpientes.

hay un idioma que solo los que tienen lenguas cortadas
pueden pronunciar. cada alba, oigo su canto. cada alba,
se hace su voz.

luz, la fruta que se pudre y se ennegrece entre mi cuerpo
y suyo.

> – *Triin Paja*
> *(Traducción, T. Warburton y Bajo y rvb)*

Bluz pod košem

Josip Razum

„Jebote, opet šutira!", rekao sam Grbi dok smo sjedili na rubovima otužnog popodneva i polako uranjali ostatke kave i ručka u duhanski dim.

Davor je bio na igralištu preko puta nas, a lopte su parale mrežicu jedna za drugom. Takav je već tjednima, pričao sam Grbi, nakon što je odjednom izašao iz kuće i počeo pucati na koš.

„Čuo sam da je to bilo nakon što se posvađao s Vanjom...?"

Da, valjda, a sada je stalno tamo, ujutro prije posla i kasno navečer, vikendima gotovo po cijele dane. Svašta se pričalo po kvartu, njegova žena je plakala na kavama s frendicama i jebala mu mater kad su izašle sve skupa. Rekla mi je Monika. Čak me i tražila da pričam s njim, ali ne bih znao što da mu kažem. Dugo se nismo čuli, još od kad smo kao klinci skupa trenirali košarku. U nekom drugom vremenu, lošem klubu s trenerima alkoholi-

The Blues Under the Hoop

Josip Razum
(tr. by J. Razum)

"Fuck it, man, he's shooting again!", I said to Grba as we sat on the edges of a gloomy afternoon, slowly immersing the remnants of our coffee and lunch in tobacco smoke.

Davor was on the playground right across us. Balls swishing through the hoop, one after another. He's been like that for weeks, I told Grba, after he suddenly went out the door and began shooting hoops.

"I heard that it happened after that argument with Vanja...?"

Yeah, I guess. Now he's there all the time. Mornings before work. Late through the evening. All weekend. Stories in the neighbourhood say his wife had a good cry over coffee with friends about his raising hell during a night on the town. Monika told me. She even asked me to talk to him...but I wouldn't know what to say.

We hadn't heard from each other for ages, probably since we'd had basketball training together. The club was really bad, coaches had major drinking problems and lot of dam-

Los Blues Bajo del Aro

Josip Razum

(traducción, T. Warburton y Bajo y rvb)

«¡A la mierda, hombre, está chutando de nuevo! », le dije a Grba, mientras nos sentábamos en los bordes de una tarde sombría, lentamente sumergiendo los restos de nuestro café y almuerzo en el humo del tabaco.

Davor estaba en el patio de recreo justo a nuestro lado... las pelotas volando a través del aro, una tras otra. Ha sido así durante semanas, le dije a Grba, después de que de repente salió de la casa y comenzó a chutar al baloncesto.

«¿Escuché que ocurrió después de ese argumento con Vanja...?»

Sí, supongo. Ahora está allí todo el tiempo, las mañanas antes del trabajo, a altas horas de la noche y durante todos los fines de semana. Los cuentos del vecindario dicen que su esposa tuvo un buen llanto mientras tomaba un café con amigas acerca de él armando un escándolo cuando salieron por la en la ciudad. Monika me dijo. También me pidió que hablara con él, pero no sabía qué decirle.

No habíamos sabido el uno del otro durante siglos, probablemente desde que habíamos entrenado

VILNIUS REVIEW

The Online Magazine for Lithuanian Literature

vilnius review
sirvydo st. 6, lt — 01101
vilnius, lithuania
vilniusreview.com

čarima, potrganim parketima i starcima koji nisu ni dolazili jer su valjda htjeli da se bavimo nogometom. Bilo je zabavno unatoč svemu, bile su to lijepe godine. Ne sjećam se više ni zašto smo prestali, bit će da smo počeli pušiti i izlaziti, bili smo klinci, kažem ti. Žao mi je u svakom slučaju. Pokrenulo se nešto u meni, Grba, i ne znam gdje mu je kraj.

Loše spavam, sanjam havajske plaže iz dokumentaraca, neke djevojke koje sam poznavao, pa onda sivilo i smrt. Budim se kraj svoje žene i osjećam se kao izdajnik u tom svijetu između snova i jave, jedinom koji mi se čini istinitim. Odlazim do sina u sobu i teško mi ga je pogledati. Shvati me, molim te.

Piljili smo jedno vrijeme tako jedan u drugoga, kiša je počela padati i zvuk kapi je punio tišinu među nama.

Izašao sam bez riječi na igralište i prišao Davoru koji je i dalje šutirao. „Hej, mogu li i ja probati?" „Samo daj, čekao sam te ovdje već neko vrijeme." Q

aged floor tiles in the hall — even our parents didn't come because they hoped we'd play soccer. We enjoyed it despite everything... those were some nice years. I don't even remember any more why we stopped, I guess we started to go out and smoke, we were kids, I'm telling you. I'm sorry, anyway.

Something's begun inside me, and I don't know where it stops. *If it stops.* I have trouble sleeping, I dream of Hawaiian beaches from documentaries, and girls I've known appear, followed by grayness and death. I wake up beside my wife and feel like a traitor caught in that world between dreams and reality, the only one that seems true to me. I'm having trouble looking at my kid in the next room. Please Grba, understand me.

We stared at each other for some time, the rain started falling and the sound of drops filled the silence between us.

Without saying anything I went and approached Davor, who was still on the playground. "Hey, can I try it too?" "Go for it pal, I've been waiting for you for some time already." Q

juntos para el básquetbol. El club era de mierda, los entrenadores eran borrachos y muchas de las azulejos en el pasillo estaban seriamente jodidos, incluso nuestros padres no vinieron porque esperaban que jugáramos al fútbol. Lo disfrutamos a pesar de todo, esos fueron algunos años agradables. Ni siquiera recuerdo por qué nos detuvimos, supongo que empezamos a salir a fumar, éramos niños, te lo digo. Lo siento, de todos modos.

Algo ha comenzado dentro de mí, y no sé dónde se detiene. Tengo problemas para dormir, sueño con playas hawaianas de documentales, y aparecen chicas que he conocido, seguidas de la grisura y la muerte. Me despierto con mi esposa y me siento como un traidor en ese mundo entre los sueños y la realidad, el único que me parece verdadero. Incluso tengo problemas para mirar a mi hijo en la habitación de al lado. Por favor, Grba, entiéndeme.

Nos miramos unos al otro durante algún tiempo, la lluvia empezó a caer, el sonido de las gotas llenó el silencio entre nosotros.

Sin decir nada salí a Davor, que todavía estaba en el patio de recreo. «Oye, ¿puedo probarlo también?» «Anímate, amigo, te estaba esperando desde hace algún tiempo». *Q*

mother foucault's bookshop

523 SE Morrison St
Portland, OR 97214

503-236-2665

Αν πυροβολούσα
το φεγγάρι

Αν πυροβολούσα το φεγγάρι
Χίλιες μικρές μπάλες από μωρά
            φεγγάρια
Θα πέφταν απ' τον ουρανό
Λερώνοντας
Τα κεφάλια μας
Με μέλι φτιαγμένο από αστέρια
            και σκόνη

Αν πυροβολούσα το φεγγάρι
Η Περσεφόνη θα
            απελευθερωνόταν
Και θα περνούσε τον ελεύθερο
            χρόνο της στην Ευρώπη
Ψάχνοντας για δουλειά
Airbnb
Και την πραγματική αγάπη

Αν πυροβολούσα το φεγγάρι
Ένα νέο λεξικό θα φτιαχνότανε
Χωρίς λέξεις για τους ποιητές τις
            νύχτες
Χωρίς λογοτεχνικά σχήματα
Και κανόνες ορθογραφίας
Για τους όρκους των εραστών
Και τον τρόπο που προφέρονται

Αν πυροβολούσα το φεγγάρι
Κανείς δε θα ρωτούσε ποτέ ξανά
Τι είναι η ομορφιά

   – Ελένη Τζατζιμάκη

If I shot the
moon

If I shot the moon
A thousand little balls of baby
            moons
Would fall from the sky
Besmearing
Our heads
With honey made of stars and
            dust

If I shot the moon
Persephone would be released
And spend her free days maybe in
            Europe
Searching for a job
An *airbnb*
And a real love

If I shot the moon
A new glossary would be made
With no words for poets in the
            night
With no tasteless literary schemes
And spelling rules
For lovers' vow(el)s

If I shot the moon
No one would ever ask again
            what beauty is

   – *Eleni Tzatzimaki*
   (tr. fr. the Greek, David
   Connolly)

Si disparara a la luna

Si me disparara a la luna
unas mil bolitas de lunas bebés
caerían del cielo
Mancillando
nuestras cabezas
con miel hecha de estrellas y
          polvo

Si me disparara a la luna
Persefone sería liberado
y pasaría sus días libres tal vez
          en Europa
buscando trabajo
un *airbnb*
y un verdadero amor

Si me disparaba a la luna
se haría un nuevo glosario
sin palabras para poetas en la
          noche
sin esquemas literarios insípidos
y reglas ortográficas
para los votos de los amantes

Si me disparara a la luna
nadie volvería a preguntar qué
          es belleza

— *Eleni Tzatzimaki*
(Traducción, T. Warburton y
Bajo y rvb)

Kad bih raznijela mjesec

Kad bih raznijela mjesec
Tisuće loptica mjesečeve
          djece
Pale bi s neba
Na naše glave
I zamrljale ih medom od
          zvijezda i prašine

Kad bih raznijela mjesec
Oslobodila bih Perzefonu
A ona bi slobodne dane
          provela
Možda u Europi
U potrazi za poslom
Smještajem preko *Airbnb-a*
I pravom ljubavi

Kad bih raznijela mjesec
Stvorio bi se novi pojmovnik
Bez riječi za pjesnike u noći
Bez jednoličnih književnih
          poredaka
I pravopisnih pravila
Za (samo)glasnike ljubavi.

Kad bih raznijela mjesec
Nitko nikad više ne bi pitao
          što je ljepota.

— *Eleni Tzatzimaki*
(prijevod s engleskoga,
Ana Katana)

Μέλμπα Ερνάντες
Ροντρίγκες

Η Μέλμπα Ερνάντες Ροντρίγκες ήταν πολύ
    όμορφη στα νιάτα της.
είχε αγαπήσει τόσο τον εαυτό της,
που ποτέ της δεν χρειάστηκε καθρέφτη.
Φορούσε αποφόρια και συχνά ξυπόλυτη
Έτρεχε νύχτα στους δρόμους της Αβάνας
Τραγουδώντας το μυστικό της ομορφιάς της
    στους φρουρούς του Μπατίστα:

Libertad

Εκείνοι τη χαζεύανε παρά τις εντολές
      άνωθεν.
Ήτανε τόσο ωραία που δεν την ερωτευόταν
    κανείς.
Μια μέρα, καλοκαίρι, πήρε από το χέρι την
      Αϊντέ Σανταμαρία,
Την πιο όμορφη φίλη της,
για να φυτέψουνε λουλούδια στη Μονκάδα
    του Σαντιάγο, κάτω από τον καυτό
      ήλιο του Ιούλη.

Μπολιάστηκαν τα φύλλα απ' τον καιρό κι
    από το αίμα το άγιο των συντρόφων
Και γρήγορα τα μπουμπούκια ανοίξανε τα
      μάτια τους
κι ευώδιασαν μια μυρωδιά ανήκουστη.

Τώρα μισοκοιμάται πλάι τους, σε βέβαιη
    νεκροφάνεια: κι αμέσως ανθίζουν.

    – *Ελένη Τζατζιμάκη*

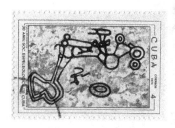

Melba Hernández
Rodriguez

Melba Hernández Rodriguez was most
      beautiful
in her youth.
She was so enamoured of herself,
that she never needed any mirror.
She wore cast-offs and often barefoot
Would run at night through the streets of
            Havana
Singing the secret of her beauty to Batista's
      guards:

Libertad

They would gape at her despite orders from
      above.
She was so lovely that no one fell in love with
      her.
One summer's day she took Haydée
        Santamaria,
Her most beautiful friend
To plant flowers together in Moncada Santiago,
      beneath the scorching July sun

The weather and the comrades' sacred blood
      imbued the leaves
And quickly the buds opened their eyes
and exuded an unprecedented fragrance.
Now she dozes beside them, in certain
       catalepsy:
and immediately they blossom.

     – Eleni Tzatzimaki
      (tr. fr. the Greek, David Connolly)

Melba Hernández Rodríguez

Melba Hernández Rodríguez fue la más hermosa
en su juventud.
Ella estaba tan enamorada de su misma,
que nunca necesitó ningún espejo.
Se vestía desechada y todas las noches corría
descalza por las calles de La Habana
Cantando el secreto de su belleza a los guardias
de Batista:

Libertad

A pesar de las órdenes de arriba, se iban a
mirarla.
Ella era tan encantadora que nadie se enamoró de
ella.
Un día de verano tomó a Haydée Santamaria, su
amiga más bella
para plantar flores juntas en Moncada Santiago,
bajo el sol abrasador de julio

El clima y la sangre sagrada de los camaradas
impregnaron las hojas
y rápidamente los brotes abrieron sus ojos
y exudaron una fragancia sin precedentes.
Ahora dormita a su lado, en cierta catalepsia: Y
de inmediato florecen.

— *Eleni Tzatzimaki*
(traducción, T. Warburton y Bajo y rvb)

Melba Hernandez Rodriguez

Melba Hernandez Rodriguez była
    najpiękniejsza
w swej młodości.
Była tak zakochana w sobie,
że nigdy nie potrzebowala lustra.
Nosiła łachmany i często boso
Biegała nocą po ulicach Hawany
Śpiewając tajemnicę swej piękności
    strażnikom Batisty:

Wolność

Gapili się na nią, mimo rozkazów z góry.
Była tak śliczna, że nie jeden się w niej nie
    zakochał.
Pewnego letniego dnia zabrała Haydee
    Santamaria,
Swą najpiękniejsza przyjaciółkę
Sadzić razem kwiaty w Moncada, w Santiago,
    w skwarze lipcowego lata

Liście wchłonęły aurę i świętą krew
    towarzyszy
Pąki wnet otworzyły oczy i wydały nieznaną
    woń.
Teraz ona drzemie przy nich w katalepsji:
a one rozkwitają.

    — *Eleni Tzatzimaki*
    (Tłumaczenie: Joanna Rosińska)

OTPAD

„Ići ću u raj", rekla je.
NE.
Ne, „ne možeš".
Nisi li rekla ono, „Napravila
    sam to i to?"
DA.
Postoji mjesto negdje gore
koje uzima otpad
i pretvara ga u dijamante.

– Kirsten Aysworth
   (prijevod na hrvatski,
   Dijana Jakovac)

BASURA

"Iré al cielo", dijo.
NO.
No, "no se puede".
¿No dijiste que hice esto y eso?
Sí.
Hay un lugar allá arriba
que toma la basura
y la transmuta en diamantes.

– Kirsten Aysworth
(Traducción, T. Warburton y Bajo
y rvb)

TRASH

"I will go to heaven", she said.
NO.
No, "you cannot".
Didn't you say that, "I did this
    and that?"
YES.
There is a place up there
that takes trash
and turn it into diamonds.

– Kirsten Aysworth

RUSL

Ég mun fara til himna,
     "sagði hún.
NEI.
Nei þú getur það ekki".
Sagðirðu ekki þetta: "Ég
     gerði hitt og þetta?"
JÁ.
Það er staður þarna uppi
sem tekur rusl
og breyta því í demöntum.

   – *Kirsten Aysworth*
    (Þýtt úr Ensku, Michael
    Lohr)

ΣΚΟΥΠΙΔΙΑ

«Θα πάω στον παράδεισο»,
    είπε εκείνη.
ΟΧΙ.
Οχι, "δεν μπορείς".
Εσύ δεν είπες, «έκανα αυτό κι
    εκείνο;»
ΝΑΙ.
Υπάρχει ένα μέρος εκεί πάνω
που παίρνει τα σκουπίδια
και τα μετατρέπει σε
    διαμάντια.

   – *Κίρστεν Άυσγουορθ*
    (μεταφρασμένο, Βασιλεία
    Οικονόμου)

---

wear a mask!

Nosite maske!

Kanna maski!

Maskenpflicht!

Vera með grímu!

Dėvėk kaukę!

носи маску!

ino se enferme, use una
máscara!

Ezrasure

On Finding Ezra Pound,
insane, locked outdoors in a
cage in Italy after WWII –
John Berryman, The Cage

This much is known: A bee winging it
at the resonance of quantum verse,
subatomic buzz weaponized
into stanzas, words in flight,
les mots juiced like wine –

can ride the fog of war from Idaho
to Pisa, then jackknife
out of the smoke into a cage
where he stings and swings
the cold bar blues.

Flying into rage, insults flying
like rain and sleet flying in the face
of reason, he's St. Francis of the wasps
and hornets, nectar held tight
                    between his knees,
praying in the sun to piss.

Unknown: how to equate
the velocity of scribbling, scrabbling
at the speed of unsound mind,
with reaching past sanity and
                    breaking off combs
until detritus of poems run sticky in
                    your hands.

– *J. Randall Brett*

Ezrasure

O pronalasku Ezre Pounda, ludog, zatvore-
nog na otvorenom u kavezu u Italiji poslije
Drugog svjetskog rata — John Berryman,
Kavez

Toliko se zna: pčela leti
u rezonanciji kvantnog stiha,
subatomsko zujanje oružano
u strofama, riječi u letu,
riječi sočne poput vina –

može jahati maglu rata od Idaha
do Pise, nož na sklapanje
iz dima u kavez
gdje bode i ljulja se
hladni takt bluesa.

Letenje u bijes, uvrede lete
poput kiše i susnježice leteći u lice
razloga, on je sveti Franjo osa
i stršljena, nektar čvrsto stisnut između
    njegovih koljena, moleći se na suncu da
      urinira.

Nepoznato: kako izjednačiti
brzinu škrabanja, škrabanja
brzinom nerazumnog uma,
s dostizanjem prošlog zdravog razuma i
    lomljenjem češlja dok krš pjesama trči
      ljepljivo u tvojim rukama.

    — J. Randall Brett
    (prijevod na hrvatski, Dijana Jakovac)

Ristraður

Þegar ég fann Ezra Pound, geðveikur,
læstur utandyra í búri á Ítalíu eftir
seinni heimsstyrjöldina – John
Berryman, búrið

Þetta er mikið vitað: býfluga vængi þess
við ómun skammtaversins,
subatomic suð vopnuð
í strofa, orð á flugi,
les mots safað eins og vín–

getur hjólað þoku stríðs frá Idaho
til Písa, þá tjaldvagn
upp úr reyknum inn í búr
þar sem hann stingur og sveiflast
kalt bar blús.

Flogið í reiði, móðganir fljúga
eins og rigning og slydda sem fljúga í
                andlitið
ástæðan, hann er St. Francis af geitungunum
og hornets, nektar haldinn þétt milli hnjána,
biðja í sólinni að pissa.

Óþekkt: hvernig eigi að jafna
hraðann á að klóra, klóra
á hraða óheilbrigðs hugar,
með því að ná framheilbrigði og brjóta af sér
                kamba
þangað til kvillur ljóða rennur fastur í
                hendurnar.

    – *J. Randall Brett*
      (*Þýtt úr Ensku, Michael Lohr*)

Ezradura

*Al encontrar a Ezra Pound, insano, encerrado
al aire libre en una jaula en Italia después de la
Segunda Guerra Mundial – John Berryman, La
Jaula*

Esto se sabe: rodillas de abeja aleteando
a la resonancia del verso cuántico,
armamento zumbido subatómico
en estrofas, palabras en vuelo,
les mots jugadas como vino –

puede montar la nube de guerra desde
              Idaho
hasta Pisa, luego plegarse como
navaja del humo en una jaula
donde balencea y pique
los *blues* de la barra fría.

Volando en cólera, insultos volando
como lluvia y aguanieve volando en la cara
por la razón, es San Francisco de las avispas
y avispas, néctar apretado entre sus rodillas,
rezando en el sol para orinar.

Desconocido: cómo dibujar la ecuación
de velocidades de garabatear, escarbar
al velocidad de mente sin sonido y poco
              sólida,
con llegar a la cordura pasada y romper
              peines
hasta que lo detritos de poemas corren
           pegajosas en sus manos.

– J. Randall Brett
(Traducción, T. Warburton y Bajo y rvb)

Grandmother Ocean

Wears the crinkled, tissue paper
skin of an old woman,
rolling swells of surf her veins,
blue and thick, protruding.

I want to take her hand in mine,
offer her comfort,
but the sea has no hand to hold,
only an undulating pulse.

Her reach is expansive, buffeting
rock-faced cliffs, while sand
welcomes the rub and scratch
of her waves. Her laugh crashes,

recedes, sighs. Repeats.
Wind whips her cry, scatters
the taste of tears. She stores
swallowed secrets in her belly:

lost souls, colorless creatures
who never see light, discards
of generations, vessels, wreckages.
We hardly know her depth.

We take her seriously
when she storms and destroys,
levels our trespass upon her edges.
Some fear her, others build walls,

attempt to contain and control.
But fading yellow light exposes
her wrinkled surface,
her ever widening girth,

advancing age and weariness,
her vulnerability.

— *Ann Farley*

Baka Ocean

Nosi zgužvanu, maramicu
koža starice,
valjaju se otekline od surfanja njezinih vena,
plave i guste, ispupčene.

Želim staviti njezinu ruku u svoju,
ponuditi joj utjehu,
ali more nema ruku koju možeš uhvatiti,
samo valoviti puls.

Njezin je domet prostran, udarajući
stjenovite hridi, dok pijesak
pozdravlja trljanje i ogrebotine
njezinih valova. Njezin se smijeh ruši,

povlači, uzdahuje. Ponavlja.
Vjetar šiba njezin plač, raspršuje
okus suza. Ona pohranjuje
progutale tajne u svom trbuhu:

izgubljene duše, bezbojna stvorenja
koja nikada ne vide svjetlost, odbacivanje
generacija, brodova, olupina.
Jedva znamo njezinu dubinu.

Mi je shvaćamo ozbiljno
kada tutnji i uništava,
izravnava naš prijelaz na njezinim rubovima.
Neki je se boje, drugi grade zidove,

pokušaj suzbijanja i kontrole.
Ali blijedo žuto svjetlo izlaže
njezinu naboranu površinu,
njezin sve širi obujam,

napredujuću dob i klonulost,
njezinu ranjivost.

> — *Ann Farley*
> *(prijevod, Dijana Jakovac)*

Mędrczyni Ocean

Nosi krepinową
skórę starej kobiety,
toczące się napęczniałe fale jej żył
błękitne, grube i wzniesione.

Chcę wziąć jej dłoń w moją
w geście ukojenia,
lecz ocean nie ma dłoni by ją trzymać
tylko falujący puls.

Jej zasieg rośnie, uderza
brzegi o skalistych twarzach, gdy piasek
wita ocieranie i drapanie
jej fal. Jej śmiech atakuje

cofa sie, wzdycha. Jeszcze raz.
Wiatr uderza w jej płacz, rozrzuca
smak łez. Ona chowa
nabrzmiałe sekrety w swym łonie:

Zagubione dusze, bezbarwne istoty
nie znające światła, złomowisko
pokoleń, statki, wraki.
Nie znamy prawie jej głębi.

Traktujemy ją poważnie
gdy wkracza i burzy
unicestwia nasze wkroczenia na swe brzegi.
Niektórzy się jej boją, inni budują mury,

próbują okiełznać, podporządkować.
A gasnące żółte światło ukazuje
jej pomarszczoną powierzchnię,
wszechrosnące ciało.

posuwający się wiek i zmęczenie,
jej bezbronność.

 – Ann Farley
  (Tłumaczenie: Joanna Rosińska)

Abuela Océano

Lleva el papel tisú arrugado
piel de una anciana,
olas ondulantes surfean por sus venas,
azules y gruesas, sobresalientes.

Quiero tomar su mano en la mía,
ofrezcar la consuelo,
pero el mar no tiene mano para sostener,
sólo un pulso ondulado.

Su alcance es amplio, azotando
acantilados de cara de roca, mientras que la arena
da la bienvenida a frotar y rasguño
de sus olas. Su risa se estrella,

retrocede, suspira. Se repite.
El viento azota su grito, dispersa
el sabor de las lágrimas. Ella almacena
secretos tragados en su vientre:

almas perdidas, criaturas incoloras
que nunca ven luz, descartes
de generaciones, vasos, escombros.
Apenas conocemos su profundidad.

La tomamos seriamente
cuando asalta y destruye,
nivela nuestra infracciones de sus fronteras.
Algunos la temen, otros construyen muros,

ensayan de contener y controlar.
Pero la luz amarilla que se desvanece expone
su arrugada superficie,
su creciente cintura,

el avance de su edad y cansancio,
su vulnerabilidad.

> — *Ann Farley*
> *(traducción, T. Warburton y Bajo y rvb)*

The Traitor, A Correspondence: The Game of Simulations

Adrian Martin & Carles Matamoros

Introduction

The mechanism is as follows: two authors exchange letters via email, for two weeks, on *The Traitor* (*Il traditore*, Marco Bellocchio, 2019); their correspondence is published here according to rules established at the outset. The game is quite simple: the opening participant proposes a title, a screenshot and a short text, which results in a response from the other author who, in turn, proposes a second title, a second screenshot and a second short text addressed to the first participant. The exchange continues with several more *moves* by both authors, Adrian Martin (AM) and Carles Matamoros (CM), who aim to share and convey their passion for the latest film of this great Italian director.

El traidor, una correspondencia
El juego de las simulaciones

Adrian Martin y Carles Matamoros
(Traducción, Cristina Álvarez López)

Introducción

El mecanismo es el siguiente: dos autores se intercambian misivas por correo electrónico durante dos semanas sobre *El traidor* (Il traditore, Marco Bellocchio, 2019) y su correspondencia se publica aquí siguiendo las normas estipuladas en la partida. El juego es muy sencillo: un participante propone un título, una captura de pantalla de la película y un texto breve, lo que da lugar a una respuesta escrita del otro autor, que, a su vez, propone un segundo título, una segunda captura de pantalla y un segundo texto breve dirigido al remitente. El intercambio sigue con varias *jugadas* más por parte de sendos autores, Adrian Martin (AM) y Carles Matamoros (CM), que aspiran a compartir su pasión por el último filme del gran cineasta italiano.

1. The Numbers (AM)

The portrait of a criminal family, a criminal network: 30 people in one frame, over-illuminated and then plunged into eerie, funereal darkness

1. Los números (AM)

El retrato de una familia criminal, una red criminal: treinta personas en un encuadre, sobreiluminadas y, después, tras el *flash* de una

by a flash bulb. Over and over: people frozen, identified (their names printed on the screen), numbered as a collateral corpse at the moment of their death. The complex opening sequence of Marco Bellocchio's *The Traitor* lays out some of the film's central motifs: an unstoppable seriality (in an image and across time) that absorbs and destroys everyone; the frozen pose that, in his cinema, always signifies death in contradistinction to the life-giving moment of joyous, Dionysiac dance. With a crucial difference, here: whenever Tommaso Buscetta (Pierfrancesco Favino) moves (from room to room, house to house, nation to nation), it is not in a sweep of pleasure, but a restless, neurotic, haunted deferment of the preordained, gridded pattern of his brutal Mafia life. The central question of the story: can Tommaso ever escape that grid – and how?

1b. The Hands (CM)

The hands of Pippo Calò (Fabrizio Ferracane) on Tommaso's back in the family photograph: they already foreshadow the unbearable burden that Bellocchio's tragic hero will carry after his Brazilian exile. Tommaso will never be able to escape from this initial imprint because their bond will be sealed with an affectionate hug under the

bombilla, sumergidas en una oscuridad escalofriante y funeraria. Una y otra vez: personas que aparecen congeladas, identificadas (sus nombres impresos en pantalla), numeradas como cadáveres colaterales en el momento de sus muertes. La compleja secuencia inicial de *El traidor* de Marco Bellocchio expone algunos de los motivos centrales del filme: una serialidad imparable (en el plano y a lo largo del metraje) que absorbe y destroza a todos; la pose congelada que, en su cine, siempre significa muerte en contraste con el momento vital de la danza alegre y dionisíaca. Con una diferencia crucial: en este film, cuando Tommaso Buscetta (Pierfrancesco Favino) se mueve (de habitación en habitación, de casa en casa, de nación en nación), no es en un impulso de placer, sino en un aplazamiento incesante, neurótico y atormentado del patrón fijo predeterminado por su brutal vida en la Mafia. La cuestión central de la historia es: ¿Puede Tommaso escapar de ese patrón? ¿Y cómo?

1b. Las manos (CM)

Las manos de Pippo Calò (Fabrizio Ferracane) sobre la espalda de Tommaso en la fotografía familiar ya presagian la carga insoportable que arrastrará el héroe trágico de Bellocchio tras exiliarse en Brasil. Tommaso nunca podrá escapar de esta estampa inicial porque sellará con un abrazo afectuoso, bajo los fuegos artificiales de Santa Rosalía, su vínculo con Pippo, a

fireworks of Santa Rosalia: Tommaso entrusts Pippo with the life of his two eldest children, Benedetto Buscetta (Gabriele Cicirello) and Antonio Buscetta (Paride Cicirello), also located in a central spot in the composition. But who then will be *the traitor* in this story? The father (Tommaso) who abandons his offspring in Italy and then betrays those who annihilate his colleagues and family to justice? Or the apparent friend (Pippo), who murders Benedetto literally *with his own hands*?

quien confiará la vida de sus dos hijos mayores, Benedetto Buscetta (Gabriele Cicirello) y Antonio Buscetta (Paride Cicirello), situados también en una posición central en la composición del plano. ¿Pero quién será entonces *el traidor* en esta historia? ¿El padre (Tommaso) que abandona a sus vástagos en Italia y luego delata ante la justicia a quienes deciden aniquilar a sus colegas y familiares? ¿O el aparente amigo (Pippo) que asesina literalmente *con sus propias manos* a Benedetto?

2. The Screens (CM)

2. Las pantallas (CM)

Bellocchio's rectangular frame is reformulated in a panoptic form in the video surveillance room belonging to the prison where the Mafia members betrayed by Tommaso are locked in. Multiple screens that individualise singular personalities and, at the same time, in the same frame, in a single *image of images*, gather various members of the earlier criminal family portrait. Pippo, of course, is again located in the centre and we have two perspectives: the close-up of his face (above) and the overhead shot of his cell (below).

El delimitado rectángulo de Bellocchio se reformula en forma de panóptico en la sala de videovigilancia de la cárcel en la que son encerrados los miembros de la Mafia delatados por Tommaso. Múltiples pantallas que individualizan personalidades singulares y al mismo tiempo aglutinan en un mismo encuadre, en una sola *imagen de imágenes*, varios integrantes de aquel retrato de la familia criminal. Pippo, evidentemente, vuelve a estar situado en el centro y contamos con dos perspectivas: el primer plano de su rostro (arriba) y el

Among the different screens that transmit *live* what is going on inside the prison, three stand out: they are broadcasting an external event, the State funeral of Giovanni Falcone (Fausto Russo Alesi), the key lawyer in the State's Maxi Trial brought against the Cosa Nostra. This media event is closely linked to the criminals trapped in the same shot, thus exemplifying two of the dialectical resources with which *The Traitor* works: the occasional integration of archival images that punctuate the fictional events; and the proliferation of scenes in which the characters follow on TV the news that impact their lives (there are even TV sets in the cells of the imprisoned Mafiosi!). The fabrication of a *political tale* in Italy as elaborated by the mass media – in response to which Bellocchio offers, in several of his historical films, alternative *re-presentations* of famous people – is more evident in the following shot of another control room: the television studio were Tommaso is interviewed.

2b. The Dreams (AM)

The dreams that punctuate the film – an essential element of Bellocchio's method since the mid 1980s – are a crucial variation on the surveillance and media screens. As externalised images, dream-visions of various sorts (memories, reveries, hallucinations), they belong to the realm of the *imaginary*, and this

plano cenital de su celda (abajo). Entre las distintas pantallas que muestran *en directo* lo que sucede en el interior de la prisión, destacan aquellas tres que emiten la señal de un evento exterior: el funeral de Estado de Giovanni Falcone (Fausto Russo Alesi), el juez instructor del macroproceso contra la *Cosa Nostra*. Un acontecimiento mediático estrechamente ligado a los criminales atrapados en el mismo plano y que ejemplifica dos de los recursos dialécticos con los que se trabaja en *El traidor*: la integración ocasional de imágenes de archivo que puntúan los hechos narrados en la ficción y la proliferación de escenas en las que los personajes miran atentamente la televisión para informarse de las noticias que marcan sus vidas (¡incluso hay pantallas en las celdas de los presos mafiosos!). La construcción de un *relato político* en Italia definido por los *mass media* –ante el que Bellocchio ofrece en varios de sus filmes históricos *representaciones* alternativas de personajes célebres– es todavía más patente en el plano justamente posterior, que nos sitúa en otra sala de control: la de un estudio televisivo donde se entrevista a Tommaso.

2b. Los sueños (AM)

Los sueños que puntúan el filme – un elemento esencial del método de Bellocchio desde mediados de los ochenta– constituyen una variante crucial de las pantallas de vigilancia y televisión. En tanto que imágenes exteriorizadas, estos sueños-visio-

imaginary is always collective and social, never merely individual. Even the openly metaphorical, Eisensteinian inserts of a tiger (prowling inside its cage) and of rats ("deserting a sinking ship", as the saying goes) have an oneiric force. Trying to sleep on the plane, Tommaso sees his now dead sons spectrally passing along the aisle and out through the back curtain: a banal invisibility that, nonetheless, sparks a Shakespearean level of guilt in him. Later, an even more terrifying apparition worthy of a *giallo* – as Tommaso lies down in his relatively comfortable and secure but still soulless holding pen – shows his entire family crowding around his open coffin, as if pressing him into the circle of death with which he is so deeply associated. Tommaso, as we are told in the final, written-on-screen detail, died in bed in April 2000, in his sleep, as he always wanted. But how could this sleep ever be peaceful? In Bellocchio, sleep is forever haunted by the ghosts of personal and political, moral and ethical accountability.

nes de todo tipo (recuerdos, ensoñaciones, alucinaciones), pertenecen al reino de lo *imaginario*; y este imaginario es siempre colectivo y social, nunca meramente individual. Incluso los insertos *eisenstenianos* abiertamente metafóricos –un tigre (merodeando dentro de su jaula) y ratas ("abandonando el barco que se hunde", como dice el proverbio)– tienen una fuerza onírica. Mientras intenta dormir en el avión, Tommaso ve a sus hijos muertos caminando espectralmente por el pasillo y desapareciendo tras la cortina: una invisibilidad banal que, sin embargo, le inyecta una buena dosis de culpa *shakespeareana*. Posteriormente, una aparición todavía más terrorífica digna de un *giallo*: mientras Tommaso se tumba en la celda (relativamente confortable y segura, pero todavía sin alma) del centro de detención, vemos a toda su familia amontonada alrededor de su ataúd abierto, como si le empujasen a ese círculo de la muerte con el que está tan profundamente asociado. Al final del filme, un texto impreso en pantalla nos informa de que Tommaso murió en su cama, en abril del 2000, mientras dormía, como siempre había querido. Pero ¿cómo pudo su sueño haber sido alguna vez pacífico? En Bellocchio, el sueño está siempre turbado por los fantasmas de crímenes cuya responsabilidad es personal y política, moral y ética.

3. The Causes & The Effects (AM)

The Traitor is a tightly organised and hyper-structured film, like the corrupt network it depicts: each moment, each incident or detail in it has an immediate correspondence or repercussion and then, further away in time and space, a wider resonance. As a deliberately hollowed-out version of a classic gangster film, it invests the most basic plot mechanics of the genre with an eerie fatalism. This process is also fundamentally cinematic, since what is at stake in the life of a gangster – and even more so, a traitor – is literally sound and image: making a noise, and/or being seen, are what will get you killed in an instant; nobody who goes public, who steps out of the silent shadows as Falcone does, will last long. The entire film, in both its form and content, is built on this dynamic principle of image and sound. Image: Tommaso, in the courtroom, is always attempting (without much success) to shield his eyes, covering his vision in dark glasses, averting his gaze from those who want to kill him, walling his whole body in glass protection. Sound: when Tommaso makes love to his wife, Cristina (Maria Fernanda Cândido), he places a hand over her mouth to stifle her cries of pleasure, and

3. Las causas y los efectos (AM)

Igual que la red criminal que retrata, *El traidor* es un filme fuertemente organizado e híper estructurado: cada momento, cada incidente o detalle tiene una correspondencia o repercusión inmediata y, luego, en otro tiempo y espacio, una resonancia más amplia. En tanto que versión deliberadamente vaciada del clásico filme de gánsteres, *El traidor* dota a los mecanismos argumentales más básicos del género de un inquietante fatalismo. Este proceso es también fundamentalmente cinematográfico, puesto que lo que está en juego en la vida de un gánster –y más aún, en la de un traidor– es literalmente el sonido y la imagen: hacer ruido y/o ser visto es lo que te mata al instante; quienes se convierten en figuras públicas y salen de las sombras silenciosas (como hace Falcone) duran poco. El filme está enteramente construido, en forma y contenido, siguiendo este principio dinámico de imagen y sonido. Imagen: Tommaso, en la sala judicial, siempre está intentando (sin mucho éxito) resguardar sus ojos, cubriéndolos con gafas oscuras, desviando la mirada de aquellos que quieren matarle, encerrándose en una cabina de cristal para proteger su cuerpo. Sonido: cuando Tommaso le hace el amor a su mujer, Cristina (Maria Fernanda Cândido), coloca una mano sobre su boca para sofocar sus gritos de placer y le ordena no hacer ruido. Pronto veremos (como en un desplazamiento onírico) a otra

instructs her to be quiet. Soon, we will see a different Cosa Nostra couple murdered (as if in a dream-displacement) naked in their beds, during sex. Even a family's most innocent outbursts – like cheering while watching a soccer match on TV – seem to immediately bring an answering tone of doom: the mysterious phone call addressed to Tommaso. For sounds not only betray presence, but also announce menace: the Sicilian folk song that sends the Buscetta family fleeing a New Hampshire restaurant is *verified*, six years later in Palermo, enigmatically and sinisterly, by Pippo singing it to Tommaso in court.

3b. The Gesture (CM)

The gesture of Tommaso to Cristina not only demonstrates the film's unstoppable sonic tension, but also the possessive character of its protagonist. We know he is able to make his enemies submit – but that is also true of his women, whether lovers, prostitutes or wives. When he is arrested at his home in Brazil, Tommaso vehemently orders Cristina to shut up in front of the police. When he remembers the past in the company of his Sicilian friend Totuccio Contorno (Luigi Lo Cascio), he evokes a time when voluptuous women *fell into their arms* – even while he was imprisoned. The character's memory of that *conqueror* phase in an idealised Cosa Nostra

pareja de la *Cosa Nostra* que es asesinada en la cama, mientras están desnudos practicando sexo. Incluso los estallidos más inocentes de una familia –los gritos de ánimo proferidos mientras ven un partido de fútbol en la televisión– parecen desencadenar, inmediatamente, un inquietante tono de respuesta: la misteriosa llamada telefónica para Tommaso. Porque los sonidos no solo delatan una presencia, sino que también anuncian una amenaza: la canción popular siciliana que hace que la familia Buscetta huya de un restaurante en New Hampshire será *verificada* (seis años después, en Palermo) por Pippo que, de manera enigmática y siniestra, se la canta a Tommaso en la sala judicial.

3b. El gesto (CM)

El gesto de Tommaso sobre Cristina no solo evidencia la incontenible tensión sonora que atraviesa *El traidor*, sino también el carácter posesivo del protagonista descrito por Bellocchio, al que sabemos capaz de someter a sus enemigos, pero también a las mujeres, ya sean amantes, prostitutas o esposas. Cuando es detenido en su casa de Brasil, Tommaso manda callar a Cristina virulentamente ante la policía y cuando rememora tiempos pasados, en compañía de su amigo siciliano Totuccio Contorno (Luigi Lo Cascio), evoca una época en la que las mujeres voluptuosas *caían en sus brazos*, incluso cuando estaba recluido en la prisión. El recuerdo del personaje sobre esa etapa de *conquistador* en una *Cosa Nostra* idealizada supone el salto abismal entre el presente –en el que Tomma-

emerges on screen in an eloquent flashback, which represents the abysmal jump between the present (in which Tommaso dyes his hair coquettishly before a mirror to camouflage his ageing) and the past (a prison in Palermo where the inmates must leave the shared dormitory so that Tommaso can be intimate with a young woman *at his service*). However, this flashback quickly adopts a sick, morbid tone – as if the character cannot escape these ghosts that haunt him, even when he recalls his *happy days*. In the conjured scene, Tommaso observes that one of the elderly prisoners remains in the cell, so he approaches the man's bed and discovers that he has died in his sleep. Discreetly, Tommaso covers the inmate's inert body with the sheet, before returning to his bed where he fucks the prostitute he has previously invited to undress. Eros and Thanatos are inseparable in his memory.

so se tiñe el cabello con coquetería ante un espejo para camuflar su envejecimiento– y el pasado –en una cárcel de Palermo en la que el resto de presos deben salir del dormitorio comunitario para que Tommaso pueda intimar con una joven a *su servicio*–. Sin embargo, esta suerte de *flashback* acaba adoptando pronto un tono mortecino, malsano, como si el personaje no pudiera escapar de los fantasmas que le atormentan, ni tan siquiera cuando piensa en sus *días felices*. En la escena evocada, Tommaso observa que uno de los presos de edad avanzada no ha abandonado la celda junto al resto, por lo que se acerca a su cama y descubre que ha muerto mientras dormía. Discretamente, cubre el cuerpo inerte del viejo con la sábana antes de volver a su lecho para follar con la prostituta a la que antes ha invitado a desnudarse: Eros y Tánatos son indisociables en su memoria.

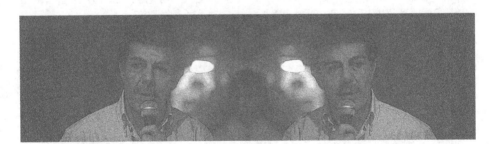

4. The Karaoke (CM)

The disquieting Sicilian melody sung by both the musician in an American restaurant and by Pippo

4. El karaoke (CM)

La inquietante melodía siciliana entonada tanto por el músico de un restaurante estadounidense

is not the only song we hear twice in *The Traitor*: the emblematic bolero "Historia de un amor" ("Story of a Love") appears in two mirroring scenes that are in dialogue with each other. First, in the celebration staged by Bellocchio of the 68th birthday of Tommaso who, in front of family and friends, sings it precariously and emotionally, in a state of drunkenness. Then, in the sequence before the final credits, where murky archival video footage of that same birthday party is revived, with the real Buscetta suddenly on stage. If we focus on the first of these musical performances, we can see how Bellocchio works with one of the most stimulating (audio)visual motifs of contemporary cinema: karaoke scenes. *The Traitor*'s scene does not take place strictly in a bar of this type: the melody is not completely pre-recorded (there's a keyboardist playing live) and there's no monitor on which the song lyrics scroll. All the same, we are absorbing a privileged moment, comparable in its form to those that emerge in works as diverse as *Lost in Translation* (Sofia Coppola, 2003), *Only God Forgives* (Nicolas Winding Refn, 2013), *HHH – A Portrait of Hou Hsiao-Hsien* (Olivier Assayas, 1999), *My Best Friend's Wedding* (P.J. Hogan, 1997), *Oasis* (Lee Chang-dong, 2002), or the final episode of the fourth season of *Better Call Saul*

(Vince Gilligan and Peter Gould, 2015–).

It is well known that karaoke scenes can lead to moments of plot inflection, where characters free themselves from their fears, show us their weaknesses, transform themselves into different people, and even bring us near the level of the transcendental. In the case of Favino's interpretation, there is a noticeable evolution that Bellocchio demonstrates in a series of shots capturing the reactions of the spectators: as the performance progresses, we pass from initial cheerful smiles to solemn expressions. The melancholic tale of this bolero – which Carlos Eleta Almarán composed in the 1950s following the death of his brother's wife – plus the changing expression in Favino's perspiring face, with a contained emotion revealed in his saddened eyes, ends up giving the scene an unmistakeable bitterness. This bitterness can be attributed to the character's lament over the passing of time, but also to the insurmountable remoteness of his native Italy, and a life overshadowed by the weight of death. It is not surprising that, in this same party, Tommaso eventually confesses that he is seriously ill, while watching from the distance the guests'

nal de la cuarta temporada de *Better Call Saul* (Vince Gilligan y Peter Gould, 2015–).

Es sabido que las escenas de karaoke pueden dar lugar a momentos de inflexión argumental en los que los personajes se liberan de sus miedos, nos muestran sus debilidades, se transforman en otras personas e incluso nos acercan a lo trascendental. En el caso de la interpretación de Pierfrancesco Favino, es perceptible una evolución que Bellocchio evidencia en una serie de planos que plasman las reacciones de los espectadores: de las sonrisas celebratorias iniciales, se pasa a los semblantes serios a medida que avanza la actuación. La melancólica letra del bolero, que Carlos Eleta Almarán compuso en los años cincuenta a raíz de la muerte de la esposa de su hermano, sumada a la expresión cambiante en el rostro sudoroso de Favino, con una emoción contenida que revelan sus ojos entristecidos, otorga a la escena una indudable amargura, que podemos atribuir al lamento del personaje por el paso del tiempo, pero también a la insalvable lejanía de su Italia natal y a una vida ensombrecida por el peso de la muerte. No resulta sorprendente que en esa misma fiesta Tommaso acabe confesando que está gravemente enfermo, mientras observa desde la distancia cómo los invitados se divierten con un animado juego de sillas en el que ya no puede participar. Las imágenes en vídeo finales otorgan un valor adicional a la escena, ya

cheerful "musical chairs" game in which he can no longer participate. The final video images give a surplus value to the scene, since they allow us to determine the similarities and differences between Bellocchio's Buscetta and the real Buscetta on the basis of their singing performances. After all, karaoke is the art of simulation, and this game of appearances finally defines what *The Traitor* is fundamentally addressing – since Pierfrancesco Favino *simulates* a historical character still very present in the imaginary of his country; and, in turn, the Italian director pursues the elusive identity of a Tommaso who is variously gangster, hero, traitor, exile and puppet of the State. Thus, an inscrutable lifetime of *simulations*, set to the rhythm of a bolero.

4b. The Cigarettes (AM)

The cigarettes form another important motif in the film, another pattern of comparisons bridging many levels. During the trial, Bellocchio places a quote from Michel Butor into the mouth of an erudite mafioso behind bars: "The gaze is the expression of reality". Butor's theory is, in fact, very close to Bellocchio's method as a filmmaker; as the writer said: "We never look at a face twice in the same way … we question it differently". So it goes with the cigarettes. The intimate (and somewhat aggressive) ritual of a shared puff is established early, when Tommaso, on their

que nos permiten especular con las similitudes y diferencias entre el Buscetta de Bellocchio y el Buscetta auténtico a partir de sus actuaciones musicales. Al fin y al cabo, el karaoke es el arte de la simulación y dicho juego de apariencias acaba siendo muy definitorio de lo que nos cuenta *El traidor*, donde el actor Pierfrancesco Favino *simula* ser un personaje histórico todavía muy presente en el imaginario de su país y, a su vez, el cineasta italiano persigue la identidad escurridiza de un Tommaso que fue mafioso, héroe, traidor, exiliado y títere del Estado. Una vida inescrutable de *simulaciones* a ritmo de bolero.

4b. Los cigarrillos (AM)

Los cigarrillos son otro motivo importante de *El traidor* y forman un patrón comparativo que enlaza varias capas del filme. Durante el juicio, Bellocchio pone en boca de un erudito mafioso esta cita de Michel Butor: "La mirada es la expresión de la realidad". La teoría de Butor es, en realidad, muy cercana al método de Bellocchio como director; tal y como dijo el escritor: "Nunca miramos un rostro dos veces del mismo modo… lo cuestionamos de forma distinta". Lo mismo sucede, en el filme, con los cigarrillos. El ritual íntimo (y un poco agresivo) de compartir un cigarrillo es instaurado al principio: cuando Tommaso, en la terraza de su casa en Brasil, toma el cigarrillo de Cristina. Luego, se convierte en un factor decisivo a la hora de es-

verandah in Brazil, takes Cristina's cigarette. Between Tommaso and Falcone, it is a major dealbreaker in establishing their rapport: Tommaso tells Falcone later that he would never have accepted a smoke from him if the pack had not already been open ... Cigarettes (like bicycles) sometimes function in the film to *make strange* certain events and situations: the mafiosi imprisoned in their cages during the trial smoke furiously (cigars or cigarettes, it becomes a legal tussle!). In one of the most striking historical footnotes presented, it is argued that importing heroin spelt the end of the old Cosa Nostra; if they had stuck with cigarettes, it all would have stayed fine! And a cigarette, lovingly smoked and discarded, also figures in the final *move* made by both the film, and by myself in this writing-game of simulations...

tablecer la confianza entre Tommaso y Falcone: más tarde, el gánster le confesará al juez que, si el paquete de tabaco no hubiese estado empezado, él nunca hubiera aceptado su cigarrillo... Los cigarrillos (como las bicicletas) a veces funcionan añadiendo extrañeza a ciertos eventos y situaciones: durante el juicio, los mafiosos encerrados en sus jaulas fuman frenéticamente (cigarros o cigarrillos, ¡se convierte en una batalla legal!). En una sorprendente nota histórica, se discute cómo la importación de heroína fue lo que precipitó el fin de la *Cosa Nostra*: ¡si hubiesen seguido negociando con tabaco todo hubiese salido bien! Y un cigarrillo, consumido con devoción y luego desechado, figura también en la última *jugada* perpetrada tanto por el filme como por mí en este juego de las *simulaciones*...

5. The End (AM)

Film narratives depend on spectators both remembering and forgetting things. We remember in order to identify (plots, faces, names, important information), to keep track of the unfolding story. We forget in order that we might, with a jolt of

5. El final (AM)

La narrativa de los films depende de que los espectadores recuerden y, al mismo tiempo, olviden cosas. Recordamos para identificar (tramas, rostros, nombres, información importante), para seguir el desarrollo de la historia. Olvi-

surprise or delight, rediscover a detail in all its ultimately revealed significance. Naturally, this game of simultaneously showing and concealing things (through underplaying or understatement), so that they can eventually be uncovered, is a measure of a filmmaker's storytelling skill: it is an art of willful *misdirection*. In a stunning game inside *The Traitor*, this misdirection comes in the form of a bold sleight-of-hand, a true magician's trick worthy of Orson Welles. At 50 minutes into the film, Tommaso begins, with theatrical deliberation, to tell a story that Bellocchio visualises in flashback. It is the story of how Tommaso, as a young man, was given a designated hit: however, this other man, sensing his fate, clutched his newly baptised baby to his chest, knowing this would avert the assassin's bullet. Then – jumping through the years – Tommaso tells us how this target never left home without his son by his side. "Then the son got married" … but, right there, Tommaso digresses in order to amplify a general point to his interlocutor, Falcone: in those days, the Cosa Nostra code meant no killing of children, women or judges. Falcone begins arguing with him about this assumption of morality and ethics. And the film pursues this point, instantly going in a new direction.

damos para poder redescubrir, en una sacudida de placer y sorpresa, un detalle cuya importancia nos es finalmente revelada. Naturalmente, este juego de mostrar y esconder cosas simultáneamente (a partir de la sutileza y el disimulo) para que puedan ser finalmente desveladas, nos sirve para medir la habilidad de un director a la hora de contar historias: es el arte de la desorientación deliberada, del desvío de la atención. En el apabullante juego perpetrado por *El traidor*, este desvío viene en forma de un audaz juego de manos, un verdadero truco de mago digno de Orson Welles. A los cincuenta minutos de metraje, Tommaso comienza a contar, con resuelta teatralidad, una historia que Bellocchio visualiza en un *flashback*. Un joven Tommaso recibe el encargo de matar a un hombre; la víctima, presintiendo su destino, se agarra a su bebé recién bautizado, apretándolo contra el pecho, pues sabe que así evitará la bala del asesino. Después –saltando a través de los años– Tommaso nos cuenta cómo su objetivo nunca abandonó la casa sin llevar a su hijo al lado. "Después el hijo se casó"… pero, justo aquí, Tommaso empieza una digresión para explicarle a Falcone cómo, en esa época, el código de la *Cosa Nostra* no permitía matar a niños, mujeres o jueces. Falcone comienza a discutir con él sobre esta premisa moral y ética. Y, siguiendo este hilo, el film rápidamente toma otra dirección.

How quickly we forget – taken up in the film's energetic, mosaic flow – that we have missed the punchline of Tommaso's story! It was simply pushed aside, just in the way that windy monologues are often interrupted in real life by impatient listeners, never reaching their conclusion. Until – a full 90 minutes of screen-time later! – Bellocchio takes us, via a transitional comparison of two moons in the night sky, to exactly that untold conclusion, now given without a narrating voice – Tommaso may be remembering or dreaming it, but he is no longer *in control* of it; Bellocchio has well and truly taken the driver's wheel. A wedding party is ending; the father embraces his son in a fond farewell; a dog lazily sleeps at the entrance of this ample courtyard. In the present – allowing a crucial ellipse in the flashback – Cristina gently removes the rifle from Tommaso's hand (he, too, now divested of his protection) and covers his sleeping body with a blanket. Back to the past: guests leave in their cars down the road behind the dog; the proud father relaxes, alone, pulls up a chair, gazes up at the moon, smokes and discards a cigarette. Then, as he stands, there is something in his eyes, his bearing, his gaze, that possibly signals that he knows exactly what is coming. Tommaso, as if magically, arrives

¡Qué rápido olvidamos –llevados por el enérgico flujo entrecruzado del film– que nos hemos perdido el *punchline* de la historia de Tommaso! Simplemente ha sido empujado a un lado, del mismo modo que, en la vida, los largos monólogos suelen ser interrumpidos por interlocutores impacientes y nunca llegan a su fin. Hasta que –¡noventa minutos más tarde!– Bellocchio nos lleva, vía una transición de dos lunas en el cielo nocturno, a la conclusión no relatada, ahora expuesta sin una voz que la narre. Puede que Tommaso la esté recordando o soñando, pero ya no tiene el control sobre ella: Bellocchio ha tomado el mando. Una fiesta nupcial está llegando a su fin: el padre se despide de su hijo con un abrazo cariñoso; un perro duerme en la entrada del jardín. En el presente, Cristina aparta el rifle de las manos de Tommaso (ahora, él también ha sido despojado de su protección) y cubre su cuerpo dormido con una manta: este inserto permite a Bellocchio ejecutar una elipsis crucial en el *flashback*. Vuelta al pasado: los invitados se van de la fiesta en sus coches, dejando atrás al perro; el padre, orgulloso, se queda solo y se relaja en una silla, mirando a la luna y fumando un cigarrillo que, finalmente, deshecha. Entonces, cuando se pone en pie, hay algo en sus ojos, en su porte, en su mirada, que señala, quizás, que sabe exactamente lo que está por venir. Tommaso, como por arte de magia, llega de

from the darkness – Bellocchio giving us now an ageless character unconstrained by strict historical chronology, this could be happening in any year – and carries out his initial command. So much about *The Traitor*'s deepest themes is implied here: the ambiguity of honour, the obedient (almost robotic) carrying out of orders (like another "simple soldier" in *The Irishman* [Martin Scorsese, 2019]), the question of what changes and what does not change with time ... As Tommaso exits, the film holds on this final, archway frame (my chosen screenshot) that recalls the opening verse of Bob Dylan's "One Too Many Mornings" (1964):

Down the street the dogs are barkin' /
And the day is a-gettin' dark./
As the night comes in a-fallin' /
The dogs'll lose their bark. /
An' the silent night will shatter /
From the sounds inside my mind. /
Yes, I'm one too many mornings /
And a thousand miles behind.

© Adrian Martin & Carles Matamoros, Dec. 2021 / English translation © Cristina Álvarez López & Adrian Martin, Dec. 2021

la oscuridad –Bellocchio nos presenta al personaje sin edad, libre de la estricta cronología histórica: esto podría estar sucediendo en cualquier año– y lleva a cabo su encargo inicial. Aquí están implícitos muchos de los temas profundos de *El traidor*: la ambigüedad del honor, el obediente (casi robótico) cumplimiento de órdenes –como haría un "simple soldado" en *El irlandés* (*The Irishman*, Martin Scorsese, 2019)–, la cuestión de qué cambia y qué no cambia con el tiempo… Mientras Tommaso abandona el lugar, el filme aguanta este último encuadre (elegido por mí) que recuerda a la primera estrofa de *One Too Many Mornings* (1964) de Bob Dylan:

En la calle los perros ladran /
Y el día se pone oscuro /
Cuando la noche venga cayendo /
El perro dejará de ladrar. /
Y la noche silenciosa estallará /
Debido a los sonidos dentro de mi
*   cabeza /*
Sí, voy demasiadas mañanas /
*   miles de millas por detrás.*

Traducción al español © Cristina Álvarez López, Diciembre 2021

CPSIA information can be obtained
at www.ICGtesting.com
Printed in the USA
LVHW081405170322
713581LV00010B/585

9 781648 714894

Gobshite Quarterly

Quadruple Trouble / Issue 40 – Summer Fall 2022

This issue is dedicated to the memory of:

Peggy Farrell (2 June, 1932 – 29 Aug., 2021)
Lee "Scratch" Perry (20 Mar., 1936 – 29 Aug., 2021)
Anne Jolliffe (17 Oct., 1933 – 27 Aug., 2021)
Carol Fran (23 Oct., 1933 – 1 Sept., 2021)(COVID-19)
Alemayehu Eshete (June 1941 – 2 Sept., 2021)
Mikis Theodorakis/Μίκης Θεοδωράκης (29 July, 1925 – 2 Sept., 2021)
Jean-Paul Charles Belmondo (9 Apr., 1933 – 6 Sept., 2021)
Pedrés (11 Feb., 1932 – 6 Sept., 2021)
Michael K. Williams (22 Nov., 1966 – 6 Sept., 2021)
George Jiří Mráz (9 Sept., 1944 – 16 Sept., 2021)[
Sarah Dash (18 Aug., 1945 – 20 Sept., 2021)
Melvin Van Peebles (21 Aug., 1932 – 21 Sept., 2021)
Valentina Malyavina/Валентина Малявина (18 June, 1941 – 30 Oct., 2021)
Emmett Chapman (28 Sept., 1936 – 1 Nov., 2021)
Dean Stockwell (5 Mar., 1936 – 7 Nov., 2021)
Sylvère Lotringer (15 Oct., 1938 – 8 Nov., 2021)
F. W. de Klerk (18 Mar., 1936 – 11 Nov., 2021)
Jay T. Last (18 Oct., 1929 – 11 Nov., 2021)
David Frishberg (23 Mar. 3, 1933 – 17 Nov., 2021)
Robert Bly (23 Dec., 1926 – 21 Nov., 2021)
David Gulpilil (1 July, 1953 – 29 Nov., 2021)
Marie-Claire Blais (5 Oct., 1939 – 30 Nov., 2021)
Greg Tate (14 Oct., 1957 – 7 Dec., 2021)
Lina Wertmüller (14 Aug., 1928 – 9 Dec., 2021)
Fjölnir Geir Bragason (5 Feb., 1965 – 11 Dec., 2021)
Anne Rice (4 Oct., 1941 – 11 Dec., 2021)
bell hooks (25 Sept., 1952 – 15 Dec., 2021)
Eve Babitz (13 May, 1943 – 17 Dec., 2021)
Jaime Comas (1936 – 21 Dec., 2021)
Joan Didion (5 Dec., 1934 – 23 Dec., 2021)
E. O. Wilson (10 June, 1929 – 26 Dec., 2021)
Betty White (17 Jan., 1922 – 31 Dec., 2021)

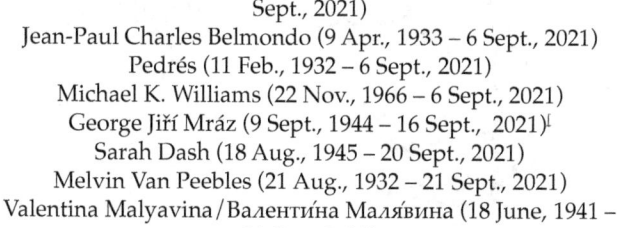

15.00 USDOL || € 13.00 EURO || £ 11.00 GBP (UK) || $ 20.00 AUD (Oz) || $19.00 CAN || ¥ 1600.00 JPY (japan yen) || 225.00 SAR (S. Africa)

Δέκα χρόνια πριν: Θα το αφήσω εδώ προς το παρόν.

Prieš dešimt metų: Kol kas čia jį pasidėsiu.

Dziesięć lat temu = Położę to tutaj na razie

Hace diez años: lo pondré aquí por ahora ...

The Usual Suspects
STAFF

Editor R. V. BRANHAM

Co-editor M.F. MCAULIFFE

Office Mgr. SOFIA SENSEI SATORI ŠOSTAKOVNA SATYAGRAHA STOLIČNIYA SASHIMI SHITKICKER

Asst. Ed. BRYAN MILLER

Assoc. Editor T. WARBURTON Y BAJO

Contrib. Editors MICHAEL LOHR *&* DOUGLAS SPANGLE

Field Correspondent MICHAEL LOHR

House Tr. T. WARBURTON Y BAJO *&* RVB (SP./TO *&* FR.), MIGUEL CAMINHÃO (PORTUGUESE), チャニング・ドッドソン (JAPANESE). Алекса Сигала *&* Андрей Сен-Сеньков (RUSSIAN), ANI GJIKA (ALBANIAN), ART TOLIN (TAGALOG), MICHAEL LOHR (SCAND.), *&* ANA KATANA *&* DIJANA JACOVAK (CROATIAN) *&* JOANNA ROSIŃSKA (POLISH) *&* A COHORT OF LITHUANIAN TRANSLATORS

House Spanish Copyediting LYDA ALVAREZ, BRYAN MILLER, M.F. MCAULIFFE

Cover Illo GRAHAM K. WILLOUGHBY *Design* T. WARBURTON Y BAJO

Cover comix & phfoto illos & franking VAR POSTAL SERVICES.

Photos (except as noted) M. F. MCAULIFFE, T. WARBURTON Y BAJO

Layout T. WARBURTON Y BAJO *&* R. V. BRANHAM

Prod. Tools INDESIGN, PHOTOSHOP (OCCASIONALLY, WHEN FUNCTIONAL), GIMP

Tech Support SAM WARD

Additional Editorial & Design Assistance DOUGLAS SPANGLE *&* M.F. MCAULIFFE

Legal PETER SHAVER

Publisher GOBQ LLC/REPROBATE BOOKS

QUADRUPLE TROUBLE FLIPBOOK ISSUES PRINTED ANNUALLY DURING COVID-19.

Post-production printing INGRAM SPARK/LIGHTNING SOURCE

Also distrib. *&* printed nationally *&* internationally through INGRAM SPARK/LIGHTNING SOURCE POD SOLD THROUGH INDEPENDENT BOOKSTORES *&* AVAILABLE THROUGH INGRAM *&* AMAZON DOT COM *&* GOBSHITEQUARTERLY DOT COM

P.R. P. H. VAZAK

Gobshite Quarterly: Quadruple Trouble, Nos. 39/40, Winter/Spring *&* Summer/Fall 2022
ISBN 978-1-64871-489-4

GobQ volunteers: Qualified candidates please send résumé to
GobQ LLC, 338 NE Roth St., Portland, OR 97211, or to gobq at yahoo dot com

*) as in *pomes penyeach*

Respectfully flip us over, as Issue 39, Winter/Spr. 2022, is a whole upsy-daisy 94 pgs away fr. the Summer/Fall 2022 issue
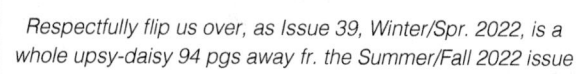

Gob Words

Meet 2021, same as 2020:

(1) Suppose that several efficacious COVID-19 vaccines were developed & given at hospitals, stadiums, & pharmacies, world-wide, but the world wide intertube paranoics persuaded a sufficient no. of people not to get vaccinated, a no. sufficient to cut short the world's summer 2021 reopening due to mutant strains arising from the global unvaccinated pool.

(2) Suppose that the Urine Soaked Putin-Sponsored Orange Cockroach, upon losing their Presidential re-election bid held a rally in DC just as Congress was certifying the electoral vote & persuaded a sufficient number of paranoics, already upset by mask mandates & other infringements, to storm the capitol, to stop what they kept labeling as *the steal*. Now, suppose that this Urine Soaked Putin-Sponsored Orange Cockroach were to be prosecuted, jailed even, for an internationally televised failed insurrection.

& of course, everyone came to their senses, got vaccinated, wore their masks, & the US, Europe, & Asia were able to lift most restrictions. & of course, the Urine Soaked Putin-Sponsored Orange Cockroach graciously conceded the election & the transition of powers, & we were able to turn the page so to speak. Those melting icecaps, cops murdering black people, both crises solved! 2022 is going to be amazing! Am I right? An Observation for 2022, for 2023, & perhaps, beyond, *Gobshite Quarterly*'ll be an annual, & feature more pages. — *rvb*

———○○○———

The Usual Suspects
CONTRIBUTORS

Miglė Anušauskaitė, cartoons & tr. essays have been in *GobQ*, & other pubs., returns w/ Lith. tr. of Dafydd Ap Gwylym's midiæval Welsh pome *Yr Wylan/Seagull/Spegillinn/Γλάρος/Galeb/Gaviota/Mewa/Žuvėdra* (Welsh/Eng./Isl./Grk./Croat./Sp./Polsk/Lith.)

Dafydd Ap Gwylym, the 14th. c. Welsh bard's *GobQ* debut is *Yr Wylan/Seagull/Spegillinn/Γλάρος/Galeb/Gaviota/Mewa/ Žuvėdra* (Welsh/Eng./Isl./Grk./Croat./Sp./Polsk./Lith.)

Μαρουσώ Αθανασίου/Marouso Athanasiou makes their *GobQ* debut w/a Grk tr. of Jenny Forrester's *I Wanna Show You My Guns: A Reasoned Rant/Θέλω να σας δείξω τα όπλα μου: Συνετό ξέσπασμα* (Eng./Sp./Grk./Isl.)

Kirsten Aysworth's *GobQ* debut is the pome *Trash/ΣΚΟΥΠΙΔΙΑ/Basur/Otpad/Rusl,* (Eng./Grk./Sp.Croat./Isl.)

Poe Ballantine, whose most recent novel is *Whirlaway*, returns fr. the plains of Nebraska w/ the short story, *Int. Bus Sta., Motel, Liq. Store. Hayes, KS/Alþj. Rúttasta., Flutningur, Mótel.../Međunarodni autobusni kolodvor, kamion, motel.../Int. Estación de autobuses camión, Motel...* (Eng./Isl./Croat./Sp.)

David Biespiel, award-winning poet & essayist, Attic Inst. founder, returns w/*Chimney Rock Rd./Trakt Kominowa Skała/Cesta Chimney Rock/Calle de roca de la chimenea* (Eng./Polsk/Croat./Sp.)

Tomislav M. Bilosnić, a freq. contrib., based in Zadar, Croatia, returns w/*Molitva Svetom Franji/A Prayer to St. Francis/Μια προσευχή στον Αγιο Φραγκίσκο/聖フランシスコへの祈り/Молитва До Святого Франциска/Sala Ya Mtakatifu Francisko/Oración a San Francisco* (Croat./Eng./Grk./Jap./Ukr./Kiswahili/Sp.)

Casey Bush's *GobQ* debut is the pome *junkpurge/šlamštoišvalymas/Usuwanie odpadów/basurapurga/ruslhreinsun/Τζανκπερτζ* (Eng./Lith./Polsk/Sp./Isl./Grk.)

Marija Dejanović, living in Larísa, Greece, runs a small press w/ Thanos Gogos. She returns w/a pome, *Zvuk/The Sound/O ήχος/*

See hääl/El Sonido/Hljóðið (Croat./Eng./Grk./Eston./Sp./Isl.). She also did the Croat. tr. for the Arturo Desimone pome *Divided Saban Night/Deild Saban Nótt/Divida noche de Sabán/ Podimeljena Sabejska noć* (Eng./Isl./Sp./Croat.), *Βασιλεία Οικονόμου/Vasileia Oikonomou's Μαθήματα Γλώσσας/Language Lessons/Lecciones de idiomas/Tungumálakennsla/Učenje jezika/Lekcje języka* (Grk./Eng.Sp./Isl./Croat./Polsk)

Иван де Монбризон/Ivan de Mobrison's *GobQ* debut fr. Paris are the pomes *Мы забываем дорогу/We forget the rd./Nos olvidamos del camino* (Eng./Russ./Sp.) & *Каменная статуя на площади/A stone statue in a sq./Un estatua se encuentra en una plaza/Ένα πέτρινο άγαλμα σε μια πλατεία/Steinstytta á torgi* (Eng./Russ./Sp./Grk./Isl.)

Arturo Desimone's *GobQ* debut is *Divided Saban Night/Deild Saban Nótt/Divida noche de Sabán/ Podimeljena Sabejska noć* (Eng./Isl./Sp./Croat.)

David Elsey returns w/ *Albert's Thurs. Night/La noche del jueves de Alberto/Albertov četvrtak navečer/Ένα βράδυ Πέμπτης του Αλμπερτ* (Eng./Sp./Croat./Grk.)

Michael Filetra & Paul Merchant return w/ their Eng. tr. of Dafydd Ap Gwylym's midiæval Welsh pome, *Yr Wylan/Seagull/Spegillinn/Γλάρος/Galeb/Gaviota/Mewa/ Žuvėdra* (Welsh/Eng./Isl./Grk./Croat./Sp./Polsk./Lith.)

Jenny Forrester returns w/*I Wanna Show You My Guns: A Reasoned Rant/ Quiero mostrarte mis pistolas: Una diatriba razonable/Θέλω να σας δείξω τα όπλα μου: Συνετό ξέσπασμα/Ég Vil Sýna Þér Byssurnar Mínar: Rökstutt gífuryrði* (Eng./Sp./Grk./Isl.)

Yannis Goumas did the Eng. tr. of *Βασιλεία Οικονόμου/Vasileia Oikonomou's Μαθήματα Γλώσσας/ Language Lessons/Lecciones de idiomas/Tungumálakennsla/Učenje jezika/Lekcje języka* (Grk./Eng.Sp./Isl./Croat./Polsk)

Dijana Jakovac returns for this *GobQ no. 39/40* w/ Croat. tr. for a goodly baker's doz. of works.

Juleen Johnson returns w/ *Sage/Szałwia/Salvia/Φαεκόμηλο* (Eng./Polsk/Sp./Grk.)

Roman Karlović returns w/an Eng. tr. of Tomislav M. Bilosnić's *Molitva Svetom Franji/A Prayer to St. Francis/Μια προσευχή στον Αγιο Φραγκίσκο/聖フランシスコへの祈り/Молитва До Святого Франциска/Sala Ya Mtakatifu Francisko/Oración a San Francisco* (Croat./Eng./Grk./Jap./Ukr./Kiswahili/Sp.)

Ana Katana, quarantining in Zagreb, returns for this *GobQ no. 39/40* w/ Croat. tr. for a goodly baker's doz. of works.

Jawrence Kiiru did the kiswahili tr. of Tomislav M. Bilosnić's *Molitva Svetom Franji/A Prayer to St. Francis/Μια προσευχή στον Αγιο Φραγκίσκο/聖フランシスコへの祈り/Молитва До Святого Франциска/Oración a San Francisco* (Croat./Eng./Grk./Jap./Ukr./Kiswahili/Sp.)

Κοντοπούλου Κωνσταντίνα/Konstopoulou Konstantina did var. Grk. tr., incl. tr. of Casey Bush's pome *junkpurge/šlamštoišvalymas/Usuwanie odpadów/basurapurga/ruslhreinsun/Τζανκπερτζ* (Eng./Lith./Polks/Sp./Isl./Grk.), Dafydd Ap Gwylym's midiæval Welsh pome *Yr Wylan/Seagull/Spegillinn/Γλάρος/Galeb/Gaviota/Mewa/ Žuvėdra* (Welsh/Eng./Isl./Grk./Croat./Sp./Polsk./Lith.), Juleen Johnson's *Sage/Szałwia/Salvia/Φαεκομηλο* (Eng./Polsk/Sp./Grk.); Casey Bush's *junk-*

purge/šlamštoišvalymas/Usuwanie odpadów/basurapurga/ruslhreinsun/Τζανκπερτζ (Eng./Lith./Polks/Sp./Isl./Grk.); Dan Raphael's *Who Changes the Weather/Los que cambian el clima/Kto zmienia pogodę/Ποιος αλλάζει τον καιρό* (Eng./Sp./Grk./Polsk)

Κορκίшко Василь/*Korkiška Vasilij* did the Ukr. tr. of Tomislav M. Bilosnić's *Molitva Svetom Franji/A Prayer to St. Francis/Μια προσευχή στον Αγιο Φραγκίσκο/*聖フランシスコへの祈り/Молитва До Святого Франциска/Sala Ya Mtakatifu Francisko/Oración a San Francisco (Croat./Eng./Grk./Jap./Ukr./Kiswahili/Sp.)

Laura Kromalcaitė did the Lith. tr. of the Casey Bush pome *junkpurge/šlamštoišvalymas/Usuwanie odpadów/basurapurga/ruslhreinsun/Junkpurge (Τζανκπερτζ)* (Eng./Lith./Polsk/Sp./Isl./Grk.)

Željka Lovrenčić did the Sp. tr. of Tomislav M. Bilosnić's *Molitva Svetom Franji/A Prayer to St. Francis/Μια προσευχή στον Αγιο Φραγκίσκο/*聖フランシスコへの祈り/Молитва До Святого Франциска/Sala Ya Mtakatifu Francisko/Oración a San Francisco (Croat./Eng./Grk./Jap./Ukr./Kiswahili/Sp.)

Michael Lohr, quarantining in Ohio, has for this *GobQ no. 39/40* done Icelandic tr. for a goodly baker's doz. of works.

Joy McDowell returns w/a short story, *Fifth Period/Peti Sat/Fimmta tímabil/Classes de conducción* (Eng./Croat./Isl./Sp.)

D.S. Maolalaí's *GobQ* debut, all the way fr. Dublin, is *The 90s/Na 90aidí/Los años mil noveciento noveinta/9. áratugurinn/ednom budala, i nikad više* (Eng./Gael./Sp./Isl./Croat.)

Adrian Martin, Oz-born & Barcelona-based essayist & film scholar returns w/an essay, or rather, a correspondence w/C. Matamoros, *The Traitor, A Correspondence: The Game of Simulations/Svikarinn, samsvörun: Leikur Hermanna* (Eng./Isl./[& on the flipside, in Eng./Sp.])

大塚真彦/*otsuka masahiko* did the Jap. tr. of Tomislav M. Bilosnić's *Molitva Svetom Franji/A Prayer to St. Francis/Μια προσευχή στον Αγιο Φραγκίσκο/*聖フランシスコへの祈り/Молитва До Святого Франциска/Sala Ya Mtakatifu Francisko/Oración a San Francisco (Croat./Eng./Grk./Jap./Ukr./Kiswahili/Sp.)

Carles Matamoros, also a Barcelona-based essayist & founder of Barcelonas online film journal *Transit*, returns w/an essay, or rather, a correspondence w/A. Martin, *The Traitor, A Correspondence: The Game of Simulations/Svikarinn, samsvörun: Leikur Hermanna* (Eng./Isl./[& on the flipside, in Eng./Sp.])

Seosamh Ó Maolalaí did the Gael. tr. of D.S. Maolalaí's pome, *The 90s/Na 90aidí/Los años mil noveciento noveinta/9. áratugurinn/ednom budala, i nikad više* (Eng./Gael./Sp./Isl./Croat.)

Βασιλεία Οικονόμου/*Vasileia Oikonomou* returns w/*Μαθήματα Γλώσσας/Language Lessons/Lecciones de idiomas/Tungumálakennsla/Učenje jezika/Lekcje języka* (Grk./Eng.Sp./Isl./Polsk); & a Grk. tr. of Ivan de Mobrison's pome Каменная статуя на площади/*A stone statue on a sq./Un estatua se encuentra en una plaza/Ενα πέτρινο άγαλμα σε μια πλατεία/Steinstytta á torgi* (Eng./Russ./Sp..Grk./Isl.)

Marjam Parve did the Eston. tr. of Marija Dejanović's pome, *Zvuk/The Sound/O ήχος/See hääl/El Sonido/Hljóðið* (Croat./Eng./Grk./Eston./Sp./Isl.) & Armin Tolentino's *In the Dunkin' Donuts Where the Virgin Mary Appeared... /Í kleinuhringjum frá Dunkin Þar sem María mey... /se Djevica

Marija pojavila... /Dunkin' Donutsis, kus Neitsi Maarja end... / En el Dunkin' Donuts donde la Virgen María apareció* (Eng./Isl./Croat./Est./Sp.)

Dan Raphael's *GobQ* debut is the pome *Who Changes the Weather/Los que cambian el clima/Kto zmienia pogodę/Ποιος αλλάζει τον καιρό* (Eng./Sp./Grk./Polsk)

Joanna Rosińska has, for this *GobQ no. 39/40.* done Polish (Polsk) tr. for a goodly baker's doz. of works.

Mark Sargent returns w/*Every Edge a Centre: OT Dream/Öll kantur í miðja: OT Draumer/Każda granica bywa środkiem: Sen o dogrywce meczu/Cada borde un centro: Sueño de horas extras* (Eng./Isl./Polsk./Sp.)

Armin Tolentino returns w/two pomes, *In the Dunkin' Donuts Where the Virgin Mary Appeared... /Í kleinuhringjum frá Dunkin Þar sem María mey... /se Djevica Marija pojavila... / Dunkin' Donutsis, kus Neitsi Maarja end... / En el Dunkin' Donuts donde la Virgen María apareció* (Eng./Isl./Croat./Est./Sp.) & *A Week's Pay Lost at the Lizard Fight/Una semana de pago perdido en la lucha de lagartos/Tjedna plaća izgubljena na borbe guštera/Viku er greitt tapað í eðlabaráttunni* (Eng./Sp./Croat./Isl.)

Χρήστος Τουμανίδης/*Chrístos Tonmaníthiz* did the Grk. tr. of Tomislav M. Bilosnić's *Molitva Svetom Franji/A Prayer to St. Francis/Μια προσευχή στον Αγιο Φραγκίσκο/*聖フランシスコへの祈り/Молитва До Святого Франциска/Sala Ya Mtakatifu Francisko/Oración a San Francisco (Croat./Eng./Grk./Jap./Ukr./Kiswahili/Sp.)

Ελένη Τζατζιμάκη/*Eleni Tzatzimaki* is a prof. jazz singer, based in Athens, Grc. Eleni's pome colls. incl. *Se poion anikei mia istoria?/Who does a story belong to?* (2015) & *The Twin Paradox* (2018); her *GobQ* debuts are *Αν πυροβολούσα το φεγγάρι/If I shot the moon/Si disparara a la luna/Kad bih raznijela mjesec* and *Μέλμπα Ερνάντες Ροντρίγκες/Melba Hernandez Rodriguez/Melba Hernandez Rodriguez/Melba Hernandez Rodriguez* (Grk./Eng./Sp./Croat.)

T. Warburton y Bajo y rvb did Sp. tr. of a goodly baker's doz. of works in this is.

Emmett Wheatfall, a local poet, makes their *GobQ* debut w/ *Once Again A Fool Never Again a Fool/Una vez tonto, nunca más tonto/Być głupcem raz – wystarczy/Jednom budala, i nikad više/Ποτέ ξανά τρελός* (Eng./Gael./Sp./Isl./Croat.)

Shannon Wheeler, whose cartoons have graced *The New Yorker* & *WIllamette Wk*, & whose *Too Much Coffee Man* became an opera, returns w/ some cartoons.

Graham Willoughby, whose artwork's adorned our covers since is. 2, returns, this time in glorious black & white!

Τώνια Τζιρίτα Ζαχαράτου//*Tonia Tzirita Zacharatou* did Grk. captions for M. Fikaris's *Altered Identity in Public Theatre Transports/τροποποιημένη ταυτότητα στο δημόσιο θέατρο των συγκοινωνιών* (Eng., w/ Croat./Dutch/Grk./Russ./Sp.); David Elsey's pome *Albert's Thurs. Night/La noche del jueves de Alberto/Albertov četvrtak navečer/Ενα βράδυ Πέμπτης του Αλμπερτ* (Eng./Sp./Croat./Grk.)

CHIMNEY ROCK ROAD

When I remembered, *Chimney
        Rock,*
I could hear the humid *whum* of
        the
Armadillo's tongue.

I imagined it
Mile by mile, the road built
Along the purling

Bayou, under slender leaves
And long twigs and deeper
Shades of willows

Like fans of stillness,
Leaves we called, *wept,*
Where everything is hurt.

In my fifty-sixth year,
I watch the cumulous
Weather that spreads out in

The big, gray drift of things,
Weighted with light, So I think to
Myself, *Chimney Rock —*

And its midsummer, next-
Door, brick-work, open-
Windowed sound of the road

Gets framed in glittered
Silence. And inside the
One-story house, in the little

Kitchen in the back, the table
Is arrayed with knives and forks
Wounded at their stems.

What do we do anymore to taste
The underbrush of any road, or
        the

Trakt Kominowa Skała *

Gdy wspomniałem Kominową
        Skałę,
Usłyszałem wilgotne „sljup"
Języka pancernika.

Wyobraziłem to sobie
Mile za milą, drogę skonstru-
        owaną
Wzdłuż leniwie szemrzącego
        strumienia,

Pod wysmukłymi liśćmi
I długimi gałązkami, głębokim
Cieniem wierzb

Jak wachlarze bezruchu,
tak zwaliśmy liście, *płaczą*,
Gdzie wszystko zranione.

W pięćdziesiątym szóstym
        roku życia
Obserwuję cumulusy
Aurę, która się rozpływa

W wielkim, szarym dryfie rze-
        czy,
Obciążonym światłem, więc
        myślę sobie
Kominowa Skała –

W otwartych oknach
Ceglanych domów sąsiedztwa,
Hałas ulicy w środku lata

Oprawiony w połyskującą
Ciszę. A wewnątrz
W parterowym domu, w małej

Kuchni w głębi domu, stół
Zdobny w noże i widelce

CESTA CHIMNEY ROCK

Kad sam se sjetio, *Chimney*
   Rocka,
Mogao sam čuti vlažni *vum*
armadilovog jezika.

Zamislio sam
Milju po milju, cestu izgrađenu
Uz riječni rukavac koji žubori,

Pod tankim lišćem i
Dugačkim granama i dubljim
Sjenama vrba

Kao lepeze mirnoće,
Lišće koje smo zvali, *plakalo je,*
Tamo gdje je sve povrijeđeno.

U svojoj pedeset šestoj godini,
Gledam oblačno
Vrijeme koje se širi

U velikim, sivim zanosima stvari,
Otežano svjetlom, Pa pomislim
   u
Sebi, *Chimney Rock* —

I sredina je ljeta, vrata
Do, cigleni dio, zvuk ceste
Kao otvoren prozor

Uokviri se svjetlucavom
Tišinom. I u jednokatnici,
U maloj

Kuhinji straga, na stolu su pore-
   dani
Noževi i vilice
Ranjenih stabljika.

Calle de roca de la chimenea

Cuando recordé, *La roca de la*
   chimenea,
Pude escuchar el tarareo húm-
   edo de la
lengua de armadillo.

Lo imaginé kilómetro a
Kilómetro, el camino construido
A lo largo de la bahía

Ondulada, bajo hojas delgadas y
Y ramitas largas y mas profun-
   das
Sombras de sauces

Como abanicos de quietud,
Las hojas a las que llamamos
   llorosas,
Donde todo está herido.

En mi quincuagésimo sexto año,
Veo el clima cumu-
loso que se extiende en

La deriva grande y gris de las
   cosas,
Pesado con la luz, Así que creo a
mí mismo, *La roca de la chimenea* —

En medio de verano, próximo-
puerta, enladrillado, por abierto-
ventana sonado de la carretera

Se enmarca con en silencio
Reluciente. Y dentro de la
casa de un piso, en la pequeña

Cocina en la parte trasera, la
   mesa
Esta arrayada con cuchillos y

First autumn floods when we

Used to float a skiff in the street
And praised the year in the
    mouth
Of the white-washed horizon

Far out into evening?
When I lived here, less than
A hint of a name,

I never expected to come back
Transparent as the dark, or be
The plowman turning round.

    – *David Biespiel*

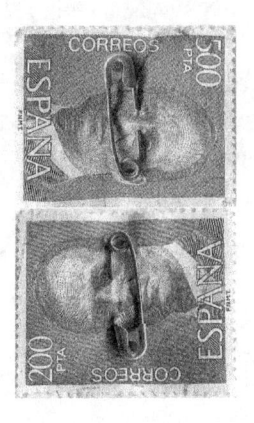

O zranionych trzonkach.

I jak więc mamy posmakować
Poszycie jakiejkolwiek drogi
Lub pierwsze powodzie jesienne
  gdy

Pływaliśmy łupiną z prądem ulicy
Chwaląc rok u wlotu do
Bielejącego horyzontu

Do późnego wieczoru?
Gdy tu mieszkałem,
Ledwie świadom siebie,

Nie przypuszczałem, że kiedyś
    wrócę
Preźroczysty jak ciemność,
Lub że zawrócę pługiem na polu.

    – *David Biespiel*
    (Tłumaczenie: Joanna Rosiń-
    ska)

*) *Trakt Kominowa Skała czyli Chimney
   Rock Road jest to obecnie ulica w mieście
   Huston, w Teksasie, w wierszu wspomina-
   na sprzed urbanizacji jako wiejska droga.*

Što još uvijek radimo da oku-
    simo
Šikaru bilo koje ceste, ili
Prve jesenske poplave kad smo

Plovili skifom po cesti
I hvalili godinu u usta
Horizonta ispranog do bjeline

Daleko u noć?
Dok sam živio ovdje, manji od
Naznake imena,

Nisam nikad očekivao da ću se
    vratiti
Providan kao mrak, ili biti
Orač koji se okreće.

    – David Biespiel
       (Prijevod, Marija Dejano-
       vić)

            tenedores
heridos en sus tallos.

¿Qué hacemos ya para probar
El sotobobosque de cualquier car-
            retera, o las
Primeras inundaciones de otoño
        cuando nosotros

Solíamos flotar un esquife en la
        calle
Y elogiamos el año en la boca
De el horizonte encalado

Hasta bien entrada la noche?
Cuando vivía aquí, a menos de
Un indicio de un nombre,

Nunca esperaba volver
Transparente como la oscuridad, o
            ser
El arado dando la vuelta.

        – David Biespiel
           (traducción, T. Warburton y
           Bajo y rvb)

Θέλω γάτα.

Noriu katino

Och, chcę kota

Quiero un gato.

"*I want a cat.*"

MOLITVA SVETOM FRANJI

Neka nam Bog udijeli mir
da ptice zemlju naslijede,
da steknemo prijateljstvo sa životi-
njama.

Neka nam Bog udijeli mir
s križem od tijela i krila
da se i po smrti družimo sa sićuš-
nim bićima.

Sveti moj Franjo, kad kreneš
putom prema gorju
neka sve ptičice s planine
dolete u polje.
Bog tako hoće, da anđeli i ptice
otvore prozore na svakoj travki
da vlati svijetle kao perje mlade zvi-
jezde

Neka me probudi cvrkut
kao otjecanje vode,
neka me uzbudi cvrkut
kao pucketanje vatre
u zagrljaju Tvojih krila

Molim te, neka ptice ne utihnu
ni s večeri kad ovce zableje.
Ne mogu izdržati sakriven u staklu,
ne mogu trpjeti jezik isplažen na
metalnoj ogradi.
Molim te, neka u pamćenju ostanu
kolibrići što poput živaca
trepere nad teškim brigama.
Neka u pamćenju ostane upisano
kako među mnoštvom ljudi
pržinom štitimo mrava.
Neka ostanu poznate moje slabosti
kao što je zajedničko buđenje crva i
leptira.
Neka se pamte moje muke
slične vjetru što njače poput magarca.

A PRAYER TO SAINT FRANCIS

May God grant us peace
that birds may inherit the earth,
and we – make friends with beasts.

May God grant us peace
by a cross of bodily wings
that, even in death, we may keep
company
with tiny creatures.

Dear Saint Francis, when you start
up the path to the hillside
may all the little mountain birds
dart to the field.
That is God's will: that angels and
birds
should open the windows on every
blade of grass
so it lights up like a young star's plu-
mage

May chirping wake me
like water draining away,
may chirping rouse me
like flames flickering
in your wings' embrace

Please, let not the birds go silent
not even at dusk, when sheep begin
to bleat.
I can't live concealed in glass,
I loathe the tongue spread out on the
metal fence.
Please, let me remember
the hummingbirds quivering like ner-
ves
over great worries.
Let there be engraved in memory
how we protect an ant with hot sand
amid a human multitude.
Let my flaws be known
as the awakening of worm and
butterfly together.
Let my torment be remembered

Μια προσευχή στον Άγιο Φραγκίσκο

Είθε ο Θεός να χαρίζει σε όλους ειρήνη,
για να μπορούν τα πουλιά να
κληρονομήσουν την Γη,
και μείς– να κάνομε φίλους τα θηρία.
Είθε ο Θεός να μας χαρίζει ειρήνη,
κι έναν σταυρό που θα είναι φτερά στο
σώμα μας,
ώστε ακόμα και στο θάνατο,
να μπορούμε να είμαστε κοντά
και στα πιο ταπεινά πλάσματα.
Αγαπητέ Άγιε Φραγκίσκο, όταν
ξεκινήσεις να ανηφορίζεις
στο μονοπάτι της βουνοπλαγιάς,
είθε όλα τα μικρά πουλιά του βουνού να
ξεχυθούν στο λιβάδι.
Είναι η επιθυμία του Θεού, πως όλοι οι
Άγγελοι και τα πουλιά
να ανοίξουνε παράθυρα στο τρυφερό
χορτάρι,
ώστε όλα τα χόρτα να λάμψουν σαν
φτερά νιογέννητου αστεριού.
Είθε να με ξυπνήσουνε
νερά που κυλάν τραγουδώντας.
Κελαϊδίσματα να με αφυπνίσουν,
σαν φλόγες που τρεμοπαίζουν
στο αγκάλιασμα των φτερών σου.
Σε ικετεύω, κάνε να μην σιωπήσουν τα
πουλιά,
ούτε την ώρα του δειλινού, τότε που
βελάζουν τα πρόβατα.
Δεν μπορώ να ζήσω κρυμμένος στη
γυάλα.
Αποστρέφομαι την γλώσσα που
απλώνεται σαν σιδερένιος φράχτης.
Άφησε με να θυμάμαι τα κολιμπρί
που τρέμουν
σαν νεύρα πάνω από τις μεγάλες
ανησυχίες.
Άφησε να χαραχτεί στην μνήμη μας, το
πως προστατεύουμε ένα μυρμήγκι,
πάνω στην άμμο την καυτή,
απ' τ' ανθρώπινο πλήθος.
Άφησε να γίνουν φανερά τα
ελαττώματα μου,
όπως το ξύπνημα του σκουληκιού και
της πεταλούδας, μαζί.
Άφησε το μαρτύριο μου να γίνει
ανάμνηση,
έτσι όπως παίρνει ο άνεμος τη φωνή του
γαϊδάρου.

聖フランシスコへの祈り

神よ、鳥が大地を受け継ぎ
われわれが生きとし生ける者との友情
を得られるような
静寂を与えてください。

神よ、身体と翼がなす十字架とともに
死してなお小さな存在たちと友好を保
てるような
静寂をわれわれに与えてください。

聖フランシスコよ、君が
丘に登る道を行くなら
その時は鳥たちがみな
野原へ舞い降りてくれると良い。
神は、天使たちが、鳥たちが
草木すべてに窓を開け放ち、その低い
茎に
若い星の羽毛のごとき光をもたらすこと
を望んでいる。

どうか、水流の音のごとく
さえずりが僕を起こすように
そしてどうか、神の翼にいだかれた火が
はぜる音のごとく
さえずりは僕をそわそわさせるように。

夜となり羊が鳴き始めても
鳥は、止むことなく歌い続けよ。
ガラスに囲まれ身を潜め続けていること
は、僕には出来ないし
金属の柵の向こうから舌を出すだけで
我慢は出来ない。
どうか、記憶に残らせよ
ハチドリが神経のごとく
重い心配に震えるのを。
どうか、大勢の人々がいる中
われわれが一匹の蟻を
砂で守ったことが記憶に刻まれるよう
に。
どうか、芋虫と蝶が一緒に目覚めるごと
く
僕の弱点が知られたままであるように。
驢馬のようにいななく風に似た
僕の苦しみが記憶されるように。

as the wind braying like a donkey.

Looking for the road you walked,
a wolf and a lamb at your side,
I saw a fish unconquerable like a bird,
I saw a donkey and a wasp suffering
    the same,
a white cloud carrying our souls to
    heaven.

What is as beautiful as the fear of the
    tiger,
as this story,
a spider at its end, weaving his web
luminous like a butterfly
rising at dawn.

May God grant us peace
may our family not lack
not even bugs —
bulls bow their bulky head
under their sway.

May God grant us such peace
that the sparrow not relent for a se-
    cond
chipping unceasingly
until we – lonely to death – hear the
    dogs bark.

May the fish inherit the earth,
may the wasp inherit the earth
and the ant
and the cicada.
May the wild horse inherit it
and the fly
that wafts lightly above our wounds.
May portly roosters
eagerly awaiting the dawn in my gar-
    den
crow like memories.

> – *Tomislav Marijan Bilosnić*
> *(Tr. fr. the Croatian, Roman*
> *Karlović)*

Κοιτάζοντας τον δρόμο που
    περπάτησες,
μ' έναν λύκο και μ' ένα αρνί στο
    πλευρό σου,
βλέπω ένα ψάρι ατρόμητο σαν πουλί,
έναν γάιδαρο και μια σφήγκα να
    υποφέρουν το ίδιο,
ένα σύννεφο άσπρο να μεταφέρει τις
    ψυχές μας στον παράδεισο.
Αυτό είναι τόσο όμορφο όσο ο φόβος
    της τίγρης,
όσο αυτή η ιστορία,
όπου μια αράχνη στο τέλος της,
    υφαίνει φωτεινό τον ιστό της,
σαν πεταλούδα που εμφανίζεται το
    ξημέρωμα.
Είθε ο Θεός να μας δίνει ειρήνη,
για να μην λείψει κάνεις από την
    οικογένεια μας,
και να μην γίνονται σφάλματα.
Οι ταύροι να σκύβουν το μεγάλο
    κεφάλι τους
με την δική τους θέληση, καθώς
    περπατούν.

Είθε ο Θεός να μας δώσει τέτοια ειρήνη,
ώστε το σπουργίτι να μην σταματήσει
    ούτε στιγμή,
να λέει το τραγούδι του,
Έως ότου εμείς – μονάχοι μες στο
    θάνατο – ν' ακούσουμε
τα σκυλιά να γαυγίζουν.
Είθε τα ψάρια να κληρονομήσουν την
    Γη.
Είθε οι σφήγκες να κληρονομήσουν την
    Γη.
Και τα μυρμήγκια.
Και τα τζιτζίκια.
Είθε τα άγρια άλογα να την
    κληρονομήσουν,
και η μύγα,
η οποία πετάει απαλά πάνω από τις
    πληγές μας.
Είθε όλοι οι πετεινοί,
ανυπόμονα να περιμένουν την αυγή
    στον κήπο μου,
και να λαλούν σαν αναμνήσεις.

> – *Τόμιλαβ Μαριάν Μπιλόσνιτς*
> *(μεταφρασμένο, Χρήστος Τουμανί-*
> *δης)*

Tražeći cestu kojom si hodio
i vuk i janje uz tebe,
vidio sam ribu neosvojivu kao pticu,
vidio sam magarca i osu na istim
    mukama,
bijeli oblak koji naše duše nosi u
    nebo.

Ima li išta ljepše od straha pred ti-
    grom,
od ove priče
na čijem kraju pauk plete mrežu
svjetlošću leptira
što se diže zorom.

Neka nam Bog udijeli mir
neka naša obitelj ne oskudijeva
niti sa insektima
pod kojima bikovi spuštaju svoje
    teške glave.

Neka nam Bog udijeli takav mir
da nam vrabac ne da mira ni trena
bez prestanka pjevajući
živ-živ, živ-živ,
dok ispaćeni samoćom ne začujemo
    lavež pasa.

Neka ribe zemlju naslijede,
neka ose zemlju naslijede,
i mravi
i cvrčci.
Neka zemlju naslijede divlji konji
i muhe
lagano lebdeći iznad naših rana.
Neka u mom vrtu
otmjeni pijevci obuzeti čekanjem
    zore
kukuriču poput sjećanja.

– *Tomislav Marijan Bilosnić*

狼も山羊も一緒に君と歩んだ
道を捜しながら、僕は
鳥のごとく、捕らえることのできない魚を
    見た
同じ苦しみを苦しむ驢馬と蜂を
われわれの霊を空へと運ぶ白い雲を見
    た。

虎を眼の前にした恐れより美しいものが
    あるだろうか
暁の訪れとともに
蝶から放たれる輝きで
蜘蛛が網を編んでいく
この物語のそんな結末よりも美しいもの
    があるだろうか。

神よ、静寂を与えてください
われわれの家庭にあっては
雄牛たちが重い頭を垂れるその上に
いつも虫たちがいますように。

神よ、静寂を与えてください
雀が、イ・キヨ、キヨキヨ、生きよ生きよ、
    と
いっときたりとも、われわれの耳を休ま
    せず
歌い続け、孤独に疲れたわれわれに
犬の吠え声がまた聞こえてくるまでは、そ
    んな静寂を。

魚がどうか大地を受け継ぐよう
蜂がどうか大地を受け継ぐよう
蟻も
蝉も。
野生の馬がどうか大地を受け継ぐよう
また、われわれの傷の上をゆるやかに飛
    び回る
蠅も。
どうかわが庭で
高貴な雄鶏が気もそぞろに暁を待ちつ
    つ
何か思い出すかのごとく高鳴きするよう。

    — トミスラフ＝マリヤン・ビロスニッチ
    (翻訳, 大塚真彦)

МОЛИТВА ДО СВЯТОГО ФРАНЦИСКА

Нехай Бог дарує нам спокій
що птахи успадковують землю,
подружитися з тваринами.

Нехай Бог дарує нам спокій
з хрестом від тіла та крил
що навіть після смерті ми асоці-
   юємося
з крихітними істотами.

Святий Франциск, коли підеш
по дорозі в гори,
пустіть з гори всіх птахів
вниз у поле.
Бог так хоче ангелів і птахів,
відкриті вікна на кожній траві,
листи яскраві, як полум'я молодої
   зірки.

Нехай щебетання мене будить
як стікає вода,
дозволь мені щебетати
наче тріскучий вогонь
в лоні твоїх крил.

Будь ласка, не дозволяйте птахам
   замовкнути
на вечері, коли вівці почнуть бе-
   кати.
Я не можу жити прихованим у
   склі,
не витримую язика
на металевому перило.
Будь ласка, зберігайте їх у своїй
   пам'яті,
колібрі як нерви тремтять від сер-
   йозних турбот.
Зберігайте це у своїй пам'яті,
як серед безлічі
людей ми захищаємо мурашок

SALA YA MTAKATIFU FRANSISKO

Mungu atubariki, tuishi kwa amani
Ndege zimerithi dunia hii,
Na sisi tufanye urafiki na wanyama
   wote.

Mungu atubariki, tuishi kwa amani
na msalaba wenye mwili na nabawa
Kwa kifo yetu tuishe pamoja na
   viumbe viote vidogo.

Mtakatifu Fransisko, ule wakati
   utaanza
matembezi yako ubavuni wa mlima
wacha ndege waishi huko mlimani
waweze kupukapuka kiwanjani.
Hiyo ni radhi ya Mungu wetu:
Malaika na ndege wafungue madi-
   risha
ya majani wote wapate mwanga
   kama
manyoya ya nyota.

Ningetaka wimbo uniamushe
kama mtirisho wa maji,
Ningetaka wimbo uniamushe kama
   moto unawakawaka
kwasababu ya kikumbatio ya ma-
   bawa yako

Tafadhali usinyamizishe ndege
hata wakati utusitusi, wakati kon-
   doo zinafanya baa baa.
Mimi siwezi kukaa maficho kwenye
   majani
Nachukia sana ulimi umepakia kwa
   ua wa metali.

Tafadhali nipe ruhusa nikumbuke
   ndege mwibaji
anaotikisa kama neva inasikia wa-
   siwasi.
Wacha nikumbuke kabisa hivyo
   tunalinda safu na mehanga moto
asikanyangwe na watu wengi wa-

ORACIÓN A SAN FRANCISCO

Qué Dios nos dé la paz
que los pájaros hereden la tierra,
para que hagamos amistad con los animales.

Qué Dios nos dé la paz
con la cruz del cuerpo
y alas
para que después de la muerte estemos en
compañía de seres diminutos.

Mi San Francisco, cuando partas
camino hacia los cerros
qué todos los pajaritos de la montaña
vuelen al campo.
Así lo quiere Dios — que ángeles y pájaros
abran ventanas en cada hierba
que sus hojas brillen como las plumas de la
estrella joven.

Qué me despierte el gorjeo
como el flujo del agua,
que me emocione como el crepitar del fuego
en el abrazo de Tus alas.
Por favor, qué no se callen los pájaros
ni en el comienzo de la noche cuando las ovejas
   balan.
No puedo soportar escondido en el cristal,
no puedo aguantar la lengua extendida en el cerco de
   metal.

Por favor, que queden en la memoria
los colibríes que como nervios
vibran bajo grandes preocupaciones.
Que en la memoria quede escrito
Como entre la multitud de gente

protegemos la hormiga en la arena diminuta.
Qué queden conocidas mis debilidades
Como el despertar conjunto de los gusanos y las
   mariposas.
Que se recuerden mis penas
parecidas al viento que rebuzna como un burro.

серед людської байдужості.
Нехай будуть відомі мої вади,
 як пробудження
черв'яка та метеликів.
Нехай запам'ятається моя туга,
 як вітер дме як осел.

Шукаєте дорогу, якою ви
 йшли,
а вовк і ягня поруч із вами.
Я побачив непереможну рибу
 як птаха.
Я побачив осла та осу що
 страждає тим же,
біла хмара яка несе наші душі
 до неба.

Чи є щось краще ніж страх пе-
 ред тигром,
з цієї історії в кінці якого павук
 в'яже сітку,
як метелик на світанку.
Нехай Бог дарує нам спокій з
 комахами,
над якими бики схиляють важ-
 кі голови.

Нехай Бог дарує нам такий
 спокій поки
ми засмучені самотністю, не
 почуємо гавкіт собак.
Нехай риба успадковує землю,
і мурашки і цвіркуни.
Нехай земля успадковується
 дикими кіньми
і летить трохи вище наших ран.
Можливо півні в саду з нетер-
 пінням чекають світанку.

— *Томіслав Мар'ян Білосніч*
(Переклад, Коркішко
Василь Анатолійович)

tembezi.
Wacha dosari zangu zijulikane kama
 uamisho wa mnyoo na kipepeo.
Wacha watu wakumbuke mateso
 yangu kama upepo
unaolia kama punda.

Nilitazama ile barabara mlichukua
 wewe
mbwa mwitu na mwanakondoo,
nikaona samaki jasiri kama ndege,
nikaona punda na nyigu wanaovumi-
 lia pamoja,
nikaona wingu mweupe uliyobeba
 roho yetu binguni.

Kuna kitu kizuri kama hofu mbele ya
 chui?
Kuliko hadithi hii mwishoni wake
buibui atenda wavu kwa mwangaza
wa kipepeo kinarukaruka asubuhi?

Mungu atubariki, amani iwe duniani
 yetu
familia yetu isiwe na ukosefu
hata wadudu –
mafahali wamishe vichwa yum-
 bayumba.

Mungu atubariki, amani duniani yetu
na yeye shorewanda asitupatie hata
 amani ndogo
wimbo wake uendelee mpaka sisi
wenye upweke – tusikie bweka wa
 umbwa.

Muwache samaki arithi dunia
muwache nyigu arithi dunia
na hata siafu
na hata nyenye.
hata farasi mwitu
hata nzi anarukaruka juu ya jeraha
wacha jogoo wanagoja mapambuziko
 dani ya banda
la kuku wawike kama kumbukumbu

— *Tomislav Marijan Bilosnić*
(tafsiri, Lawrence Kiiru)

Buscando la carretera que pasaste
y el lobo y el cordero contigo,
vi el pez inconquistable como el pájaro,
vi al burro y a la avispa con las mismas
    penas,
la nube blanca que nuestras almas lleva
    al cielo.
Hay algo más hermoso que el miedo
    frente al tigre,
de este cuento
en cuyo final la araña teje la telaraña
con luz de mariposa
que se levanta a la madrugada.

Qué Dios nos dé la paz
que nuestra familia no carezca
ni de los insectos
bajo los que los toros inclinan sus
    pesadas cabezas.

Qué Dios nos dé tanta paz
que el gorrión no nos deje en paz
 ni un momento
cantando sin cesar
pío-pío, pío-pío,
mientras mortificados por la soledad no
    escuchemos el ladrido de
de los perros.

Qué los peces hereden la tierra,
qué las avispas hereden la tierra,
Y las hormigas
y los grillos.

Qué hereden la tierra
los caballos salvajes y
las moscas
flotando levemente sobre nuestras
    heridas.

Qué en mi huerto
los nobles gallos ensimismados
    esperando el alba
canten como los recuerdos.

– *Tomislav Marijan Bilosnić*
    (Traducción, Željka Lovrenčić)

3ʳᵈ printing, 2017

REPROBATE / GobQ BOOKS

ISBN 9781935662341

$13.

Order on-line @
http://www.gobshitequarterly.com
or from Amazon.com

also available at Portland area independent booksellers, incl.: Mother Foucault's Books, Powell's Books

junkpurge

This is a serious chicken and egg conundrum.
Use the brain to step out of your mind.
 Obstinate antechambers organically con-
   joined:
good and evil, east and west, light and dark,
apples and oranges, rich and poor, time and
space. You might ask from which fiendish
event horizon do such cosmic motes emanate?
What do they really want from us? Perceive,
conceive, distinguish, evoke. Embrace that
ascendant spiraling epiphany. It may not be
necessary to straighten out the convolutions
of your cerebral cortex. Petulant chanteuse
hurls brickbats against the pretext of lucidity.
Violinist continues to raise the bow after
reaching a score's finale, maintaining the
audience's attention while careful not to
perturb the instrument's hushed filaments.
 You must keep pace with those mad dogs
chasing the tires of cars which they dare not
seize with their teeth.

  — *Casey Bush*

šlamštoišvalymas

Tai yra rimtas vištos ir kiaušinio galvosūkis.
Naudok smegenis, kad išliptum iš savo proto.
Užsispyrę prieškambariai organiškai
    sujungti:

gera ir bloga, rytai ir vakarai, šviesa ir tamsa,
obuoliai ir apelsinai, turtingi ir vargšai, laikas ir
erdvė. Galėtum klausti, iš kurio demoniško
įvykių horizonto sklinda tokios kosminės dulkės?
Ko jos iš tikrųjų iš mūsų nori? Suvokti,
suprasti, atskirti, sužadinti. Priimk tą
kylantį spiralinį nušvitimą. Galbūt
nebūtina ištiesinti tavo smegenų
žievės persisukimų. Nekantri giedotoja
svaido plytas į aiškumo pretekstą.
Smuikininkas vėl kelia stryką po to,
kai pasiekia finalą, išlaikydamas
publikos dėmesį, neužgaudamas
nutildytų instrumento gijų.

Tu privalai neatsilikti nuo tų pasiutusių šunų,
besivaikančių mašinų padangas, kurių jie
nedrįsta sugriebti dantimis.

— Casey Bush
(iš lietuvių kalbos vertė Laura Kromalcaitė)

Usuwanie odpadów

To jest poważny dylemat, jajka i kury.
Mózg zatrudniony by wyjść z umysłu.
Uparte przedsionki naturalnie połączo-
    ne:

dobro — zło, wschód — zachód, światło — ciemność,
przeciwstawne kategorie, bogactwo — bieda, czas —
przestrzeń. Spytać by można, z jakiego diabelskiego
horyzontu zdarzeń emanują takie pyłki kosmiczne?
Czego naprawdę od nas chcą? Postrzeganie,
wyobrażanie, wyróżnianie, przywołanie.
Akceptowanie spiralnie rosnące w siłę — nagłe
olśnienie. Może nie trzeba prostować zwojów kory
mózgowej. Natrętna wokalistka kamienuje pretekst
jasnowidzenia. Skrzypaczka unosi coraz wyżej
smyczek po zakończeniu partytury, utrzymując
uwagę widowni, nie zakłócadi
c zamilkłych strun
instrumentu.

Trzeba dotrzymywać kroku tym
szalonym psom goniącym koła samochodu, których
nie ważą się dotknąć zębami.

— Casey Bush
(Tłumaczenie: Joanna Rosinska)

basurapurga

Este es un serio enigma de pollo y huevo.
Utilice el cerebro para salir de su mente.

Antecámaras obstinadas orgánicamente unidas:
bueno y mal, este y oeste, claro y oscuro,
manzanas y naranjas, ricos y pobres, tiempo y
espacio. ¿Podrías preguntarte de qué diábolo
horizonte evento emanan tales motas cósmicas?
¿Qué quieren realmente de nosotros? Perciba,
conciba, distinga, evoce. Abrace esa epifanía
ascendente en espiral. Es posible que no sea
necesario enderezar las circonvoliciones de su
corteza cerebral. La chanteuse petulante lanza
pasteles de mierda contra el pretexto de la lucidez.
Violinista continúa levantando el arco después de
llegar al final de una partitura, manteniendo la
atención de la audiencia mientras se cuida de no
perturbar los filamentos silenciosos del instrumento.

Debes seguir el ritmo de esos perros rabiosos
persiguiendo los neumáticos del coche que no se atre-

ven
acarajar con los dientes.

— *Casey Bush*
(*Traducción, T. Warburton y Bajo y rub*)

ruslhreinsun

Þetta er alvarleg kjúklinga- og eggjaráða.
Notaðu heilann til að stíga út úr huga þínum.

Þrjósk forhólf lífrænt samtengd:
gott og illt, austur og vestur, ljós og myrkur,
epli og appelsínur, ríkur og fátækur, tími og
pláss. Þú gætir spurt af hvaða djöfulsins
Sjóndeildarhringur atburða myndast slíkar
geimmyndir? Hvað vilja þeir okkur eiginlega?
kynja, hugsa, greina, vekja. Tek undir það
scendant spiraling skýringarmynd. Það er
kannski ekki nauðsynlegt til að rétta út
hvolfið af heilaberki þínum. Snilldar söngur
kastar brickbats gegn yfirskini skýrleika.
Fiðluleikari heldur áfram að lyfta boganum
á eftir að ná lokapunkti stigs, viðhalda athygli
áhorfenda á meðan gætt er að gera það ekki
trufla þögla þræði hljóðfærisins.

Þú verður að halda í við þessa vitlausu
hunda elta dekk bíla sem þeir þora
ekki grípa með tönnum.

— *Casey Bush*
(*Þýtt úr Ensku, Michael Lohr*)

Junkpurge *

Αυτό είναι ένα σοβαρό αίνιγμα κότας και
αυγού. Χρησιμοποιήστε τον εγκέφαλο για
να βγείτε από το μυαλό σας. Επίμονοι προθάλαμοι
    οργανικά ενωμένοι:
καλό και κακό, ανατολή και δύση, φως και
σκοτάδι, μήλα και πορτοκάλια, πλούσιοι
και φτωχοί, χρόνος και χώρος. Μπορείς
να ρωτήσεις από ποιον διαβολικό ορίζοντα
γεγονότων εκπορεύονται τέτοιες κοσμικές
μύτες; Τι πραγματικά θέλουν από εμάς;
Αντιλαμβάνομαι, κυοφορώ, διακρίνω,
προκαλώ. Αγκαλιάστε την ανοδική
σπειροειδής επιφάνεια. Μπορεί να μην
είναι απαραίτητο για την εξομάλυνση των
συνελίξεων του εγκεφαλικού σας φλοιού.
Θλιβερή καντάδα εκτοξεύει ρόπαλα με το
πρόσχημα της διαύγειας. Ο βιολιστής
συνεχίζει να σηκώνει το τόξο μετά
φτάνοντας στο φινάλε ενός αποτελέσ-
ματος, διατηρώντας την προσοχή του
κοινού ενώ προσέχει να μην διαταράξει
τα σιγασμένα νήματα του οργάνου. Πρέπει
να συμβαδίσεις με αυτά τα τρελά σκυλιά
Που κυνηγούν τα λάστιχα των αυτοκινήτων
που δεν τολμούν πιάσουν με τα δόντια τους.

—Κέισι Μπους
    (μετάφραση Κοντοπούλου Κωνσταντίνα)

*) Nota del editor: Τζανκπερτζ (como Набóков)

Yr Wylan

Yr wylan deg ar lanw, dioer,
Unlliw ag eiry neu wenlloer,
Dilwch yw dy degwch di,
Darn fal haul, dyrnfol heli.
Ysgafn ar don eigion wyd,
Esgudfalch edn bysgodfwyd.
Yngo'r aud wrth yr angor
Lawlaw â mi, lili môr.
Llythr unwaith lle'th ariannwyd,
Lleian ym mrig llanw môr wyd.

Cyweirglod bun, cai'r glod bell,
Cyrch ystum caer a chastell.
Edrych a welych, wylan,
Eigr o liw ar y gaer lân.
Dywaid fy ngeiriau dyun,
Dewised fi, dos hyd fun.
Byddai'i hun, beiddia'i hannerch,
Bydd fedrus wrth fwythus ferch
Er budd; dywaid na byddaf,
Fwynwas coeth, fyw onis caf.

Ei charu'r wyf, gwbl nwyf nawdd,
Och wŷr, erioed ni charawdd
Na Merddin wenithfin iach,
Na Thaliesin ei thlysach.
Siprys dyn giprys dan gopr,
Rhagorbryd rhy gyweirbropr.

Och wylan, o chai weled
Grudd y ddyn lanaf o Gred,
Oni chaf fwynaf annerch,
Fy nihenydd fydd y ferch.

— *Dafydd Ap Gwylym*

Seagull

White gull (my God!) above waves,
the color of snow, of silver moon,
bearer of beauty without a blemish,
sun's gleam, gauntlet of sea-spray.
Weightless, drifting over deep waters,
so fleet and haughty, fine fish-forager,
agile in air, anchored to oceans,
we touch fingers, wave-foam lily,
shining sheet silver with script,
pure as a nun in her salt cell.

The girl I sing, her fame will spread
far about, to castle and keep.
Sharp-eyed gull, swoop to see
a maid in her eyrie, another Igraine.
Speak this single phrase of friendship:
let her love Dafydd. Go to the girl,
if you see her alone, dare to greet her.
Use all your wit, for she's a wise one,
to win her over. Say these words:
this captive lad can't live without her.

I love her, I make no bones about it.
No man ever desired so deeply.
I think neither Merlin, the honey-
   tongued,
not true Taliesin wooed dearer damsel.
This tall girl's curls are spun copper,
such grace she has, in such sweet guise.

Ah gull, when you come to contemplate
the prettiest cheek in Christendom,
unless she send me a tender message,
this girl will earn me an early grave.

— *Dafydd Ap Gwylym*
(tr., Paul Merchant & Michael Filetra)

Spegillinn

Ég hugsaði ekki, ég sagði svima,
Láttu andlit mitt vera sanngjarnt
       og gott,
Þarna varð ég sýnilega hissa
Í speglinum; drepið vondan!
Svo loksins sandur
Spegillinn sem ég er ekki frábær
     í að horfa á.
Öskraðu í augnablik Luned
Húðin, stór er trú mín.

Gler er gróteski sælkerinn,
Og smjörgult gulgrátt.
Það gæti örugglega ekki verið
     óvinur
Gefið langt nef; þetta er leitt.
Hamingjusamar pöndur sem
     eru glöð augu
Blind heit holur?
Og dúnkenndu áfengisflúan
Hver handfylli þeirra sagði og
     féll.

Frábært hjá mér, skaðlegt stökk:
Einn, að mínu mati,
Er ég garðgúrú,
Slæmt eðli, eða ekki spegillinn.
Ef ég geri það, þekki ég
     tilfinningu um þrá,
Sökin er, láttu hina látnu deyja!
Ef á spegilblettinum núna
Það hefur verið að kenna lífsins
     vefur.

— *Dafydd Ap Gwylym*
   *(Þýtt úr Ensku, Michael
   Lohr)*

Γλάρος

ένας λευκός γλάρος (Θεέ μου!) πάνω από τα
    κύματα,
το χρώμα του χιονιού,
του ασημένιου φεγγαριού,
φορέας ομορφιάς δίχως ψεγαδιασμένα σχήματα,

η λάμψη του ηλίου, γάντι θαλάσσιας σταγόνας
Αβαρές, παρασυρόμενο από βαθιά νερά,
τόσο γοργό και αγέρωχο, άριστο ψαροβόλο,
ευκίνητο στον αέρα, στους ωκεανούς αγκυρο-
    βόλο
Αγγίζουμε τα δάχτυλα μας, αφρού κυμάτων
    κρίνο
λαμπρό σεντόνι , ασημένιο με γραμμένο κείμενο
αγνό, σαν μοναχή στο αλατοκελί της.

Για το κορίτσι που τραγουδώ, η φήμη θα εξα-
    πλωθεί
μακριά, σε ένα κάστρο θα κρατηθεί
έναν γλάρο με κοφτερά μάτια, σκύψε να δεις
μια κόρη με το βλέμμα της, μια άλλη Igraine.
Πείτε αυτή τη μοναδική φράση φιλίας:
αφήστε την να αγαπήσει τον Dafydd.
Πήγαινε στο κορίτσι,
αν τη δεις μόνη, τόλμα να την χαιρετήσεις.
Χρησιμοποίησε όλη σου την εξυπνάδα,
καθώς είναι σοφή, για να την κερδίσεις.
Πες αυτά τα λόγια:
αυτό το αιχμάλωτο παλικάρι δεν μπορεί να ζή-
    σει χωρίς αυτήν.

Την αγαπώ, ως τα κόκκαλα, δεν το αμφισβητώ
Κανένας άνθρωπος δεν ένιωσε πιο εκ βαθέων το
    «επιθυμώ»
Νομίζω ότι ούτε ο Μέρλιν, τούτος ο γλωσσικός
    μελίτης,
δεν είναι αλήθεια ότι ο Ταλιέσιν επιθύμησε πιο
    αγαπημένο κορίτσι.
Οι μπούκλες αυτού του ψηλού κοριτσιού είναι
    χάλκινο τοπίο
έχει τόση χάρη, με το γλυκό της προσωπείο
Αχ γλάρε, σαν έρθεις στη συλλογιστική σου
    δύνη
το πιο όμορφο μάγουλο σ' όλη τη Χριστιανοσύ-
    νη,
αν δε μου στείλει ένα τρυφερό μήνυμα,
αυτό το κορίτσι θα με στείλει πρόωρα στο μνή-
    μα.

– *Ντάφιντ απ Γκουίλιμ*
   (μεταφρασμένο, Κοντοπούλου Α. Κωνσταντίνα)

Gaviota

Gaviota blanca *(¡Dios mío!)* sobre las olas,
color de nieve, de luna plateada,
portador de belleza sin defecto, brillo del
sol, guante de rociado de mar. Sin peso,
a la deriva sobre aguas profundas, tan
veloz e impertinente, de peces buen for-
    rajero
ágil en el aire, anclado a océanos, tocamos dedos, lirio de espuma de ola,
brillante hoja de plata con escritura,
puro como una monja en su celda de sal.

la chica a la que canto, su fama se ex-
    tiende
por lejos, a castillo y fortaleza. Gaviota
de ojos afilados, cale para ver a una
criada en su aguilera, otra Igraine. Diga
esta única frase de amistad: dejala amar
a Dafydd. Vaya a ella, si está sola,
atrévale a saludarla. Utilize todo su
ingenio (por que ella es sabia) para
ganar su amor. Diga estas palabras:
este chico cautivo no puede vivir sin ella.

La amo, no acepto ninguna discusión.
Ningún hombre jamás deseó tan pro-
    fundamente.
Creo que ni Merlín en tono miel o
Taliesin verdadero cortejaba una don-
    cella más rara. Los rizos de esta
chica alta son de cobre hilado, con tan-
ta gracia, con tan aspecto dulce. Ah

gaviota, cuando llega a contemplar la
cara más bonita de la cristiandad, de
menos que ella envíe un mensaje tierno,
esta chica me enviará a una tumba tem-
    prana.

— *Dafydd Ap Gwylym*
(traducción, T. Warburton y Bajo y rvb)

Gaviota

Gaviota blanca (¡Dios mío!) sobre las olas,
color de nieve, de luna plateada,
portador de belleza sin defecto, brillo
del sol, guante de rociado de mar.
Sin peso, a la deriva sobre aguas profundas,
tan veloz e impertinente, de peces buen for-
    rajero
ágil en el aire, anclado a océanos,
tocamos dedos, lirio de espuma de ola,
brillante hoja de plata con escritura,
puro como una monja en su celda de sal.

la chica a la que canto, su fama se extiende
por lejos, a castillo y fortaleza.
Gaviota de ojos afilados, cale para ver a
una criada en su aguilera, otra Igraine.
Diga esta única frase de amistad:
deja la a amor a atrévale a Dafydd. Vaya
a ella, si está sola, a saludarla.
Utilize todo su ingenio (por que ella es sa-
    bia)
para ganar su amor. Diga estas palabras:
este chico cautivo no puede vivir sin ella.

La amo, no acepto ninguna discusión.
Ningún hombre jamás deseó tan profunda-
    mente.
Creo que ni Merlín en tono miel
o Taliesin verdadero cortejaba una doncella
    más rara.
Los rizos de esta chica alta son de cobre
    hilado,
con tanta gracia, con tan aspecto dulce.

Ah gaviota, cuando llegua a contemplar
la cara más bonita de la cristiandad,
de menos que ella envíe un mensaje tierno,
esta chica me enviará a una tumba tem-
    prana.

— *Dafydd Ap Gwylym*
(traducción, T. Warburton y Bajo y rvb)

Mewa

Biała mewa (o Boże!) ponad falami
kolor śniegu, księżyca srebrnego.
odziana w piękność bez skazy,
fragment słońca, kiść rozbryzganej
    morskiej wody.
Nieważka, dryfująca nad głębiną,
zwinna i dumna, zręczna łowczyni ryb,
wdzięczna w powietrzu, zakotwiczona
    w oceanach,
dotyk palców, lilią piany na fali,
byszczącą kopertą posłaniem
    usrebrzoną,
czysta jak mniszka w swej słonej celi.
Dziewczynę, której ten pean chwałę
    głosi
wkoło daleko, otoczę opieką.
Sokoloka mewa, zapętla w locie by
    ujrzeć
pannę w swym gnieździe na skale,
    drugą Igrane.
Powiedz jej jedno ciepłe słowo:
nich pokocha Dafydda. Idź do
    dziewczyny,
jeśli ujrzysz ją samą, ośmiel się powitać.
Użyj swej mądrości, bo ona jest mądra,
by ją sobie zaskarbić. Powiedz jej to:
oczarowany nią młodzieniec nie może
    bez niej żyć.
Kocham ją, nie ukrywam tego.
Żaden człowiek nie pożądał tak
    dołębnie.
myślę, że ani Merlin, proroczego słowa,
ani dusza Taliesina nie adorowała
    bardziej kochanej damy.
Loki tej wysokiej panny miedzią utkane,
tak wdzięczna, w miłym przebraniu.

O mewo, gdy poznasz
te najpiękniejsze lica w Christendom,
jeśli nie odpowie mi przyjazną wieścią,
dziewczyna wpędzi mnie do mogiły
    wcześnie.

– Dafydd Ap Gwylåm
(Tłumaczenie: Joanna Rosińska)

Žuvėdra

Balta žuvėdra sklendžianti vir-
    šum vandens
Bespalvė, o gal spindinti mėnu-
    lio sidabru,
Ji neša grožį be jokios dėmės,
Saulės žvilgesį ir sūrymą van-
    dens.
Praslysdama paviršiumi bangos
Žuvis ji veja, lydi nuolatos
Vikri ore, prie jūros pririšta,
Ranka manojoje, jūros lelija,
Raštas, kartą suderėtas,
Lyg druskos celėje vienuolė
    tyras.

Tyrumo lopas, šauksmas iš toli,
Keliauja lig tvirtovės ir pilies.
Žuvėdra aštriaake, pamatyk
Mergelę, spalvą švariame lauke.
Ir vieną mano frazę jai ištark,
„Pasirink mane," ir eik pas ją,
Pasveikink, jei ji bus pati viena,
Klasta padės tau ją laimėti,
Sakyki šiuos žodžius, sakyk:
„Jis be tavęs gyvent negali".

Aš myliu ją, to pripažint negėda,
Joks vyras niekada nėra sutikęs
    mielesnės,
Nei Merlinas saldžialiežuvis,
Nei Taliesinas savo giesmėse.
Jos garbanos tarytum varis
    spindi
Tokia grakšti jinai, tokia daili.

Žuvėdra, ak, tik pažiūrėk –
Skaisčiausi skruostai krikščio-
    nijoj –
Ir jeigu ji ištars man „ne",
Verčiau kapai priglaus mane.

— Dafydd Ap Gwylym
(lietuvių kalbą vertė, Miglė
Anušauskaitė)

I Wanna Show You My Guns: A Reasoned Rant

Jenny Forrester

Said: posted on Facebook
Reposted: as reposted by the person who said:posted on Facebook

The man I kissed when we were young at Homecoming said: "What's it called when the people doing the fact checking are controlled by the same people doing the lying?" and the woman my brother kissed at Homecoming a different year said: "Democrats/left wing/idiots." Reposted from Megan Maria D'Andrea.

And then the man I kissed when we were young at Homecoming said: "If you're sending men with "weapons of war" to take my "weapons of war", then I'm fairly certain that's what's called an act of war…and the definition of tyranny… which coincidentally is the reason for the second amendment in the first place." Reposted from Mike Emerick.

He posts from Jeff Brands: "This is my gun permit…it's a seal, created to look official. The 2nd amendment. Caption: "This is my gun permit." Wording from Jeff Brands: "FOR THOSE WHO DON'T UNDERSTAND."

I read in the New York Times about one of the terrorists, a white male insurrectionist, who stormed the capitol building attempting to overthrow the government, murder public officials such as the Speaker of the House, Nancy Pelosi. The in-

Quiero mostrarte mis pistolas: Una diatriba razonable

Jenny Forrester
(traduccion, T. Warburton y Bajo y rvb)

publicado en Facebook
Publicado de nuevo: como republicado por la persona que dijo: publicado en Facebook

El hombre al que besé en el baile de *Homecoming* cuando éramos jóvenes preguntó: «¿Cómo se llama cuando las personas que hacen la verificación de hechos están controladas por las mismas personas que mienten? » y la chica que mi hermano besó en *Homecoming* otro año dijo: «Demócratas/izquierdistas/idiotas». – Publicado de Megan Maria D'Andrea. Entonces el hombre al que besé en *Homecoming* cuando éramos jóvenes dijo: «Si envías a hombres con «armas de guerra» a tomar mis «armas de guerra», entonces estoy bastante seguro de que llamamos a eso un acto de guerra y lo definimos como tiranía, por casualidad es la razón de la segunda enmienda en primer lugar».– Republicado de Mike Emerick.

El publica de Jeff Brands: «Este es mi permiso de armas... es un sello, creado para parecer oficial. La segunda enmienda». Leyenda: «Este es mi permiso de armas». Redacción de Jeff Brands: «Para ellos que no entienden».

Leí en el New York Times sobre uno de los terroristas, un insurreccionista blanco, que asaltó el edificio del capitolio tratando de derrocar al gobierno, asesinar a funcionarios públicos como la presidenta de la Cámara de Representantes, Nancy Pelosi. El insurreccionista, cuyo nombre no se pronunciará, escrito aquí, solía ser un hombre liberal de boca fuerte, un hombre que avergonzaba a los amigos que votaron

Θέλω να σας δείξω τα όπλα μου: Συνετό ξέσπασμα

Jenny Forrester
(Μετάφραση από τα Αγγλικά, Μαρουσώ Αθανασίου)

Είπε/δημοσίευσε στο Facebook
Αναδημοσίευση/όπως κοινοποιήθηκε από το άτομο που το είπε/δημοσίευσε στο Facebook

Ο άντρας που φίλησα όταν ήμασταν μικροί στον χορό της αποφοίτησης είπε: «Πώς λέγεται όταν οι άνθρωποι που εξακριβώνουν τα γεγονότα ελέγχονται από τους ίδιους ανθρώπους που λένε τα ψέματα;» και η γυναίκα που φίλησε ο αδελφός μου στον χορό της αποφοίτησης μια άλλη χρονιά είπε: «Δημοκρατικοί/αριστεροί/ηλίθιοι». Αναδημοσίευση από την Megan Maria D'Andrea.

Και τότε ο άντρας που φίλησα όταν ήμασταν μικροί στον χορό είπε: «Αν στέλνεις άντρες με «οπλισμό πολέμου» για να πάρουν τον δικό μου «οπλισμό πολέμου», τότε είμαι αρκετά σίγουρος ότι αυτό λέγεται πολεμική πράξη... και ο ορισμός της τυραννίας...που συμπτωματικά είναι και ο λόγος που υπάρχει η δεύτερη τροπολογία εξαρχής». Αναδημοσίευση από τον Mike Emerick.

Αναδημοσίευση από τον Jeff Brands: «Αυτή είναι η άδεια οπλοφορίας μου...είναι μια σφραγίδα, φτιάχτηκε για να μοιάζει νόμιμη. Η 2η τροπολογία. Λεζάντα: «Αυτή είναι η άδεια οπλοφορίας μου». Συντάχθηκε από τον Jeff Brands: «ΓΙΑ ΌΣΟΥΣ ΔΕΝ ΚΑΤΑΛΑΒΑΪΝΟΥΝ».

Διάβασα στους New York Times για έναν από τους τρομοκράτες, έναν λευκό εξτρεμιστή, ο οποίος εισέβαλε στο κτίριο του Καπιτωλίου επιχειρώντας να ανατρέψει την κυβέρνηση, να δολοφονήσει δημόσιους αξιωματούχους, όπως την πρόεδρο της Βουλής των Αντιπροσώπων, Nancy Pelosi. Ο εξτρεμιστής, το όνομα του οποίου δεν θα αναφερθεί/γραφτεί εδώ, ήταν ένας μεγαλοφωνάριος φιλελεύθερος άνδρας, ένας άνδρας που

Ég Vil Sýna Þér Byssurnar Mínar: Rökstutt gífuryrði

Jenny Forrester
(Þýtt úr Ensku, Michael Lohr)

Sagði: birt á Facebook
Endurbirt: eins og endurbirt var af þeim sem sagði: birti á Facebook

Maðurinn sem ég kyssti þegar við vorum ung á Heimkoma sagði: „Hvað heitir það þegar fólkið sem rannsakar staðreyndir er stjórnað af sama fólkinu sem ljúga? og konan sem bróðir minn kyssti á Homecoming annað ár sagði: „demókratar/vinstri væng/fífl. Endurbirt frá Megan Maria D'Andrea.

Og svo sagði maðurinn sem ég kyssti þegar við vorum ung í Heimkomu: „Ef þú ert að senda menn með „stríðsvopn" til að taka „stríðsvopnin mín", þá er ég nokkuð viss um að það sé það sem kallast stríðsaðgerð... og skilgreininguna á harðstjórn... sem fyrir tilviljun er ástæðan fyrir seinni breytingunni í fyrsta lagi. Endurbirt frá Mike Emerick.

Hann skrifar frá Jeff Brands: „Þetta er byssuleyfið mitt...þetta er innsigli, búið til til að líta opinbert út. 2. breytingin. Myndatexti: „Þetta er byssuleyfið mitt." Orðalag frá Jeff Brands: "FYRIR ÞA SEM SKILJA EKKI."
Ég las í New York Times um einn hryðjuverkamannanna, hvítan karlkyns uppreisnarmann, sem réðst inn í höfuðborgabygginguna og reyndi að steypa ríkisstjórninni af stóli, myrti opinbera embættismenn eins og forseta húsið, Nancy Pelosi. Uppreisnarmaðurinn, en nafn hans verður ekki sagt; skrifað

surrectionist, whose name won't be spoken, written here, used to be a loud-mouth liberal man, a man who shamed friends who voted for the 45th President of the United States, according to his friends who voted for the 45th President of the United States. His brother and friends and everyone were surprised he'd turned, become so right-wing, his having been so liberal before. It was the second amendment, he'd said. The capitol-stormer, liberal turned conservative turned because someone called him a fascist, a Nazi because he loved his guns.

I know a lot of these loud-mouth liberal men. I've lived in Portland, Oregon.

One day, a family member sent me a text, "If you've heard about the shooting in Boulder, I'm safe at home."

A 21-year-old man carried out a mass shooting at King Soopers in Boulder, Colorado, where I've lived, where some family members still live or work. We've all shopped at that King Soopers. The shooter killed ten people, injured many others in countless ways.

The man I kissed when we were young posted a meme by Callon R. Tonner: "Anyone ever notice how when congress is trying to introduce more gun control laws, that mass shootings just coincidentally start happening? Yeah me neither."

This post by the man I kissed when we were young at Homecoming is a gut-punch.

So the loudmouth liberal men who never admit to being gut-punched begin their postings:

por el 45° presidente de los E.U., según sus amigos que votaron por el 45° presidente de los E.U. Su hermano y sus amigos y todos se sorprendieron de que se había vuelto, se convertido en tan derechista, que hubiera sido tan liberal antes. Era la segunda enmienda, dijo. El asaltante del capitolio, liberal convertido en conservador, se convirtió en el asalto al capitolio porque alguien lo llamó fascista y nazi porque amaba sus armas.

Conozco a muchos de estos hombres liberales de boca fuerte. He vivido en Portland, Oregon.

Un día, un miembro de la familia me envió un mensaje de texto: «Si te enteraste del tiroteo en Boulder, estoy a salvo en casa».

Un hombre de 21 años llevó a cabo un tiroteo masivo en King Soopers en Boulder, Colorado, donde he vivido, donde los miembros de la familia todavía viven o trabajan.

Todos hemos comprado en ese King Soopers. El tirador mató a diez personas, hirió a muchos otros de innumerables maneras.

El hombre al que besé cuando éramos jóvenes publicó un meme de Callon R. Tonner: «¿Alguien notó alguna vez que cuando el Congreso intenta introducir más leyes de control de armas, los tiroteos masivos comienzan a ocurrir casualmente? Sí, yo tampoco».

Esta publicación del hombre al que besé cuando éramos jóvenes en *Homecoming* es un golpe de tripa.

Así que los hombres liberales de boca fuerte que nunca admiten ser golpeados de tripa comienzan sus publicaciones.

Un hombre liberal que conozco y amo y que vive en Portland publicó una foto de un arma larga del siglo XVII y dijo: «Por favor, dirija sus argumentos razo-

κατέκρινε τους φίλους του που ψήφισαν τον 45ο Πρόεδρο των Ηνωμένων Πολιτειών, σύμφωνα με τους φίλους του που ψήφισαν τον 45ο Πρόεδρο των Ηνωμένων Πολιτειών. Ο αδελφός του και οι φίλοι του και όλοι έμειναν έκπληκτοι που είχε αλλαξοπιστήσει, που είχε γίνει τόσο δεξιός, αφού πριν ήταν τόσο φιλελεύθερος. Ήταν η δεύτερη τροπολογία, είχε πει. Ο φιλελεύθερος του Καπιτωλίου έγινε συντηρητικός επειδή κάποιος τον αποκάλεσε φασίστα και ναζιστή επειδή αγαπούσε τα όπλα του.

Γνωρίζω πολλούς τέτοιους φιλελεύθερους άντρες με μεγάλο στόμα. Έχω ζήσει στο Πόρτλαντ του Όρεγκον.

Μια μέρα, ένα μέλος της οικογένειάς μου μού έστειλε ένα μήνυμα: «Αν έμαθες για τους πυροβολισμούς στο Μπόλντερ, είμαι σπίτι κι είμαι καλά».

Ένας 21χρονος άνδρας επιτέθηκε με μαζικά πυρά στο King Soopers στο Μπόλντερ του Κολοράντο, όπου έχω ζήσει, όπου ζουν ή εργάζονται ακόμη κάποια μέλη της οικογένειάς μου. Όλοι έχουμε ψωνίσει από αυτό το King Soopers. Ο δράστης σκότωσε δέκα άτομα και τραυμάτισε πολλά άλλα με αμέτρητους τρόπους.

Ο άντρας που φίλησα όταν ήμασταν μικροί δημοσίευσε ένα meme του Callon R. Tonner: «Έχει παρατηρήσει ποτέ κανείς πώς όταν το Κογκρέσο προσπαθεί να θεσπίσει περισσότερους νόμους για τον έλεγχο της οπλοκατοχής, ότι αρχίζουν κατά σύμπτωση και οι μαζικοί πυροβολισμοί; Ναι ούτε κι εγώ».

Αυτό το ποστ από τον άνδρα που φίλησα όταν ήμασταν μικροί στον χορό της αποφοίτησης είναι μια γροθιά στο στομάχι.

Έτσι αρχίζουν τις αναρτήσεις τους οι λεβέντες φιλελεύθεροι άνδρες που δεν παραδέχονται ποτέ ότι έχουν πληγωθεί:

Ένας φιλελεύθερος άνδρας που γνωρίζω και συμπαθώ και ζει στο Πόρτλαντ, δημοσίευσε μια φωτογραφία ενός μακρύκαννου όπλου από το 1700 και είπε: «Παρακαλώ, γράψτε τα συνετά σας επιχειρήματα σχετι-

hér, var áður hávær frjálslyndur maður, maður sem skammaði sig vinir sem kusu 45. forseta Bandaríkjanna, að sögn vina hans sem kusu 45. forseta Bandaríkjanna. Bróðir hans og vinir og allir voru hissa á því að hann hefði snúist við, orðið svo hægrisinnaður, hann hafði verið svo frjálslyndur áður. Þetta var önnur breytingin, sagði hann. Höfuðborgarstormurinn, frjálshyggjumaðurinn, sem varð íhaldssamur, sneri sér vegna þess að einhver kallaði hann fasista, nasista vegna þess að hann elskaði byssurnar sínar.

Ég þekki marga af þessum háværu frjálshyggjumönnum. Ég hef búið í Portland, Oregon.

Einn daginn sendi fjölskyldumeðlimur mér skilaboð: „Ef þú hefur heyrt um skotárásina í Boulder, þá er ég öruggur heima.

21 árs gamall maður gerði fjöldaskot á King Soopers í Boulder, Colorado, þar sem ég hef búið, þar sem sumir fjölskyldumeðlimir búa enn eða vinna. Við höfum öll verslað í King Soopers. Skotmaðurinn drap tíu manns, særði marga aðra á ótal vegu.

Maðurinn sem ég kyssti þegar við vorum ung birti meme eftir Callon R. Tonner: „Tar einhver nokkurn tíma eftir því hvernig þegar þing er að reyna að innleiða fleiri byssueftirlitslög, þá byrja fjöldaskotárásir bara fyrir tilviljun? Já ég ekki heldur. "

Þessi færsla eftir manninn sem ég kyssti þegar við vorum ung á Heimkoma er magnað.

Þannig að hinir háværu frjálshyggjumenn sem aldrei viðurkenna að hafa verið slegnir í gegn byrja færslur sínar:

A liberal man I know and love who lives in Portland posted a photo of a long gun from the 1700's and said: "Please direct your reasoned arguments about the Second Amendment and your right to own an AR here."

A man I don't know answered the call with a dick joke: "Well, I have a very tiny dick and it just makes me feel more manly, that's all. Please don't take my manhood away from me…I'm begging you…please, it's all I've got…please."

A very, very loud-mouthed liberal man I know and don't love at all: "We should require gun owners be a member of a militia. The militias should be well regulated. Including requirements to register their weapons and to also have insurance for each weapon. And you can get kicked out of if you commit a weapon crime, like threatening someone."

Someone else: "I grew up with guns…"

I didn't finish that bullshit sentence starter that always comes up in these conversations, and I grew up with guns, too, and I wanna show them all my guns, my gun that shoots statistics, my gun that shoots reality checks, my gun that shoots articles and opinions by actual experts, people who study and work and create policy.

I posted in the comments of the liberal man I know and love who lives in Portland. I posted a NYT article by David Leonhardt in "The Morning: Five Key Facts We Know About Gun Violence." Everything in the article disproves, disqualifies, or throws into question everything everyone

nados sobre la segunda Enmienda y su derecho a poseer una AR aquí».

Un hombre que no conozco respondió a la llamada con una broma de polla: «Bueno, tengo una polla muy pequeña y me hace sentir más varonil, eso es todo. Por favor, no me quites mi hombría... Te lo ruego... por favor, es todo lo que tengo... por favor» .

Un hombre liberal muy, muy ruidoso que conozco y no amo en absoluto: «Deberíamos exigir que los propietarios de armas sean miembros de una milicia. Las milicias deben estar bien reguladas. Incluyendo requisitos para registrar sus armas y también tener un seguro para cada arma. Y puedes ser expulsado si cometes un crimen con armas, como amenazar a alguien».

Alguno más: «Crecí con armas...»

No terminé ese iniciador de frases de mierda que siempre aparece en estas conversaciones, y crecí con armas, también, y quiero mostrarles todas mis armas: una que dispara estadísticas, una que dispara verificaciones de la realidad, una que dispara artículos y opiniones de expertos reales, personas que estudian y trabajan y crean políticas.

Publiqué en los comentarios del hombre liberal que conozco y amo que vive en Portland. Publiqué un artículo de David Leonhardt NYT, «La mañana: Cinco hechos que sabemos sobre la violencia con armas». Todo en el artículo refuta, descalifica o pone en duda todo lo que todos publicaron sobre el problema de las armas. Entonces dije: «Publiqué esto porque no puedo soportar leer todos los comentarios que he escuchado durante todas mis décadas, y nada cambia».

El hombre liberal que conozco y amo que vive en Portland le dio a mi comentario y palabras un poco de

κά με τη Δεύτερη Τροπολογία και το δικαί-ωμά σας να κατέχετε ένα AR εδώ».

Ένας άντρας που δεν τον ξέρω, απά-ντησε στο κάλεσμα με ένα αστειάκι για το πουλί του: «Λοιπόν, έχω πολύ μικρό πουλί και αυτό με κάνει να νιώθω πιο άντρας, αυτό είναι όλο. Σας παρακαλώ, μην μου πάρετε τον ανδρισμό μου... σας ικετεύω... σας παρακαλώ, είναι το μόνο που έχω... σας παρακαλώ».

Ένας πολύ πολύ φωνακλάς φιλελεύθε-ρος άνδρας που γνωρίζω και δεν τον συ-μπαθώ καθόλου: «Θα πρέπει να απαιτή-σουμε από τους οπλοκράτες να φτιάξουν μια πολιτοφυλακή. Οι πολιτοφυλακές θα πρέπει να είναι καλά οργανωμένες. Θα χρειάζεται, μεταξύ άλλων, να καταγρά-φουν τα όπλα τους και να έχουν ασφάλεια για κάθε όπλο. Και να μπορείς να σε διώ-ξουν αν διαπράξεις οποιοδήποτε αδίκημα με όπλο, όπως το να απειλήσεις κάποιον».

Κάποιος άλλος: «Μεγάλωσα με όπλα...»

Δεν τελείωσα αυτή την ηλίθια εναρκτή-ρια πρόταση που υπάρχει πάντα σε αυτές τις συζητήσεις, κι εγώ μεγάλωσα με όπλα και θέλω να τους δείξω όλα τα όπλα μου, το όπλο μου που πυροβολεί στατιστικές, το όπλο μου που πυροβολεί ελέγχους εγκυρό-τητας, το όπλο μου που πυροβολεί άρθρα και γνώμες από ειδήμονες, ανθρώπους που μελετούν και εργάζονται και δημιουρ-γούν πολιτικές.

Έγραψα στα σχόλια του φιλελεύθερου ανθρώπου που γνωρίζω και συμπαθώ και ζει στο Πόρτλαντ. Ανέβασα ένα άρθρο των NYT του David Leonhardt «Πέντε βασικά στοιχεία που γνωρίζουμε για την οπλοκα-τοχή». Τα πάντα στο άρθρο διαψεύδουν, αποκλείουν ή θέτουν υπό αμφισβήτηση όλα όσα ο καθένας πόσταρε σχετικά με το πρόβλημα των όπλων. Στη συνέχεια είπα: «Το ανέβασα αυτό γιατί δεν αντέχω να διαβάζω σχόλια που ακούω σ' όλη μου τη ζωή και τίποτα δεν αλλάζει ποτέ». Ο φιλελεύθερος άνθρωπος που γνωρίζω και συμπαθώ και ζει στο Πόρτλαντ έβαλε στο

Frjálslyndur maður sem ég þek-ki og elska og býr í Portland birti mynd af langri byssu frá 1700 og sagði: „Vinsamlegast bendi rök-studdum rökum þínum um seinni breytinguna og rétt þinn til að eiga AR hér.

Maður sem ég þekki ekki svaraði símtalinu með gríni: „Jæja, ég er með mjög lítinn pikk og mér líður bara karlmannlegri, það er allt og sumt. Vinsamlegast ekki taka karl-mennskuna frá mér ... ég bið þig ... plís, það er allt sem ég á ... vinsam-legast. "

Mjög, mjög hávær frjálslyndur maður sem ég þekki og elska alls ekki: „Við ættum að krefjast þess að byssueigendur séu meðlimir vígamanna. Hersveitunum ætti að vera vel stjórnað. Þar á meðal krö-fur um að skrá vopn sín og að hafa einnig tryggingu fyrir hvert vopn. Og þú getur verið rekinn út ef þú fremur vopnaglæp, eins og að hóta einhverjum."

Einhver annar: „Ég ólst upp við byssur... "

Ég kláraði ekki þennan kjaftæðis-setning sem kemur alltaf upp í þess-um samtölum, og ég ólst líka upp við byssur, og ég vil sýna þeim al-lar byssurnar mínar, byssuna mína sem skýtur tölfræði, byssuna mína sem skýtur raunveruleikaeftirliti, byssuna mína sem skýtur greinum og skoðunum eftir raunverulega sérfræðinga, fólk sem lærir og vin-nur og skapar stefnu.

Ég skrifaði í athugasemdum frjáls-lynda mannsins sem ég þekki og elska sem býr í Portland. Ég birti NYT grein eftir David Leonhardt í „Morgunn Fimm Lykilstaðreyndir Sem Við Vitum um Byssuofbeldi".

posted regarding the gun problem. Then I said: "I posted this because I can't take reading all the comments I've heard all my decades, and nothing ever changes." The liberal man I know and love who lives in Portland gave my comment and words a little Facebook heart. He cares about me, knows about my family's proximity that day.

These liberal men of Portland aren't saving any lives any more than the man I kissed when we were young at Homecoming.

That's the way of it. I've reasoned it out. I hope you see this reasoning through the images, through the story of it, through the way of people on Facebook.

They're all pointing out the other side's stupidity, the other side's bad grammar, the other side's side and have pointed at the dick sizes of everyone else when what we need is to get off Facebook, get some facts straight, listen to the experts, educate ourselves, reach out to people who're hurting, protect people we can protect, appreciate that dick size doesn't have anything to do with heart size, and we need to love more than we think we can or should have to. It sucks that we should have to love so much. It really, really sucks except when it doesn't. Except when it changes everything.

Love: Love: Love *Q*

NOTE: Grammatical errors, typos and misinformed opinions contained in everyone's Facebook posts are left as-is/are for a purpose

corazón de Facebook. Él se preocupa por mí, sabe de la proximidad de mi familia ese día.

Estos hombres liberales de Portland no están salvando ninguna vida más que el hombre que besé cuando éramos jóvenes en *Homecoming*.

Así es. Lo he razonado. Espero que veas este razonamiento a través de imágenes, a través de la historia, a través de cómo la gente está en Facebook. He dejado todos los errores tipográficos y errores gramaticales y opiniones mal informadas de los hombres liberales y no he traducido el lenguaje y la cosmovisión del hombre que besé en *Homecoming* o las mujeres que mi hermano besó cuando todos éramos jóvenes para la gente de la ciudad (liberal, progresista, tan performativa).

Todos señalan la estupidez del otro lado, la mala gramática del otro lado, el lado del otro lado y los tamaños de polla de todos los demás cuando lo que necesitamos es salir de Facebook, obtener algunos hechos, escuchar a expertos, educarnos, ayudar a esas personas con dolor, proteger a las personas que podemos proteger, apreciar que el tamaño de la polla no tiene nada que ver con el tamaño del corazón, y necesitamos amar más de lo que pensamos que podemos o deberíamos tener que hacerlo. Chupa mierda que tengamos que amar tanto. Realmente, realmente chupa, excepto cuando no lo hace. Excepto cuando lo cambia todo.

Amor: :Amor: :Amor *Q*

NOTA: Los errores gramaticales contenidos en las publicaciones de Facebook de todos se dejan tal cual son/son con un propósito

σχόλιό μου καρδούλα. Νοιάζεται για μένα, γνωρίζει ότι ήταν κοντά η οικογένειά μου εκείνη τη μέρα.

Αυτοί οι φιλελεύθεροι άντρες του Πόρτλαντ δεν σώζουν ζωές, ούτε ο άντρας που φίλησα όταν ήμασταν μικροί στον χορό της αποφοίτησης.

Έτσι είναι τα πράγματα. Το σκέφτηκα λογικά. Ελπίζω να δείτε αυτή τη συλλογιστική μέσα από τις εικόνες, μέσα από την ιστορία της, μέσα από τον τρόπο των ανθρώπων στο Facebook. Έχω αφήσει όλα τα τυπογραφικά λάθη και τις παραπλανητικές απόψεις των φιλελεύθερων ανδρών και δεν έχω μεταφράσει τη γλώσσα και την κοσμοθεωρία του άντρα που φίλησα στον χορό ή των γυναικών που φίλησε ο αδελφός μου όταν ήμασταν μικροί στον χορό της αποφοίτησης των κατοίκων της πόλης (φιλελεύθεροι, προοδευτικοί, με υψηλές επιδόσεις).

Όλοι επισημαίνουν τη βλακεία της άλλης πλευράς, την κακή γραμματική της άλλης πλευράς, την άλλη πλευρά της άλλη πλευράς και δείχνουν το μέγεθος του πουλιού όλων των άλλων, ενώ αυτό που χρειαζόμαστε είναι να βγούμε από το Facebook, να βάλουμε τα πράγματα στη θέση τους, να ακούσουμε τους ειδικούς, να μορφωθούμε, να πλησιάσουμε τους ανθρώπους που πονάνε, να προστατεύσουμε τους ανθρώπους που μπορούμε να προστατεύσουμε, να αντιληφθούμε ότι το μέγεθος του πουλιού δεν έχει καμία σχέση με το μέγεθος της καρδιάς και ότι πρέπει να αγαπάμε περισσότερο από όσο νομίζουμε ότι μπορούμε ή ότι πρέπει να αγαπάμε. Είναι απαίσιο που πρέπει να αγαπάμε τόσο πολύ. Είναι πραγματικά άθλιο, εκτός από όταν δεν είναι. Εκτός από τη στιγμή που αλλάζει τα πάντα.

Αγάπη/Αγάπη/Αγάπη Q

Allt í greininni afsannar, ógildir eða dregur allt í efa allt sem allir settu inn varðandi byssuvandann. Þá sagði ég: „Ég setti þetta inn vegna þess að ég þoli ekki að lesa öll ummælin sem ég hef heyrt alla mína áratugi og ekkert breytist. Frjálslyndi maðurinn sem ég þekki og elska og býr í Portland gaf athugasemd minni og orðum smá Facebook-hjarta. Honum þykir vænt um mig, veit um nálægð fjölskyldu minnar þann daginn Þessir frjálslyndu menn í Portland eru ekki að bjarga neinum mannslífum frekar en maðurinn sem ég kyssti þegar við vorum ung á Heimkoma.

Það er leiðin. Ég hef rökstutt það. Ég vona að þú sjáir þessa röksemdafærslu í gegnum myndirnar, í gegnum söguna um það, í gegnum hátt fólks á Facebook.

Þeir eru allir að benda á heimsku hinnar hliðarinnar, slæma málfræði hinnar hliðarinnar, hliðina á hinni hliðinni og hafa bent á pikkstærð allra hinna þegar það sem við þurfum er að hverfa af Facebook, fá staðreyndir á hreint, hlusta á sérfræðingana , fræða okkur, ná til fólks sem er sárt, vernda fólk sem við getum verndað, meta að pikkstærð hefur ekkert með hjartastærð að gera og við þurfum að elska meira en við höldum að við getum eða ættum að þurfa að gera. Það er leiðinlegt að við skulum þurfa að elska svona mikið. Það er virkilega, virkilega sjúskað nema þegar það gerist ekki. Nema þegar það breytir öllu.

Ást: Ást: Ást Q

Who Changes the Weather

Last night's full moon a pink
　　smear
this morning's drizzle glossed
　　the street but couldn't
make it through the oak and
　　beech to the driveway

I'm the support system for my
　　hands, eyes and brain
whether my mind needs protec-
　　tion or is affected by gravity
even constant motion isn't per-
　　fect, salted & peppered
with the tiniest hesitations, a
　　10th.-step backwards
turning to look around cause of
　　something almost heard,
a soft déjà vu, a blip in the still-
　　ness i think i can create
putting up signs no one needs
　　to read
curve swoop, winding jiggle, a
　　red octagon
slowly draining & rounding

Waiting for trucks the size of
　　billboards, impossible float-
　　ing curtains
to block my view or what I
　　thought the sky opens to re-
　　veal
the machinery we're travelling
　　inside, hinged ribs to access
the clockwork circuitry within,
　　energy instead of blood,
artificial neurons so much less
　　efficient than the real thing
with my meat brain replaced by

Los que cambian el clima

La luna llena de anoche una mancha
　　rosa
la llovizna de esta mañana brilló la
　　calle, pero no pudo
pasar a través del roble y haya a la
　　entrada
Soy el sistema de apoyo para mis
　　manos, ojos y cerebro
si mi mente necesita protección o se
　　ve afectada por la gravedad
incluso el movimiento constante no
　　es perfecto, salado y
salpicado
con vacilaciones más pequeñas, un
　　paso décimo atrás
mirando por algo casi escuchado,
un déjà vu suave, un destello en la
　　quietud creo que puedo construir
colocando letreros que nadie debe
　　leer
una curva en picado, sinuoso zango-
　　teo, un octágono rojo
lentamente drenando y redonde-
　　ando

Esperando camiones del tamaño de
　　vallas publicitarias, imposibles
　　cortinas flotantes
para bloquear mi vista o lo que pen-
　　sé que el cielo se abre para revelar
la maquinaria en la que hemos via-
　　jado, costillas articuladas para
　　acceder a
los circuitos de relojería interior, en-
　　ergía en lugar de sangre,
neuronas artificiales mucho menos
　　eficientes que lo real
con mi cerebro de carne

Kto zmienia pogodę

Pełnia księżyca ostatniej nocy jak
  rozmazany róż
Dziś rano kapuśniaczek
  nabłyszczył ulicę
lecz nie przesiąkł przez dębinę
  i buczynę na podjeździe do
  domu

Jestem systemem
  podrzymującym moje ręce, i
  oczy i mózg
gdy mój umysł potrzebuje
  ochrony, czy podlega
  grawitacji
nawet ruch ciągły nie jest
  doskonały, popstrzony i
  okraszony
maleńkimi wahaniami, 10-ty
  krok w tył—
zawracam by rozejrzeć sie wkoło
  jakbym coś słyszał,
delikatne *déjà vu*, plusk w ciszy,
  którą mogę stworzyć
ustawiając znaki przydrożne,
  których nikt nie musi czytać
skręcona pętla, meandrująca
  galareta, czerwony oktagon
powoli cieknący i okrąglejący

czekając na tiry rozmiaru reklam,
  nieprawdopodobne, płynące
  zasłony
by zakryć mi widok tego— co
  myślałem ukazują otwierajace
  się niebiosa—
machinerię, w której
  podróżujemy— żebra na
  zawiasach by sięgnąć

Ποιος αλλάζει τον καιρό

Η χθεσινή πανσέληνος ένα ροζ
  επίχρισμα
το ψιλόβροχο του πρωινού γυάλισε
  το δρόμο αλλά δεν τα κατάφερε
να περάσει μέσα από τη βελανιδιά
  και την οξιά στον κεντρικό
  δρόμο
Είμαι το σύστημα υποστήριξης
  για τα χέρια, τα μάτια και τον
  εγκέφαλό μου
αν το μυαλό μου χρειάζεται
  προστασία ή επηρεάζεται από
  τη βαρύτητα
ακόμα και η συνεχής κίνηση δεν
  είναι τέλεια, αλατισμένη και
  πιπερωμένη
με τους πιο μικροσκοπικούς
  δισταγμούς, ένα 10ο βήμα προς
  τα πίσω
γυρίζοντας να κοιτάξω γύρω μου
  γιατί κάτι σα να ακούστηκε,
ένα απαλό déjà vu, ένα χτύπημα
  στην ακινησία, νομίζω ότι
  μπορώ να δημιουργήσω
τοποθετώντας σημάδια που δεν
  χρειάζεται να διαβάσει κανείς
καμπύλη εφόρμησης,
  στριφογυριστή τίναγμα, κόκκινο
  οκτάγωνο
που σιγά σιγά στραγγίζεται και
  στρογγυλοποιείται

Περιμένοντας φορτηγά στο
  μέγεθος των διαφημιστικών
  πινακίδων, αδύνατες
  αιωρούμενες κουρτίνες
να μπλοκάρουν τη θέα μου ή αυτό
  το οποίο νόμιζα ότι ανοίγει ο
  ουρανός για να αποκαλύψει

chips
can I rent out the extra skull
    space
or is that how i'm paying for
these involuntary improve-
    ments
taxed from the inside, toxed ev-
    ery way else

    — *Dan Raphael*

reemplazado por chips de
ordenar
puedo alquilar el espacio
adicional del cráneo
o es que cómo estoy pagando por
estas mejoras involuntarias
gravadas desde el interior,
    toxificadas de todas formas.

    — *Dan Raphael*
    (traducción, T. Warburton y
    Bajo y rvb)

Orlando, Fla.

TRASH

"I will go to heaven",
    she said.
NO.
No, "you cannot".
Didn't you say that, "I
    did this and that?"
YES.
There is a place up there
that takes trash
and turns it into dia-
    monds.

    – *Kirsten Aysworth*

ΣΚΟΥΠΙΔΙΑ

«Θα πάω στον παράδεισο», είπε
    εκείνη.
ΟΧΙ.
Οχι, "δεν μπορείς".
Εσύ δεν είπες, «έκανα αυτό κι εκεί-
    νο;»
ΝΑΙ.
Υπάρχει ένα μέρος εκεί πάνω
που παίρνει τα σκουπίδια
και τα μετατρέπει σε διαμάντια.

    – *Κίρστεν Αυσγουορθ*
    (μεταφρασμένο, Βασιλεία
    Οικονόμου)

do mechanizmu obwodów
   wewnętrznych— energia
   zamiast krwi.
Sztuczne neurony — jakże
   mniej sprawne od
   prawdziwych,
mięso mego mózgu
   zastąpione czipami;
czy mogę odnająć wolne
   miejsce w czaszce
czy też jest to moja należność
za te narzucone usprawnienia
opodatkowany od wewnątrz,
   zatruty w każdy inny
   sposób.

> – Dan Raphael
> (Tłumaczenie: Joanna
> Rosińska)

τα μηχανήματα μέσα στα οποία
   ταξιδεύουμε
με αρθρωτές νευρώσεις για πρόσβαση
το κύκλωμα του ρολογιού μέσα,
   ενέργεια αντί για αίμα,
τεχνητοί νευρώνες τόσο λιγότερο
   αποτελεσματικοί από τους
   πραγματικούς
με τον κρεάτινο εγκέφαλό μου να
   αντικαθίσταται από κυκλώματα
   τσιπ
μπορώ να νοικιάσω τον περαιτέρω
   χώρο στο κρανίο μου
ή έτσι πληρώνω
αυτές τις ακούσιες βελτιώσεις
   φορολογημένος εκ των έσω,
   δηλητηριασμένος με κάθε άλλον
   τρόπο.

> – Ντάνιελ Ράφαελ
> (μεταφρασμένο, Κοντοπούλου Α.
> Κωνσταντίνα)

BASURA

"Iré al cielo", dijo.
NO.
No, "no se puede".
¿No dijiste "hice esto y
       eso"?
SÍ.
Hay un lugar allá ar-
       riba
que toma la basura
y la transmuta en dia-
       mantes.

> – Kirsten Aysworth
> (Traducción, T. War-
> burton y Bajo y rvb)

OTPAD

„Ići ću u raj", rekla je.
NE.
Ne, „ne možeš".
Nisi li rekla ono,
   „Napravila sam to i
   to?"
DA.
Postoji mjesto negdje
gore
koje uzima otpad
i pretvara ga u
dijamante.

> – Kirsten Aysworth
> (prijevod na hrvatski,
> Dijana Jakovac)

RUSL

Ég mun fara til himna,
       "sagði hún.
NEI.
Nei þú getur það ekki".
Sagðirðu ekki þetta:
"Ég gerði hitt og þetta?"
JÁ.
Það er staður þarna uppi
sem tekur rusl
og breyta því í demöntum.

> – Kirsten Aysworth
> (Þýtt úr Ensku,
> Michael Lohr)

DIVIDED SABAN NIGHT

A sadness that fills like lightning:
emperor noise is dead,
wine conquers heaven
  the muse, she is here, strongest
    without music.
Sadness is the state of love
in waiting,
stationed at terminal, where mu-
    sic is
an unsent letter.
I wait for a train from Buenos Ai-
    res to Bratislava.
Sadness is in the wine from light-
    ning
until heaven and moon, like
    ships, conquer.
Light the lamps of my mosque of
    absences,
light my inventories of empty
    brothels
that fill the heart-unamputated-
    mind like the sun fills
    lakes.
And I am awakened alone at
    night by rush of light-
    ning
against rapid-eye-movement lids,
so I can write away absences,
about lovers awakened
by the thunder-nocturne.

— *Arturo Desimone*

DEILD SABAN NÓTT

Sorg sem fyllist eins og elding
keisarinn hávaði er dauður,
vín sigrar himininn
Muse, hún er hér, sterkust án
    tónlistar.
Sorgin er ást ástandsins
í bið
staðsett í flugstöðinni, þar sem
    tónlist er
ó sent bréf.
Ég bíð eftir lest frá Buenos Aires
    til Bratislava
Sorgin er í víni eldingarinnar
þar til himinn og tungl eins og
    skip sigra
kveikja á lampa í fjarveru minni
og birgðir mínar af tómum
    vændishúsum
sem fylla hjarta-unamputated-
    huga eins og sólin fyllir
    vötn.
og ég er vakinn einn á nóttunni
    af eldingum
gegn skjótum
    augnahreyfingum,
svo ég geti afskrifað fjarvistir,
um elskendur vakna
af þrumunni-nocturne.

— *Arturo Desimone*
  (*Þýtt úr Ensku, Michael Lohr*)

DIVIDIDA NOCHE
DE SABÁN

La tristeza se llena como relám-
    pago
el ruido del emperador está
    muerto,
y vino conquista el cielo
la musa, ella está aquí, más
    fuerte sin música.
La tristeza es el estado de amor
en espera
estacionado en la terminal,
    donde la música es
una carta no enviada.
Espero un tren de Buenos Aires a
    Bratislava
La tristeza está en el vino del
    rayo
hasta que el cielo y la luna como
    barcos conquistan
encienden las lámparas en mi
    mezquita de ausencias
e inventarios de burdeles vacíos
que llenan la mente aún conecta-
    da al corazón como el sol llena
    los lagos.
Me despierto solo por la noche
relámpago contra mis párpados
    soñadores,
así que puedo escribir ausencias,
sobre amantes agitados
por la nocturnidad del trueno.

    – Arturo Desimone
    (Traducción, T. Warburton y
    Bajo y rvb)

PODIJELJENA SABEJSKA
NOĆ

Tuga koja ispunjava kao munja:
car buka je mrtav,
vino pokorava raj
muza, ona je tu, najjača bez glaz-
    be.
Tuga je stanje ljubavi
u čekanju,
smještene na terminalu, gdje je
    glazba
neposlano pismo.
Čekam vlak iz Buenos Aires a za
Bratislavu.
Tuga je u vinu munje
dok raj i mjesec ne pokore kao
    brodovi.
Upali lampe moje džamije od-
    sutnosti,
zapali moje popise praznih bor-
    dela
koji ispunjavaju um od kojeg
    srce nije amputirano kao što
    sunce
ispunjava jezera.
I probudi me samog u noći nalet
munje
nasuprot vjeđa brzih pokreta
    očiju,
tako da mogu otpisati odsustva,
o ljubavnicima koje je probudio
nokturno groma.

    –Arturo Desimone
    (Prijevod, Marija Dejanović)

SZAŁWIA

Czy szałwia mnie uchroni przed wilgocią?
Nic mnie nie uchroni.

Natrzyj ciało solą
Niech cię sól obserwuje.

Bezpieczny?
Nie, nikt nie jest.

Przytłum tę lek-
komyślność

Niektórzy ludzie są latarniami ulicznymi
Niektórzy ludzie są spadającymi gwiaz-
dami.

Przywiąż notatki do czerwonych balonów
wskrześ zmarłych

Pióra są pozbawione ptaków
Bez cienia

— Juleen Johnson
(Tłumaczenie: Joanna Rosińska)

SAGE

Will sage keep me dry?
Nothing will.

Rub salt on your body
Let it observe you.

Safe?
No, no one.

Hold this reckless-
ness down

Some people are streetlights.
Some people are shooting stars.

Tie notes to red balloons
bring back the dead.

Feathers are birdless
Without shadows

— Juleen Johnson

SALVIA

¿La salvia me mantendrá seco?
Nada lo hará.

        Frote la sal en su cuerpo
        Deje que lo observe.

Seguro?
No, nadie.

        Sujetar esta imprud-
          encia

    Algunas personas son farolas.
      Y algunas son estrellas fugaces.

Atar unas notas a globos rojos
traer de vuelta a los muertos.

      Las plumas no tienen pájaros
        Ni sombras

— *Juleen Johnson*
(Traducción, T. Warburton y Bajo
y rvb)

ΦΑΣΚΟΜΗΛΟ

Το φασκόμηλο θα με κρατήσει στεγνό;
Τίποτα δεν θα το κάνει.

    Τρίψτε αλάτι στο σώμα σας
    Αφήστε το να σας παρατηρήσει.

Ασφαλής;
Όχι, κανένας.

    Κρατήστε
    αυτή η απερισ-
    κεψία χαμηλά.

    Μερικοί άνθρωποι είναι φώτα του δρό-
    μου.
    Μερικοί άνθρωποι είναι πεφταστέ-
    ρια.

Δέστε σημειώματα σε κόκκινα μπαλόνια
φέρτε πίσω τους νεκρούς.

    Τα φτερά είναι χωρίς πουλιά
    Χωρίς σκιές.

— *Τζουλίν Τζόνσον*
(μεταφρασμένο, Κοντοπούλου Α. Καν-
σταντίνα)

EVERY EDGE A CENTRE: OT DREAM: So we gotta get up in the middle of the night for Mirella's taxi to Venizelos and I'm having a cool dream till the alarm. It's the NCAA hoop tournament, March Madness, and after several overtimes the score is tied, 101-101, I think Florida State was one of the teams, and through some unknown protocol, after so many OTs, they have what resembles a soccer shootout only it isn't the players but their entourage starting with the cheer leaders, then through the band: trumpets, tubas, saxophones, drums and they're all lined up on the court waiting to shoot free throws. How many get to shoot? It's not clear and after the bands maybe more will join the queue: the coaches and assistants, the physical therapists, maybe the university presidents, the Board of muthafucking Trustees? And the mascots, they must be in there somewhere. And, of course, some of them can't shoot worth a shit, missing the hoop entirely. And the crowd is watching in stunned silence. Where does it end? Then the alarm on Mirella's phone, which is very disconcerting as it is the same droning ring we used to remind me to take my chemo pills – four years distant and still staying ahead of the big C. Maybe this is

ÖLL KANTUR Í MIÐJA: OT DRAUMUR: Svo við verðum að standa upp um miðja nótt fyrir leigubíl Mirellu til Venizelos og mig dreymir svalan draum þar til viðvörunin kemur. Það er NCAA hringamótið, March Madness, og eftir nokkrar framlengingar er staðan jöfn, 101-101, ég held að Flórída-ríki hafi verið eitt af liðunum, og í gegnum einhverja óþekkta siðareglur, eftir svo marga OT, hafa þeir það sem líkist fótboltakeppni aðeins það eru ekki leikmennirnir heldur föruneyti þeirra sem byrja á hressa leiðtogunum og síðan í gegnum hljómsveitina: lúðra, túpur, saxófónar, trommur og þeim er öllum stillt upp á vellinum og bíður þess að skjóta vítaskot. Hversu margir fá að skjóta? Það er ekki ljóst og eftir að hljómsveitirnar koma kannski fleiri í biðröðina: þjálfararnir og aðstoðarmennirnir, sjúkraþjálfararnir, kannski háskólaforsetarnir, stjórn móðurfokk trúnaðarmanna? Og lukkudýrin, þau hljóta að vera þarna einhvers staðar. Og að sjálfsögðu geta sumir þeirra ekki skotið skít virði og vantar alveg hringinn. Og mannfjöldinn fylgist með í töfrandi þögn. Hvar endar það? Svo vekjaraklukkan í símanum Mirellu, sem er mjög áhyggjufullur þar sem það er sami drónahringurinn og við notuðum til að minna mig á að taka lyfjatöflurnar

Każda granica bywa środkiem: Sen o dogrywce meczu: Więc mamy wstać w środku nocy, bo przyjeżdża po Mirellę taksówka do Venizelos, a ja mam fajny sen aż do pobudki. Są rozgrywki koszykówki Narodowego Związku Sportu Akademickiego (NCAA) tak zwane Marcowe Szaleństwo. Po kilku dogrywkach mamy wynik 101:101. Chyba Uniwersytet Florydzki jest jedną z drużyn i według jakichś nieznanych przepisów mają tam coś w rodzaju rzutów karnych w piłce nożnej, tyle że nie zawodnicy je egzekwują ale ich świta. Zaczyna się od "cheerleaderów", potem orkiestra dęta uniwersytetu maszerująca w paradzie przed meczem: trąbki, tuby, saksofony, bębny, wszyscy ustawiają się w kolejce do rzutów osobistych. Ilu wykonało rzuty? Nie wiadomo. Po orkiestrach może nawet więcej dołączy do kolejki: trenerzy i ich pomocnicy, fizjoterapeuci drużyn, może nawet zarząd uniwersytetów i, kurwa, nawet grono ich doradców finansowych! No i ludzie przebrani za maskotki drużyn—co pewnie gdzieś w pobliżu się szwendają. Rzecz jasna, niektórzy z nich za żadne skarby nie potrafią strzelić kosza, ba, nawet go dotknąć. Publiczność patrzy w niemym zaskoczeniu. Dokąd to zmierza?

Wtedy dzwoni budzik w telefonie Mirelli, co jest dość niepokojące bo

CADA BORDE UN CENTRO: SUEÑO DE HORAS EXTRAS: Así que tenemos que levantarnos en medio de la noche para el taxi de Mirella a Venizelos y estoy teniendo un sueño genial hasta la alarma. Es el torneo de aro de la NCAA, *March Madness*, y después de varios horas extras el marcador estaba empatado, 101-101, creo que Florida Estado fue uno de los equipos, y a través de un protocolo desconocido, después de tantos HEs,* tienen lo que se parece a un tiroteo de fútbol, solo que no son los jugadores pero su entorno empezando por los líderes alegres, luego a través de la banda: trompetas, tubas, saxofones, tambores, todos están alineados en la cancha esperando para disparar tiros libres. ¿Cuántos van a disparar? No está claro y después de a las bandas tal vez más se unirán a la cola: entrenadores y asistentes, fisioterapeutas, tal vez presidentes de universidades, Junta de hijoputa Fideicomisarios? Y las mascotas, deben estar allí en algúna parte. Y, por supuesto, algunos de ellos no pueden disparar vale la pena una mierda, perdiendo el aro por completo. Y la multitud observa en un silencio aturdido. ¿Dónde termina? Luego la alarma en el teléfono de Mirella, que es muy desconcertante porque es el mismo anillo de zum-

my overtime? I don't think I've reached the shootout impasse point. And who would shoot for me? An interesting question, who would queue up? And who would I want to queue up, if being able to shoot was the priority, rather than a willingness to try? I love ya, sister, but have you ever made a foul shot? In the dream world they must still be shooting, maybe the fans are finally getting their chance.

– *Mark Sargent*
  Sparti, Greece, 27 May, 2020
  Q

mínar - fjögur ár fjarri og vera enn á undan stóru C. Kannski er þetta yfirvinna mín? Ég held að ég sé ekki kominn í ógöngustig skotbardaga. Og hver myndi skjóta fyrir mig? Áhugaverð spurning, hver myndi standa í biðröð? Og hvern myndi ég vilja standa í biðröð ef það væri forgangsatrið að geta skotið frekar en vilji til að prófa? Ég elska þig, systir, en hefur þú einhvern tíma gert rangt skot? Í draumaheiminum hljóta þeir samt að skjóta, kannski eru aðdáendur loksins að fá sitt tækifæri.

– *Mark Sargent*
  Sparti Grikklandi, 27. maí 2020
  (Þýtt úr Ensku, Michael Lohr)
  Q

to ten sam dźwięk, którego używaliśmy by przypomnieć mi o pigułce chemioterapii -- cztery lata minęły i dalej się nie daję rakowi. Może to jest moja dogrywka. Nie sądze bym osiągnął swój punkt impasu. Kto by strzelał kosze w mojej drużynie? Interesujące, kto by zgłosił się do kolejki? I kogo bym chciał w mojej kolejce, jeśli najważniejsze byłoby celne wrzucenie piłki do kosza a nie gotowość do spróbowania. Kocham cię siostrzyczko, ale czy ty kiedykolwiek celnie rzuciłaś do kosza?

W świecie mojego snu oni pewnie dalej strzelają kosze, może nawet i fani w końcu dostali się do kolejki.

— *Mark Sargent*
  (Tłumaczenie: Joanna Rosinska)
  Q

bido utilizado para recordarme que tome mis pastillas de quimio – a cuatro años de distancia y todavía me quedo por delante de la gran C. ¿Tal vez estas son mis horas extras? No creo que haya llegado al punto de impasse del tiroteo. ¿Y quién dispararía por mí? Una pregunta interesante, ¿quién haría cola? ¿Y a quién le gustaría hacer cola, si poder disparar fuera la prioridad, en lugar de estar dispuesto a intentarlo? Te amo, hermana, ¿pero alguna vez has hecho un tiro sucio? En el mundo de los sueños todavía deben estar disparando, tal vez los fanáticos finalmente estén teniendo su oportunidad.

– *Mark Sargent,*
  Sparti, Grecia, 27 Mayo, 2020
  (Traducción, T. Warburton y Bajo
  y rvb)
  Q

In the Dunkin' Donuts
Where the Virgin Mary
Appeared on an Apple
Fritter

Every day since that report
    I've ordered a fritter
        and sat by the window

    to inspect its frosting
for Teresa's laugh lines,
    Jesus' beard,

anything to prove
    there's more for me today

    than coffee and subways
and a burned-out porchlight
    I've yet to fix.

God didn't have to make it so hard,
    you know,
    if he wanted me to believe.

He didn't have to let
    miracles run dry
        in my century.

    Another weekday,
Another secular fritter.
    From the window,

    I see a boy chase
a lost ball into a bush.
    Thank God it's not burning.

    — *Armin Tolentino*

**Í kleinuhringjum frá
Dunkin Þar sem María
mey birtist á epli fritter**

Á hverjum degi síðan skýrslan
  Ég hef pantað fritter
    og settist við gluggann

    að skoða frosting þess
  fyrir hláturlínur Teresa,
      Skegg Jesú,

  hvað sem er til að sanna
      það er meira fyrir mig í dag

    en kaffi og neðanjarðarlestir
  og útbrunnið verkljós
      Ég er ekki enn búinn að laga.

Guð þurfti ekki að gera það svo erfitt,
              þú veist,
  ef hann vildi að ég myndi trúa.

Hann þurfti ekki að láta
      kraftaverk verða þurrt
        á mínum öld.

          Annar virkur dagur,
  Annar veraldlegur fritter.
        Úr glugganum

    Ég sé strák elta
  týndur bolti í runna.
      Guði sé lof að það brennur ekki.

  — Armin Tolentino
  (Þýtt úr Ensku, Michael Lohr)

U Dunkin's Donuts gdje se Djevica Marija pojavila na kolačićima od jabuka

Svaki dan od tog izvještaja
naručio sam kolačić
i sjeo pokraj prozora.

proučavajući njegovu
šećernu glazuru
Terezine linije smijeha,
Isusovu bradu,

bilo što da mogu dokazati
da ima više za mene danas

od kave i podzemnih
i izgorjele lampe na trijemu
koju još trebam
popraviti.

Bog mi nije trebao tako otežati,
znaš,
ako je želio da vjerujem.

Nije trebao dopustiti
da se sva čuda iskoriste
u mojem stoljeću.

Drugi dan u
tjednu,
Drugi laički kolačić.
S prozora,

vidim dječaka kako
juri
za izgubljenom loptom u
grmlju.
Hvala Bogu da ne gori.

— *Armin Tolentino*
(prijevod, Dijana Jakovac)

Dunkin' Donutsis, kus Neitsi Maarja end õunasõõrikul ilmutas

Sellest uudisest peale olen iga päev
tellinud õunasõõriku
ja istunud akna äärde,

et otsida selle glasuurist
Teresa naerukortse,
Jeesuse habet,

ükskõik mida, mis tõestaks,
et mulle on täna midagi enamat

kui kohv ja metroo
ja verandalaterna läbipõlenud pirn,
mida ma pole jõudnud
vahetada.

Jumalal poleks olnud vaja asju nii
raskeks ajada,
eks ole,
kui ta tahtnuks, et mul usku
oleks.

Tal poleks olnud vaja lasta
minu sajandil
imedest kuivaks joosta.

Järjekordne tööpäev,
järjekordne ilmalik sõõrik.
Aknast näen,

kuidas üks poiss jookseb
plehku pannud pallile põõsasse
järele.
Jumal tänatud, et põõsas
ei põle.

—*Armin Tolentino*
(Inglise keelest tõlkinud, Mirjam Parve)

**En el Dunkin' Donuts donde
la Virgen María apareció en
un buñuelo de manzana**

Cada día desde ese informe
      He ordenado un buñuelo
         y me senté junto a la ventana

              para inspeccionar su azúcar glaseado
      para las líneas de risa de Teresa,
la barba de Jesús,

cualquier cosa para probar que
        hoy en día hay más para mí

        que el café yel metro
y una luz del porche quemada
   que aún no he arreglado.

Dios no tenía que hacerlo tan duro,
        ya sabes,
   si quería que creyera.

No tuvo que dejar que
      milagros se secaran
         en mi siglo.

     Otro día de la semana,
Otro buñuelo secular.
     Desde la ventana,

       Veo a un chico perseguir a
una bola perdida en un arbusto.
     Gracias a Dios que no se está
         quemando.

— *Armin Tolentino*
   (traducción, T. Warburton y Bajo y rvb)

ZRAKOPLOVOM
PAR AVION

A Week's Pay Lost at the Lizard Fight

You drop your roll of Friday bills
on the purple one with a thick
              black
tongue, because its yellow eyes
haven't shifted from its opponent,
a green skink clawing at the walls
of the box, cold-footed gladiator
wetting its corner.
But when the fight ends
with your pick split open,
neck to rectum, organs spilt
like pink confetti, you'll wander
              home,
thinking how to win it all back.

Even at six you'd ask your dad
what could kill what: Great white
              or gorilla?
Cobra or buffalo? Neanderthal or
Green Beret? Everything eyed
as potential death matches. Every
              day
you find yourself standing across
another new monster eager to
              empty your torso.
You'll get lost, circle the city,
forget your way home as you
              dream
of a box big enough to fit
you in one corner
and the entire world in the other

              — *Armin Tolentino*

Una semana de pago perdido en la lucha de lagartos

Se deja caer el rollo de billetes del
              viernes
en el púrpura con una gruesa
lengua negra, porque sus ojos
              amarillos
no se han desplazado de su oponente,
un lagarto verde en las paredes de la
              caja,
gladiador de pies fríos
que moja su esquina.
Pero cuando la lucha termine
con tu campeón partido abierto,
de cuello a culo, órganos derramados
como confeti rosado, te irás a casa,
pensando cómo recuperarlo todo.

Incluso a la edad de seis le
              preguntabas a tu padre
qué podría matar qué: ¿gran tiburón
              blanco o gorila?
Cobra o búfalo? Neandertal o
Zapatista? Todo miraba como
posibles combates de muerte. Cada día
te encuentras frente otro nuevo
monstruo ansioso por vaciar tu torso.
Te perderás, rodeando la ciudad,
olviderás tu camino a casa mientras
              sueñas con
una caja bastante grande para
encajarte
en una esquina
y el mundo entero en el otro

              — *Armin Tolentino*
              (traducción, T. Warburton y Bajo y rvb)

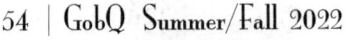

Tjedna plaća izgubljena na borbe guštera

Svoj bunt zarađenih novčanica
polažeš na ljubičastog s debelim
crnim jezikom, jer
   njegove se žute oči
ne miču s protivnika,
zelenog rovaša koji grebe
zidove kutije, hladnonogog gla-
   dijatora koji
moči svoj kut.
No kad borba završitvoj odabir
   je rasporen
od vrata do rektuma, organi mu
rasuti k'o roza konfete, ti odlaziš
   kući
razmišljajući kako vratiti izgub-
   ljeno.

Čak kao šestogodišnjak pitao si
   tatu
što može ubiti što. Bijela psina
   ili gorila?
Kobra ili bizon? Neandertalac ili
Zelena Beretka? Sve si gledao
   kao moguću borbu na smrt.
   Svaki se dan
suočavaš s novim čudovištem
koje jedva čeka da ti prospe or-
   gane.
Gubiš se, kružiš gradom,
zaboravljaš put kući dok sanjaš
o kutiji toliko velikoj da
u jedan kut staneš ti
a u drugi čitav svijet.

   — Armin Tolentino
   (prijevod s engleskoga, Ana
   Katana)

Viku er greitt tapað í eðlabaráttunni

Þú sleppir hlutanum af
   föstudagsreikningum
á fjólubláa með þykka svörtu
tungu, vegna þess að gulu augu þess
hefur ekki vikið frá andstæðingi
   sínum,
grænt skink kló við veggi
á kassanum, kaldfótur skylmingakappi
væta hornið.
En þegar baráttunni lýkur
með skiptingu þínum opinn,
háls að endaþarmi, líffæri hella niður
eins og bleikar konfettí, þá ferð þú
   heim,
að hugsa hvernig á að vinna allt aftur.

Jafnvel klukkan sex myndirðu spyrja
   föður þinn
hvað gæti drepið hvað: Stórhvítur eða
   górilla?
Kóbra eða vísundur? Neanderthal eða
Græn Beret? Allt augað
sem hugsanleg dauðafæri. Daglega
þér finnst þú standa þvert á
annað nýtt skrímsli sem er fús til að
   tæma búkinn.
Þú villtist, hringðu um borgina,
gleymdu leiðinni heim eins og þig
   dreymir
af kassa nógu stórt til að passa
þú í einu horninu
og allur heimurinn í hinni

   — Armin Tolentino
   (Þýtt úr Ensku, Michael Lohr)

The 90s

1997 –
yes, perhaps
that;
the last year
we'll ever
nostalgise.

like how
they did it properly,
before,
with the american
50s;
happy days
and du-wop,
leather jackets
and johnny rockets
(eddie's over here)
after war tore up the
    40s
and the decades that
    followed
full of chaos, sudden
civil rights
and children kicking
    their legs out,
learning to struggle.

the 90s
are going to be that
all again –
the last time
we had,
pre-internet
and just the very start,
before
the whole '01 thing

Na 90aidí

1997
is ea, b'fhéidir
é sin;
an bhliain dheireannach
ariamh
go ndéanfaimid cumhadh
    uirthi.

sa chaoi
a rinne siad i gceart é,
roimhe,
leis na 50aidí
meiriceánacha;
laethanta sona
agus dú-op,
casóga leathair
agus *johnny rockets*
(tá eddie thall anseo)
i ndiaidh don chogadh na
    40aidí
a stracadh as a chéile
agus na deich mblianta a
    lean
lán cíor thuathail, go
    tobann
cearta sibhialta
agus páistí ag sín-ciceáil
    amach a gcosa,
strachailt á fhoghlaim.

na 90aidí
mar sin a bheidh
go huile arís –
an ré dheireannach
a bhí againn,
roimh an idirlíon

Los años mil novecientos noventa

mil novecientos noventa siete –
sí, tal vez
eso; el
último añon de que
    vamos
alguna vez
ser nostálgicos.

como lo
hicieron correctamente,
antes, con
los años mil novecientos
cincuenta de Estados
    Unidos;
días felices
y *doo-wop*,
hay chaquetas de cuero
y los *johnny rockets*
(y eddie esta allí)
después de la guerra
    arrancó
los años años mil
    novecientos cuarenta
y las décadas que
    siguieron a
lleno de caos, de repente
derechos civil, y
los niños que echan
    puntapié,

9. áratugurinn

1997 –
já, kannski
það;
síðasta árið
við munum alltaf
fortíðarþrá.

eins og hvernig
þeir gerðu það
    almennilega,
áður,
við Ameríkana
50s;
gleðilegra daga
og du-wop,
leðurjakka
og johnny
    eldflaugum
(Eddie er hérna)
eftir stríð reif 40s
og áratugina sem
    fylgdu
fullur af ringulreið,
    skyndilega
borgaraleg réttindi
og börn sparka
    fótunum út,
að læra að glíma.

90. áratugurinn
ætla að verða það
allt aftur –
síðasta skiptið
við höfðum,

90-e

1997 —
da, možda
to;
posljednja godina
kada ćemo
čeznuti.

kao kako
napravili su kako
    treba,
prije,
s američkim
50-ima;
sretni dani
i *du-wop*,
kožne jakne
i johnny rakete
(eddie je ovdje)
nakon rata koji je
    uništio 40-e
i desetljeća koja su
    uslijedila
puna kaosa,
    iznenadna
građanska prava
i djeca izbacujući
    svoje noge,
učeći se boriti.

90-e
će biti to sve
iznova—
zadnji put
imali smo

blew up
and later,
realising
what the internet
　　would become.

things
seemed pretty simple.
I'm sure they weren't,
but that's the past:
getting further away
the longer you look
　　at it.

　　　　　　– D.S. Maolalaí

agus díreach an fíor thús,
sular
phléasc
an rud sin is uile '01
agus níos déanaí,
ag teacht chun tuisceana
ar cén sort rud a bheadh san
　　idirlíon.

bhí cuma sách simplí
ar rudaí.
tá mé cinnte nach raibh siad,
ach sin é an t-am atá caite:
ag imeacht níos faide uait
fad a fhéachann tú air.

　　　　　　– D.S. Maolalaí
　　　　　　(Seosamh Ó Maolalaí, a
　　　　　　d'aistrigh go Gaeilge)

aprendiendo a luchar.

los años mil novecientos
noventa van a ser así
de nuevo,
la última vez
que tuvimos,
antes-internet
y sólo el comienzo,
antes de todo
la cosa del año dos mil
uno explotó
y más tarde,
realización lo
de qué sería Internet.

las cosas
parecían bastante sim-
    ples.
Estoy seguro de que no
    lo eran,
pero eso es el pasado:
alejarse más
cuanto más lo mires.

    – D.S. Maolalaí
      (Traducción, T.
       Warburton y Bajo
       y rvb)

fyrirfram internetið
og bara byrjunin,
áður
allt '01 hluturinn
sprengdi sig
og síðar,
að átta sig
hvað internetið yrði.

hlutir
virtist frekar einfalt.
Ég er viss um að
    það voru það
    ekki,
en það er fortíðin:
að komast lengra
því lengur sem þú
    horfir á það.

    – D.S. Maolalaí
      (Þýtt úr Ensku,
      Michael Lohr)

prije interneta
i sam početak
prije nego se
cijela '01 stvar
raznijela
i kasnije,
shvaćajući
što će internet postati.

stvari
su izgledale prilično
    jednostavne.
siguran sam da nisu
    bile,
ali to je prošlost:
odlazeći i nestajući
što dulje gledaš u to.

    – D.S. Maolalaí
      (prijevod, Dijana
      Jakovac)

Once A Fool Never Again
A Fool

Only once have I ever considered myself
a fool,
after having scampered about in ravenous
rainfall,
finding shelter under a tree bearing the
marks of
violent lightning strikes: whereto, I
marked the
spot for future fools.

– *Emmett Wheatfall*

Una vez tonto nunca
más tonto

Solo una vez me he considerado tonto,
después de haber correteado bajo una
lluvia voraz,
encontrar refugio bajo un árbol con las
marcas de
violentos relámpagos: en donde,
marqué el
lugar para tontos futuros.

– *Emmett Wheatfall*
(Traducción, T. Warburton y Bajo y rɔɒb)

**Być głupcem raz –
wystarczy**

Raz tylko pomyślałem o sobie
że jestam głupcem,
gdy biegając pośród ulewnego
deszczu,
znalazłem schronienie pod
drzewem noszącym
znamiona
gwałtownych uderzeń
piorunów: które to
miejsce oznaczyłem
dla przyszłych głupców.

— *Emmett Wheatfall
(tłumaczenie: Joanna
Rosińska)*

**Jednom budala, i
nikad više**

Samo sam jednom zbilja ispao
budala
kad sam bježao od
strahovita pljuska,
i sklonio se pod stablo obilježeno
ožiljcima
silovitih udara groma:
time sam obilježio mjesto
za sve buduće budale.

— *Emmett Wheatfallă
(prijevod s engleskoga, Ana
Katana)*

**Ποτέ ξανά
τρελός**

Μόνο μια φορά θεώρησα ποτέ τον
εαυτό μου τρελό,
αφότου έτρεξα μέσα σε καταιγίδα
μανιασμένη,
βρήκα καταφύγιο κάτω από ένα
δέντρο που έφερε
από οφθαλμούς κεραυνούς: εκεί,
σημάδια
σημείο για τους επόμενους τρελούς.

— *Έμετ Γουίτφολ
(Μετάφραση, Βασιλεία
Οικονόμου)*

We forget the road.
Here is a green and large forest,
There are so many birds flying
    between the trees.
The world stands on one leg,
All the dead take each others' hands.
And I forgot you a long time ago.

— *Ivan de Monbrison*
(tr. fr. the Russian, I. de M.)

Мы забываем дорогу.
Вот зеленый и большой лес,
между деревьями летает так
    много птиц.
Мир стоит на одной ноге,
мертвые берутся за руки,
и я забыл тебя надолго.

— *Иван де Монбризон*

AUSTRALIA
Blue Devil
Eryngium pinnatifidum
$1

Nos olvidamos del camino.
Aquí hay un bosque verde y
    grande,
hay tantas aves volando entre los
    árboles.
El mundo se apoya en una
    pierna.
Todos los muertos se toman del
    mano.
Y te olvidé hace mucho tiempo.

— *Ivan de Monbrison*
(traducción, T. Warburton y
Bajo y rʊb)

Ένα πέτρινο άγαλμα σε μια πλατεία.
Στο δρόμο πεζοί, αυτοκίνητα,
Ο θόρυβος που δεν σταματά ποτέ.
Και φωνές γυναικών και ανδρών
βγαίνουν από τα παράθυρα,
Αλλά δεν ανήκουν σε κανέναν

— Ιβάν ντε Μόνμπριζον
(μεταφρασμένο, Βασιλεία Οικονόμου)

Steinstytta á torgi.
Á götunni eru gangandi
vegfarendur, bílar,
Hávaðinn sem aldrei hættir.
Og raddir kvenna og karla
koma út um gluggana,
En ekki tilheyra neinum

— Ivan de Monbrison
(Þýtt úr Ensku, Michael Lohr)

Una estatua de piedra se
encuentra en una plaza.
En la calle hay peatones, coches,
El ruido que nunca se detiene.
Y las voces de mujeres y
hombres
salen de las ventanas,
Pero no pertenecen a nadie

— Ivan de Monbrison
(traducción, T. Warburton y
Bajo y rob)

A stone statue in a square.
On the street there are
pedestrians, cars,
The noise that never stops.
And voices of women and men
come out of the windows,
But don't belong to anyone

— Ivan de Monbrison
(tr. fr. the Russian, I. de M.)

Каменная статуя на площади.
На улице пешеходы, машины,
Шум который никогда не ути-
хает.
И голоса женщин и мужчин
выходят из окон,
но не принадлежат никому.

— Иван де Монбризон

Fifth Period

Joy McDowell

The picture told the entire story. Corpse here, smashed automobile there, corpse's head between bent front fender and oak tree.

Jordan glanced over at Carolyn. She looked ill. The film about fatal accidents was supposed to put the fear of God into the fifteen and sixteen-year-old students in the Driver's Ed class.

The instructor, with his dated film, was boring. Everyone in class had seen worse in popcorn movies and on TV. A headless corpse popped up about once a week on forensic series.

Jordan already had a license, but needed the class to lower his insurance rate.

A scrapping noise.

Carolyn fought to free herself from her desk. Then she vomited in the classroom aisle.

The instructor almost looked pleased as he rang the office to summon a janitor.

Several students left the room. Jordan patted Carolyn on the back as he ushered her to the door. Having a girlfriend hurl in class was not cool, but she was a girl.

Once out in the hallway,

Peti sat

Joy McDowell
(prijevod, Ana Katana)

Slika govori tisuću riječi. Ovdje leš, ondje smrskan automobil, glava leša uklještena između prednjeg blatobrana i hrastova debla.

Jordan baci pogled prema Carolyn. Izgledala je bolesno. Film o smrtnim nesrećama trebao je usaditi bogobojaznost u petnaestogodišnjake i šesnaestogodišnjake koji slušaju pripremna predavanja za pohađanje autoškole.

Predavač je dosadan, kao i njegov zastarjeli film. Svi prisutni vidjeli su mnogo gore stvari u igranim filmovima i na televizoru. Obezglavljeno truplo prikazuje se barem jednom tjedno u poznatoj seriji o forenzičarima.

Jordan već ima vozačku dozvolu, no pohađa predavanja ne bi li smanjio premiju osiguranja.

Šuštanje.

Carolyn se pokušava osloboditi sa svojeg mjesta. Zatim povraća između redova klupa.

Dok poziva domara, predavač djeluje zadovoljno ishodom.

Nekoliko učenika napustilo je učionicu. Jordan potapše Carolyn po leđima prateći je van. Nije neka fora kad tvoja djevoj-

Fimmta tímabil

Joy McDowell
(Þýtt úr Ensku, Michael Lohr)

Myndin sagði alla söguna. Lík hér, mölvaður bíll þar, höfuð líksins á milli beygðrar framhliðar og eikartrés.

Jordan leit yfir á Carolyn. Hún leit illa út. Kvikmyndin um banaslys átti að koma guðsótta inn í fimmtán og sextán ára nemendur í Driver's Ed bekknum.

Leiðbeinandinn, með dagsettri kvikmynd sinni, var leiðinlegur. Allir í bekknum höfðu séð verra í poppmyndum og í sjónvarpi. Höfuðlaust lík skaust upp um það bil einu sinni í viku á réttarrannsóknarþáttum.

Jordan hafði þegar leyfi, en þurfti bekkinn til að lækka tryggingarhlutfallið sitt.

Skrapphljóð.

Carolyn barðist við að losa sig frá borðinu sínu. Svo ældi hún í skólastofunni.

Leiðbeinandinn virtist næstum ánægður þegar hann hringdi á skrifstofuna til að kalla til húsvörð.

Nokkrir nemendur yfirgáfu stofuna. Jordan klappaði Carolyn á bakið þegar hann leiddi hana til dyra. Að vera með kærustu í bekknum var ekki flott, en hún var stelpa.

Þegar hún var komin út á ganginn, flúði Carolyn á salerni stúlkunnar. Jordan gat aðeins ímyndað sér

Clases de conducción

Joy McDowell
(Tradicción, T. Warburton y Bajo y rvb)

La imagen contaba toda la historia. Cadáver aquí, coche destrozado allá, cabeza de cadáver entre guardabarros delantero doblado y roble.

Jordan miró a Carolyn, que parecía enferma. Una película sobre accidentes fatales diseñada para poner el temor de Dios en los jóvenes de quince y dieciséis años en la Educación del conductor.

El maestro, con su película anticuada, era aburrido. Todo el mundo había visto algo peor en programas de televisión y películas de éxito. Un cadáver sin cabeza aparecía aproximadamente una vez a la semana en programas policiales.

Jordan tenía una licencia, pero necesitaba la clase para reducir su seguro de coche.

Un ruido de raspado.

Carolyn luchó para liberarse de su escritorio. Luego vomitó.

El maestro sonrió cuando llamó para convocar a un conserje.

Varios estudiantes abandonaron la sala. Jordan le dio unas palmaditas en la espalda a Carolyn mientras la llevaba a la puerta. Tener una novia vomitando en clase no era fresco o genial, pero ella estaba chica.

Desde el pasillo, Carolyn huyó al baño de las chicas. Jordan apenas

Carolyn fled to the girl's restroom. Jordan could only imagine what went on behind that swinging door. He had heard that bulimic girls were rotting the school plumbing with their purged stomach acid. Anorexia, menstruation, even girl tears were jungles of comprehension that Jordan was struggling to sort into understanding.

The drivers' education instructor had been a sub in wood shop class. Jordan hated the bastard. Now he had another reason.

Upsetting Carolyn might get the instructor's green Ford keyed in the staff parking area.

Carolyn emerged from the restroom looking pale.

"Let's skip sixth period. I need some pop to settle my stomach."

Jordan opened the door of his parents' aged-out Malibu and placed his books and Carolyn's on the rear seat. His foot pressed the accelerator. The tires bit and jerked forward as he piloted the rocket ship along a country road that snaked away from their school. He eased his foot off the gas. He could not get that black and white movie scene out of his mind. The headless corpse wore a skirt and sturdy shoes, just like his grandmother. *Q*

ka bljuje usred sata, no djevojke su takve.

Čim su izišli u hodnik, Carolyn pojuri u ženski toalet. Jordan je samo mogao zamisliti što se događa iza tih vrata. Čuo je da su bulimične djevojke uništile školske cijevi svojom želučanom kiselinom. Anoreksija, menstruacija, pa čak i ženske suze bile su nerazumljiva džungla s kojom se Jordan jedva nosi.

Predavač je zapravo bio učitelj iz drvodjelstva na zamjeni. Jordan mrzi tog kretena, i upravo je dobio još jedan razlog za to.

Uzrujao je Carolyn, i time će si možda priskrbiti ogrebotine od ključa na zelenom Fordu parkiranom na parkiralištu za osoblje.

Carolyn izlazi iz toaleta blijeda lica.

"Markirajmo šesti sat. Treba mi malo gaziranog soka da smirim želudac."

Jordan otvori vrata prastarog Chevrolet Malibua svojih roditelja te stavi svoje i Carolynine knjige na stražnje sjedalo. Pritisne papučicu gasa. Gume zagrizu i potegnu naprijed, a on svojom raketom pilotira vijugavim seoskim putom, što dalje od škole. Skida nogu s papučice. Ne može izbiti crno – bijeli prizor iz glave. Obezglavljeni leš imao je suknju i čvrste cipele, baš kao njegova baka. *Q*

hvað gerðist á bak við þessar sveifluhurð. Hann hafði heyrt að bulimískar stúlkur væru að rotna skólapípuna með hreinsuðu magasýrunni. Lystarleysi, tíðir, jafnvel stelputár voru frumskógur skilnings sem Jordan átti erfitt með að raða í skilning.

Kennari ökumanna hafði verið undirmaður í tréverkstæðistíma. Jordan hataði ræfillinn. Nú hafði hann aðra ástæðu.

Carolyn í uppnámi gæti fengið græna Ford leiðbeinandann inn á bílastæði starfsmanna.

Carolyn kom út af klósettinu og leit föl út.

„Sleppum sjötta leikhluta. Ég þarf smá popp til að jafna magann.“

Jordan opnaði hurðina á gamla Malibu foreldra sinna og setti bækur hans og Carolyn í aftursætið. Fótur hans þrýsti á bensíngjöfina. Dekkin bitu og kipptist áfram þegar hann stýrði eldflaugaskipinu eftir sveitavegi sem sneri sér frá skólanum þeirra. Hann létti fótinn undan bensíninu. Hann gat ekki losað sig við þessa svarthvítu kvikmyndasenu. Höfuðlausi líkið var í pilsi og traustum skóm, alveg eins og amma hans. Q

imaginó lo que sucedía detrás de esa puerta oscilante. Había oído que las chicas bulímicas estaban pudriendo la plomería de la escuela con su ácido estomacal. La anorexia, la menstruación, incluso las lágrimas de las niñas eran selvas de emoción que Jordan luchaba por comprender.

El maestro había sido un subalterno en la clase de carpintería. Jordan ya odiaba al bastardo. Ahora tenía otra razón.

Molestar a Carolyn podría hacer que el Ford verde del maestro sea vandalizado en el estacionamiento del personal.

Carolyn salió del baño, pálida.

"Saltémonos el sexto período. Necesito *Fanta* para arreglar mi estómago".

Jordan abrió la puerta del antiguo Malibú de sus padres, puso sus libros y los de Carolyn en el asiento trasero. Su pie apretó el acelerador. Los neumáticos mordieron, se sacudieron hacia adelante, mientras pilotaba la nave espacial a lo largo de un camino rural que serpenteaba lejos de la escuela. Aliviando su pie del acelerador. No podía quitarse esa película de su cabeza. La falda del cadáver sin cabeza y llevó una falda y zapatos resistentes, al igual que su abuela. Q

Language Lessons

Mother always said i should talk
    nicely
She taught me how to say
Ceaseless
Biddable
Affable

Are these words hard to learn?

Now try to say
Goodbye

— *Vasileia Oikonomou*
(Tr. fr. the Greek, Yannis Goumas)

Μαθήματα Γλώσσας

Να μιλάς όμορφα
έλεγε η μάνα μου
Μου μάθαινε να λέω
Ατέρμονος
Ευπροσήγορος
Προσηνής

Είναι δύσκολες αυτές οι λέξεις;

Τώρα, δοκίμασε να πεις,
    Αντίο

— *Βασιλεία Οικονόμου*

Lecciones de idiomas

Madre siempre decía que
    debería hablar bien
Me ensañó a decir
Sin cesar
Maleable
Amable

¿Son difíciles de aprender
    estas palabras?

Ahora tratar de decir
Adiós

— *Vasileia Oikonomou*
(Traducción, T.
Warburton y Bajo y
rob)

Lekcje języka

Matka zawsze mawiała, że powinnam ład-
    nie mówić
Nauczyła mnie jak powiedzieć
Nieustannie
Grzeczna
Uprzejma

Czy są to trudne do nauki słowa?

A teraz spróbuj powiedzieć
Do widzenia

– *Vasileia Oikonomou*
(Tłumaczenie: Joanna Rosińska)

Učenje jezika

Lijepo se izražavaj
govorila je moja majka
Naučila me reći
Beskrajan
Poslušan
Ljubazan

Jesu li te riječi teške?

Sada probaj reći
Zbogom

– *Vasileia Oikonomou*
(Prijevod, Marija Dejanović)

Tungumálakennsla

Móðir sagði alltaf að ég
ætti að tala fallega
Hún kenndi mér hvernig á
að segja
endalaust
Tilboðshæft
Vingjarnlegur

Er erfitt að læra þessi orð?

Reyndu nú að segja
Bless

– *Vasileia Oikonomou*
(Þýtt úr Ensku,
Michael Lohr)

INT. BUS STA., TRUCK, MOTEL, LIQUOR STORE. HAYS, KS

Poe Ballantine

It was raining naturally in Hays, Kansas, when I got down at the bus station to learn that my suitcase had been lost. The girl half my age at the counter was friendly, beauâtiful and unafraid of me, as it is often *not* theâ case with young women who encounter unshaven middle-aged unemployed homeless vagabonds without suitcases who announce an intent to stay in their small town for a spell.

This was her father's depot, she explained, and she had Jethro Tull on her player, a band that had its heyday many years before she was born. She wore green low-heeled velvet shoes like dancing shoes with complex designs embossed on the toe and she seemed not only pleased that I was waiting out the rain all alone with her in this depot but she called around to find the best motel rates and then when she found one suitable she gave me a ride. Her father by now had shown up and sat in the backseat glowering with disapproval.

The motel was called the Villa, thirty a night. It was out on the edge of town not far from a highway restaurant called Al's Chickenette, which fascinated me. The Chickenette had one of those old light-bulb signs with the yellow turned-under arrow common in the 1950s, a

ALÞJ. RÚTTASTA., FLUTNINGUR, MÓTEL, ÁFENGIS-VERSLANIR. HAYS, KS

Poe Ballantine
(*Þýtt úr Ensku, Michael Lohr*)

Það rigndi náttúrulega í Hays, Kansas, þegar ég kom niður á rútustöðina til að komast að því að ferðataskan mín hefði týnst. Stúlkan sem var hálf gömul við afgreiðsluna var vinaleg, falleg og óhrædd við mig, enda er það oft ekki raunin með ungar konur sem lenda í órakuðum miðaldra atvinnulausum heimilislausum ferðatöskum flakkara sem tilkynna að þeir hyggist dvelja í smábænum sínum í kl. stafa.

Þetta var geymsla föður síns, útskýrði hún, og hún hafði Jethro Tull á spilaranum sínum, hljómsveit sem átti blómaskeið sitt mörgum árum áður en hún fæddist.

Hún var í grænum lághæluðum flauelsskóm eins og dansskóm með flóknum hönnun upphleyptum á tána og hún virtist ekki bara ánægð með að ég væri að bíða eftir rigningunni ein með henni í þessari geymslu heldur hringdi hún í kring til að finna bestu verð á mótelinu og svo þegar hún fann einn við hæfi gaf hún mér far. Faðir hennar var nú búinn að mæta og sat í aftursætinu og glotti af vanþóknun.

Mótelið var kallað Villa, þrjátíu á nóttu. Það var úti í jaðri bæjarins ekki langt frá veitingastað sem heitir Al's Chickenette, sem heillaði

MEĐUNARODNI AUTOBUSNI KOLODVOR, KAMION, MO- TEL, TRGOVINA ALKOHOL- NIH PIĆA. HAYS, KS.

Poe Ballantine
(prijevod na hrvatski, Dijana Jakovac)

Kišilo je u Haysu, Kansasu, kada sam sišao na auto- busni kolodvor i shvatio da sam izgubio kofer.

Djevojka upola mlađa od mene bila je ljubazna na šalteru, prekrasna i nije me se bojala, što *nije* čest slučaj s mladim ženama koje se susreću s neobrijanim sredovječnim nezaposlenim beskućnicima skitnicama koji najavljuju namjeru da će os- tati u njihovom malenom gradu kratko vrijeme.

Ovo je bilo skladište njezina oca, objasnila je, a Jethro Tull svirao je na njezinom playeru, bend koji je imao svoj proc- vat mnogo godina prije nego što se rodila. Nosila je zelene baršunaste cipele s niskom pot- peticom poput plesnih cipela složenih dizajna utisnutih na nožnom prstu i činila se ne samo zadovoljnom što sam iščekivao kišu sam s njom u ovom skladištu, već se i raspitivala kako bi pronašla najbolje cijene mote- la i onda kada je pronašla jedan prikladan, povela me. Njezin se otac do tada već pojavio i sjedio na zadnjem sjedištu užaren od neodobravanja.

Motel se zvao Villa, trideset dolara za noć. Bio je na rubu

INT. ESTACIÓN DE AUTOBU- SES, CAMIÓN, MOTEL, LICO- RERÍA. HAYS, KS

Poe Ballantine
(Traducción, T. Warburton y Bajo y rvb)

Llovía por supuesto en Hays, Kan- sas, cuando bajé por la estación de autobuses para encontrar que mi maleta se había perdido. La chica en el mostrador que tenía la mitad de mi edad era bastante amable, bonita y sin miedo de mí, a menudo no es el caso de mujeres jóvenes que se encuentran vagabundos de mediana edad sin afeitar sin hogar sin maletas que declaran una intención de quedarse en su pequeña ciudad por un rato.

Era la estación de su papá, dijo. Tenía a Jethro Tull en su iPod, una banda cuyo apogeo había ocurrido muchos años an- tes de su nacimiento. Ella usaba zapatos verdes de terciopelo con tacones bajos que podrían haber sido confundidos con zapatos de baile, con diseños complejos grabados en la punta, y ella no sólo pare- cía contente que esperaba la lluvia solo con ella en este estación, sino que tam- bién llamó a encontrar las mejores tarifas de motel, y en la búsqueda de uno ade- cuado que me dio un paseo. Su padre, ya habiendo llegado, brillaba desde el asien- to de atrás con desaprobación.

El motel se llamaba *La Villa*, treinta por cada noche. En el borde de la ciu- dad no muy lejos de un restaurante de la autopista llamado Pollería Alberto, lo que me fascinó. El Pollería tenía viejos letreros de bombilla con la flecha amari-

feature that looked like a new addition compared to the building itself. The tantalizing scent of fried chicken and baking pies hung in the air.

When I went down to the liquor store to get two large bottles of beer I asked the clerk how long Al's Chickenette had been there. The clerk was about sixty-five, flesh of the cheeks and nose patterned with gin blossoms.

Oh, he said, longer than I have. Been through three owners.

Business good? I asked.

Oh yes, he said. They do real well. Only place I know of where they fry the chicken to order. Takes about forty-five minutes. You sit down and have a salad and you're looking around. Good mashed potatoes and gravy, too.

Real mashed potatoes? I asked.

Yep, he said, those are hard to find.

Don't I know it, I said, caught up in the mystique of Al's Chickenette. I vowed to have dinner there one day before I left, though at the moment I couldn't afford to eat in restaurants and I had food left over from a trip to a grocery store in Plainview, Texas, so I picked up a newspaper and returned with my beer and chicken fantasies to the Villa Motel.

It was too late to go out and look for work or a cheaper living arrangement so I basked in the novelty of the new start, good omens abounding and all hell in a twisted distant pile behind me, though I could see it rising and reforming like an evil, self-repairing robot to soon pursue me again.

mig. The Chickenette var með eitt af þessum gömlu ljósaperuskiltum með gulu snúin ör sem var algeng á fimmta áratugnum, einkenni sem leit út eins og ný viðbót miðað við bygginguna sjálfa. Spennandi ilmurinn af steiktum kjúklingi og bökunarböku hékk í loftinu.

Þegar ég fór niður í áfengisbúðina til að ná í tvær stórar bjórflöskur spurði ég afgreiðslumanninn hversu lengi Al's Chickenette hefði verið þar. Afgreiðslumaðurinn var um sextíu og fimm ára, hold af kinnum og nefi með ginblómum.

Ó, sagði hann, lengur en ég hef. Gengið í gegnum þrjá eigendur.

Viðskipti góð? Ég spurði.

Ó já, sagði hann. Þeir standa sig virkilega vel. Eini staðurinn sem ég veit um þar sem þeir steikja kjúklinginn eftir pöntun. Tekur um fjörutíu og fimm mínútur. Þú sest niður og færð þér salat og þú ert að skoða þig um. Góð kartöflumús og sósu líka.

Ekta kartöflumús? Ég spurði.

Já, sagði hann, þetta er erfitt að finna.

Veit ég það ekki, sagði ég, upptekin af dulúðinni í Al's Chickenette. Ég hét því að borða kvöldmat þar einum degi áður en ég fór, þó að í augnablikinu hefði ég ekki efni á að borða á veitingastöðum og ég átti mat afgang eftir ferð í matvöruverslun í Plainview, Texas, svo ég tók upp dagblað og kom aftur með bjór- og kjúklingafantasíurnar mínar á Villa Mótel.

Það var of seint að fara út að

grada nedaleko restorana na autocesti zvanog Al's Chickenette, koji me fascinirao. Chickenette je imao jedan od onih starih znakova žarulje sa žutom okrenutom strelicom uobičajenom za 1950-e, novi dodatak u usporedbi sa samom zgradom. Zamamni miris pržene piletine i pita za pečenje visio je u zraku.

Kada sam sišao u trgovinu alkoholnih pića po dvije velike boce piva, pitao sam blagajnika koliko dugo Al's Chickenette već postoji. Blagajnik je imao oko šezdeset i pet godina, mesnatih obraza i nosa s uzorcima cvjetova džina.

O, kaže, duže nego što ja. Imao sam tri vlasnika.

Posao dobar? pitao sam.

O, da, kaže. Stvarno im dobro ide. Jedino mjesto za koje znam da prže piletinu po narudžbi. Potrebno je oko četrdeset i pet minuta. Sjednete, uzmete salatu i gledate oko sebe. Dobar pire krumpir i umak, također.

Pravi pire krumpir? pitao sam.

Da, rekao je, takvog je teško pronaći.

Zar to ne znam, rekao sam, uhvaćen u mističnosti Al's Chickenettea. Zavjetovao sam se da ću ondje večerati jednoga dana prije nego što sam otišao, iako si trenutno nisam mogao priuštiti da jedem u restoranima i ostalo mi je hrane od putovanja do trgovine mješovite robe u Plainviewu u Teksasu, pa sam uzeo novine i vratio se sa svojim fantazijama o pivu i piletini do motela Villa.

Bilo je prekasno izaći i po-

lla invertida de la década de 1950, una característica que parecía una nueva adición en comparación con el edificio en sí. El olor atractivo de pollo frito y pasteles de cocción colgaba en el aire.

Cuando fui a la licorería por dos grandes botellas de cerveza le pregunté al empleado cuánto tiempo había estado allí Pollería Alberto. El empleado tenía aproximadamente unos sesenta y cinco, su cara modelada con flores de ginebra. Dijo, más tiempo que yo. He pasado por tres dueños.

¿Bien para negocio?, pregunté.

Sí, dijo. Lo hacen muy bien. El único lugar que conozco donde fríen el pollo por encargo especial. Necesita unos cuarenta y cinco minutos. Te sientas y comes una ensalada y estás mirando a tu alrededor. Buena puré de patatas y salsa, también.

¿Verdadero puré de patatas?, pregunté.

Sí, dijo, aquellos son difíciles de encontrar.

Como no lo sé, dije, atrapado en la mística del Pollería Alberto. Juré de cenar allí antes de irme, aunque por el momento no podía permitirme restaurantes y todavía tenía comida por un viaje a una tienda de comestibles en Plainview, Texas. Así que conseguí un periódico y volví con mi cerveza y fantasías de pollo al motel Villa.

Era demasiado tarde para ir a buscar trabajo o un arreglo de vida más barato, así que me basé en la novedad de un nuevo principio, buenos augurios en la vida y todo el infierno en un montón distante torcido muy detrás de mí, aunque pude verlo levantarse y

You don't have to *stay*, I reminded myself though I was so skittery with thinning confidence and an inclination to nervous bowels and a keen awareness that a flop here might result in me living under a bridge and foraging for hackberries and aluminum cans, so I decided it would probably be best if I threw down my anchor here. I caught up on notes and jotted down thoughts and ideas for stories including a sketch of a novel about a guy addicted to traveling who only feels good arriving in the new place which wears off in a few days so he picks up again.

Soon the rain turned to snow, tumbling past the windows. One day I was well aware every one of my deeds and dreams would be dust. A proper idea, I thought, new starts for us all. For now I watched the snow, savored its crystalline glow. This time in the new place before the job is always the sweetest. And **misery** is never so bad when you can see its end. Q

leita sér að vinnu eða ódýrara búsetufyrirkomulagi svo ég næddi mér í nýjunginni í nýju byrjuninni, góðir fyrirboðar gnótt og allt helvíti í brengluðri fjarlægri hrúgu á bak við mig, þó ég gæti séð það rísa og endurbæta sig eins og illt, sjálfviðgerðar vélmenni til að elta mig fljótlega aftur.

Þú þarft ekki að vera, minnti ég sjálfan mig þó að ég væri svo skrítinn með þynnandi sjálfstraust og hneigð til taugaþörma og meðvitund um að flopp hér gæti leitt til þess að ég bjó undir brú og leitaði að járnberjum og áldósum, svo Ég ákvað að það væri líklega best ef ég kastaði niður akkerinu mínu hér. Ég náði mér í minnispunkta og skrifaði niður hugsanir og hugmyndir að sögum, þar á meðal skissu af skáldsögu um gaur sem er háður ferðalögum sem líður bara vel við að koma á nýja staðinn sem hverfur eftir nokkra daga svo hann tekur sig upp aftur.

Fljótlega breyttist rigningin í snjó, veltist fram hjá gluggunum. Einn daginn var ég vel meðvitaður um að öll verk mín og draumar yrðu ryk. Aldeilis hugmynd, fannst mér, ný byrjun fyrir okkur öll. Í bili horfði ég á snjóinn, naut kristallaðs ljóma hans. Þessi tími á nýja staðnum fyrir starfið er alltaf sá ljúfasti. Og eymdin er aldrei svo slæm þegar þú getur séð fyrir endann á henni. Q

tražiti posao ili jeftiniji životni aranžman pa sam se naslađivao s novostima novoga početka, pregrštom dobrih predznaka i čitavim paklom na uvijenoj dalekoj hrpi iza mene, iako sam ga mogao vidjeti kako se diže i reformira poput zlog, samopopravljajućeg robota koji će me uskoro ponovno progoniti.

Ne trebaš *ostati*, podsjetio sam se premda sam bio toliko nemiran s tankim samopouzdanjem i sklonošću nemirnim crijevima i oštrom sviješću da bi neuspjeh ovdje mogao rezultirati time da živim ispod mosta tražeći hackberry i aluminijske limenke, pa sam odlučio da bi vjerojatno bilo najbolje da se ovdje usidrim. Uhvatio sam bilješke i zabilježio misli i ideje za priče, uključujući skicu romana o tipu ovisnom o putovanju koji se osjeća dobro samo kada stigne na novo mjesto što se brzo istroši za nekoliko dana pa se ponovno podiže.

Ubrzo se kiša pretvorila u snijeg, rušeći se pored prozora. Jednoga dana bio sam jako dobro svjestan da će svako moje djelo i snovi biti prašina. Prikladna ideja, pomislio sam, novi početak za sve nas. Za sada sam promatrao snijeg, uživao u njegovom kristalnom sjaju. Ovaj put na novom mjestu prije posla uvijek je najslađe. A bijeda nikada nije tako loša kada joj se vidi kraj. *Q*

reformarse como un robotico malvado y auto-reparador para volver a perseguirme.

No tienes que *quedarte*, me recordé a mí mismo aunque estaba tan tembloroso con la confianza que merma y una inclinación a las entrañas nerviosas y una aguda conciencia de que un fracaso aquí podría resultar en vivir debajo de un puente, buscando bayas y latas de aluminio, así que decidí que probablemente era mejor si tiré mi ancla aquí. Me puse al corriente con notas, pensamientos e ideas anotado para historias, incluyendo una novela sobre un tipo adicto a viajar que sólo se siente bien al llegar al nuevo lugar que desaparece en unos días por lo que recoge de nuevo.

Pronto la lluvia se convirtió a nieve, cayendo por delante de las ventanas. Un día estaba bien consciente de que cada una de mis obras y sueños se convertiría en polvo. Una idea apropiada, pensé, nuevas aventuras para todos nosotros. Por ahora miré la nieve, saboreó su brillo cristalino. Ese tiempo en el nuevo lugar antes de un trabajo es siempre el más dulce. Y la miseria nunca es tan mala cuando se puede ver su final. *Q*

Šūdas tas gyvas bendravimas   *

W Realnym Życiu (IRL) jest
beznadziejnie!

¡El IRL apesta! /
¡La Vida Real apesta!

Η πραγματική ζωή είναι χάλια!

*) or maybe, if we're referencing lifting of covid restrictions: Šūdas tas kontaktinis

"IRL sucks."

SHANNON WHEELER

Οδηγός

*Πολύ νωρίς κατάλαβα
πως
τον άνθρωπο τον πλάθει
η αντίστασή του στο
περιβάλλον του –
ΜΑΞΙΜ ΓΚΟΡΚΙ*

Να γίνεσαι ο στόχος.
Στην κάννη του όπλου να κρέμε-
σαι βαρύς
Μέχρι να σε κρατήσει
Χέρι με θάρρος.

Αυτά που έχουμε ανάγκη είναι
πανάκριβα.
Ισορροπούμε ανάμεσα σε αντε-
γκλήσεις
Ιστορικισμούς
Μύδρους
Και καταθέσεις στην τράπεζα.
Κυκλοφορούμε όλοι ανάμεσά
μας
Ανήμποροι
Στα γέλια των παιδιών,
Παιδιά ακόμη,
Στο χρέος των μεγάλων.

Στον τηλεοπτικό μας αντικατο-
πτρισμό,
Τώρα πια γίνεται η μνήμη,
θέμα και θύμα.

Και για κάποιους παραμένει θύ-
της η ανάμνηση.

– Ελένη Τζατζιμάκη

Instructions

*Very early I understood that man
is shaped by his resistance to his
environment – Maxim Gorky*

Become the target.
Hang heavy on the gun's barrel
Till you're held
By a bold hand.

The things we need are costly.
We balance between
recriminations
historicism
Strictures
And bank deposits.
We all move among each other
Powerless
Before children's laughter,
Still children,
Before the grown-ups' debt.

In our televised reflection,
Memory now becomes,
Both topic and victim.

For some, recollection remains the
culprit.

*– Eleni Tzatzimaki
(tr. fr. the Greek, David
Connolly)*

Leiðbeiningar

*Mjög snemma skildi ég að
maðurinn er mótaður
með andstöðu sinni við
umhverfi sitt – Maxim
Gorky*

Verða skotmarkið.
Hangðu þungt á byssuhlaupinu
Þangað til þú ert haldinn
Með djörfum hendi.

Hlutirnir sem við þurfum eru
      dýrir.
Við jafnvægi á milli ásakana
sagnfræði
Þvinganir
Og bankainnstæður.
Við flytjum öll sín á milli
Valdalaus
Á undan hlátri barna,
Enn börn,
Fyrir skuldir fullorðinna.

Í sjónvarpshugleiðingunni
      okkar,
Minnið verður nú,
Bæði umræðuefni og
      fórnarlamb.

Fyrir suma er endurminningin
      enn sökudólgurinn.

   – *Eleni Tzatzimaki*
    *(Þýtt úr Ensku, Michael
    Lohr)*

Instrucciones

*Muy temprano entendí que
el hombre está formado por
su resistencia a su entorno –
Maxim Gorky*

Convértese en el blanco.
Colgar pesado en el cañón de la
      pistola
Hasta que está agarrado
Por una mano audaz.

Las cosas que necesitamos son
      costosas.
Equilibramos entre
      recriminaciones
Historicismo
Censuras
Y depósitos bancarios.
Nos movemos todos entre
      nosotros
Impotentes
Adelante de la risa de los niños,
Que todavía son niños,
Antes de la deuda de adultos.

En nuestra reflexión televisada,
Memoria ahora se convierte en
Tanto tema como víctima.

Para algunos, el recuerdo se
      queda lo culpable.

   – *Eleni Tzatzimaki*
    *(traducción, T. Warburton y
    Bajo y rvb)*

Albert's Thursday Night

Albert's father is an empty wine
    bottle on the warped floor.
His brother and sister sleep,
he listens to their even
      breathing
down the hallway,
he drinks his father's wine.
Out of work and needing a
    shave
Albert waits for a single day
that will make sense by
      nightfall,
that will listen to his voice
muttering some kind of prayer.
His father drinks at the bar until
  closing,
then drinks at his buddy's place
  till dawn.
His father will arrive
when the sun spreads up the
    sides of houses,
he will be a pair of thick legs
wobbling down the hall,
a lump falling into a twin bed.
And then Albert will sleep
in a darkness blacker
than the nights he runs from.

    – David Elsey

La noche del jueves de Alberto

El padre de Alberto es una
    botella de vino vacía en el
    piso deformado.
Su hermano y hermana duer-
    men,
escucha su respiración uni-
    forme
desde el pasillo,
bebe el vino de su padre.
necesitando trabajo y un af-
    eitado
Alberto espera un día solo
que tendrá sentido por la caída
      de la noche,
que escuchará su voz
murmurando algún tipo de
    oración.
Su padre bebe en el taberna
    hasta la hora de cerrar,
luego bebe en el lugar de su
      amigo hasta el amanecer.
Su padre llegará
cuando el sol se extienda por
      los lados de las casas,
sólo un par de piernas gruesas
tambaleándose por el pasillo,
un bulto cayendo por cama
    doble.
Y entonces Alberto dormirá
en una oscuridad más negra
que las noches de las que huye.

    – David Elsey
    (Traducción, T. Warburton
    y Bajo y rvb)

Albertov četvrtak
navečer

Albertov otac prazna je boca
vina na izvitoperenu
podu.
Njegovi brat i sestra spavaju,
Sluša njihovo smireno disanje
koje dopire niz hodnik,
pije očevo vino.
Nezaposlen, neobrijan
Albert čeka baš onaj dan
koji će do večeri dobiti
smisao,
koji će poslušati njegov glas
kako mrmlja nekakvu
molitvu.
Njegov otac pije u kafiću do
zatvaranja,
a onda kod prijatelja sve do
zore.
Otac će stići
Kad se sunce popne uza
zidove kuća,
doći će kao zdepaste noge
koje teturaju hodnikom,
hrpa mesa koja se ruši na
bračni krevet.
Tad će Albert zaspati
u tami crnjoj
nego noć od koje bježi.

– David Elsey
(prijevod s engleskoga,
Ana Katana)

Ένα βράδυ Πέμπτης
του Άλμπερτ

Ο πατέρας του Άλμπερτ είναι ένα
άδειο μπουκάλι
κρασί στο σκεβρωμένο πάτωμα.
Ο αδελφός και η αδελφή του κοιμού-
νται,
αφουγκράζεται τη σταθερή τους
αναπνοή
από τον διάδρομο,
πίνει το κρασί του πατέρα του.
Ένας άνεργος που χρειάζεται ξύρι-
σμα
ο Άλμπερτ περιμένει έστω μια μέρα
που ώσπου να νυχτώσει θα βγάζει
νόημα
που θα ακούσει τη φωνή του
να μουρμουρίζει κάποιου είδους
προσευχή.
Ο πατέρας του πίνει στο μπαρ μέχρι
το κλείσιμο,
έπειτα πίνει στο σπίτι του φίλου του
ως το ξημέρωμα.
Ο πατέρας θα επιστρέψει
όταν ο ήλιος θα επεκτείνει τις πλευ-
ρές
των σπιτιών,
θα είναι ένα ζευγάρι βαριά πόδια
που παραπαίουν στο διάδρομο,
ένας γρόμπος που πέφτει πάνω σε
δυο κρεβάτια.
Και τότε ο Άλμπερτ θα κοιμηθεί
σε ένα σκοτάδι πιο μαύρο
από τις νύχτες απ' τις οποίες προσπαθεί να ξεφύγει.

– Ντέιβιντ Έλσεϊ
(Μετάφραση, Τώνια Τζιρίτα
Ζαχαράτου)

Tri Krezube Vještice

Njezin je pogled nož zaboden
 u kruh.
Zatvorila je oči da se ne otruse
posivjele uspomene
sa njezinih zjenica.
Stavila sam joj dva zlatnika na
 vjeđe
i rekla: spavaj, sigurno si
 umorna.

Jučer je ujutro okrhnula zub.
Spremila je krunu u kutiju i
 okopnila.
Godinama sam vjerovala da je
 ona šumska
da su njezini zubi klanci za
 lješnjake i orah

i možda su doista bili.
Od dana kad se izgubila viđam
kako na svakom od stolova
 stoji kruh
i u njemu nož.

U našoj je sobi previše kuća.
U svakoj je kući stol.
Na svakom stolu tri krezube
 vještice
grizu šiljasti kut.

— *Marija Dejanović*

Three Toothless Witches

Her gaze is a knife plunged into
 bread.
She closed her eyes not to shed
faded memories
from her pupils.
I placed two shiners on her eyelids
and said: sleep, you must be tired.

Yesterday morning she chipped a
 tooth.
She put her crown into a box and
 withered.
For years I believed that she was a
 forest,
that the slopes of her teeth hid
 hazelnuts

and maybe they did.
From the day she vanished, I have
 been seeing
a loaf of bread on each table
and a knife stuck in it.

There are too many houses in our
 room.
There is a table in each house.
Around each table, three toothless
 witches
gnaw at the narrow end.

— *Marija Dejanović*
 (tr. fr. the Croatian, Hana
 Samaržija)

Tres brujas sin dientes

Su mirada como cuchillo
          hundido en pan.
Cerró los ojos para no derramar
recuerdos descoloridos
de sus pupilas.
Puse dos reales en sus párpados
          y
dije: duerme, debes estar
          cansada.

Ayer por la mañana se astilló un
          diente.
Ella puso su corona en una caja y
          se marchitó.
Durante años asumí que era un
          bosque,
las cuestas de sus dientes
          escondieron avellanas

y tal vez lo hicieron así.
Desde el día en que desapareció,
          he visto
hogazas de pan en cada mesa y
cuchillo pegado en cada uno.

Hay demasiadas casas en nuestra
          cuarto.
Hay una mesa en cada casa.
Alrededor de cada mesa, tres
          brujas sin dientes
royendo en el extremo más
          delgado.

    – *Marija Dejanović*
    (Traducción, T. Warburton y
    Bajo y rvb)

Trys bedantės raganos

Jos žvilgsnis – į duonos kepalą
          įsmeigtas peilis.
Užmerkė akis, kad iš vyzdžių
neišbėgtų visi
nykstantys atsiminimai.
Uždėjau ant vokų dvi monetas
ir pasakiau: miegok, turbūt
          pavargai.

Vakar ryte jai nuskilo dantis.
Įsidėjo karūnėlę dėžutėn ir
          nudžiūvo.
Metų metus tikėjau, kad ji
          miškas,
kad šios dantų kalvos slepia
          lazdyno riešutus,

gal taip ir buvo.
Nuo tos dienos kai išėjo, ant
          kiekvieno stalo
matydavau duonoje
įstrigusį peilį.

Mūsų kambaryje per daug
          namų.
Kiekviename name po stalą.
Prie kiekvieno stalo trys
          bedantės raganos
graužia siaurąjį galą.

    – *Marija Dejanović*
    („Trys bedantės raganos". Į
    lietuvių kalbą vertė Aušra
    Kaziliūnaitė)

The Traitor, A Correspondence: The Game of Simulations

Adrian Martin & Carles Matamoros

Introduction

The mechanism is as follows: two authors exchange letters via email, for two weeks, on *The Traitor* (*Il traditore*, Marco Bellocchio, 2019); their correspondence is published here according to rules established at the outset. The game is quite simple: the opening participant proposes a title, a screenshot and a short text, which results in a response from the other author who, in turn, proposes a second title, a second screenshot and a second short text addressed to the first participant. The exchange continues with several more *moves* by both authors, Adrian Martin (AM) and Carles Matamoros (CM), who aim to share and convey their passion for the latest film of this great Italian director.

Svikarinn, samsvörun: Leikur Hermanna

Adrian Martin & Carles Matamoros
(Þýtt úr Ensku, Michael Lohr)

Kynning

Fyrirkomulagið er eftirfarandi: tveir höfundar skiptast á bréfum í tölvupósti, í tvær vikur, um *The Traitor* (*Il traditore*, Marco Bellocchio, 2019); bréfaskipti þeirra eru birt hér samkvæmt reglum sem settar voru í upphafi. Leikurinn er nokkuð einfaldur: þátttakandi í upphafi leggur til titil, skjámynd og stuttan texta, sem skilar sér í svari frá öðrum höfundinum sem síðan leggur til annan titil, annað skjámynd og annan stuttan texta beint til fyrsti þátttakandi. Skiptin halda áfram með nokkrum fleiri hreyfingum beggja höfunda, Adrian Martin (AM) og Carles Matamoros (CM), sem miða að því að deila og koma á framfæri ástríðu sinni fyrir nýjustu kvikmynd þessa frábæra ítalska leikstjóra.

1. The Numbers (AM)

The portrait of a criminal family, a criminal network: 30 people in one frame, over-illuminated and then plunged into eerie, funereal darkness by a flash bulb.

1. Tölurnar (AM)

Andlitsmynd glæpsamlegs fjölskyldu, glæpasamtaka: 30 manns í einum ramma, yfirlýstir og steyptu síðan í skelfilegt, útfararlegt myrkur með leifturljósi. Aftur og aftur: fólk

Over and over: people frozen, identified (their names printed on the screen), numbered as a collateral corpse at the moment of their death. The complex opening sequence of Marco Bellocchio's *The Traitor* lays out some of the film's central motifs: an unstoppable seriality (in an image and across time) that absorbs and destroys everyone; the frozen pose that, in his cinema, always signifies death in contradistinction to the life-giving moment of joyous, Dionysiac dance. With a crucial difference, here: whenever Tommaso Buscetta (Pierfrancesco Favino) moves (from room to room, house to house, nation to nation), it is not in a sweep of pleasure, but a restless, neurotic, haunted deferment of the preordained, gridded pattern of his brutal Mafia life. The central question of the story: can Tommaso ever escape that grid – and how?

1b. The Hands (CM)

The hands of Pippo Calò (Fabrizio Ferracane) on Tommaso's back in the family photograph: they already foreshadow the unbearable burden that Bellocchio's tragic hero will carry after his Brazilian exile. Tommaso will never be able to escape from this initial imprint because their bond will be sealed with an affectionate

frosið, auðkennt (nöfn þeirra prentuð á skjánum), númeruð sem tryggingarlíki á andláti sínu. Hin flókna opnunarröð „The Traitor" frá Marco Bellocchio leggur fram nokkur aðal myndefni myndarinnar: óstöðvandi myndaröð (í mynd og í gegnum tíðina) sem tekur upp og eyðileggur alla; frosinn sitja sem í kvikmyndahúsi hans merkir alltaf dauðann í mótsögn við lífgefandi stund gleðigjafans, Dionysiac dans. Hér skiptir sköpum máli: hvenær sem Tommaso Buscetta (Pierfrancesco Favino) flytur (frá herbergi til herbergi, hús til hús, þjóð til þjóðar), það er ekki í sóun af ánægju, heldur eirðarlaus, taugaveikluð, áleitin frestun á fyrirfram táknaðri, grinduðu mynstri hrottafenginna mafíulífs hans. Mið spurning sögunnar: getur Tommaso einhvern tíma sloppið við það rist – og hvernig?

1b. Hendur (CM)

Hendur Pippo Calò (Fabrizio Ferracane) á baki Tommaso á fjölskyldumyndinni: Þeir sjá þegar fyrir óbærilegri byrði sem hörmuleg hetja Bellocchio mun bera eftir brasilíska útlegð hans. Tommaso mun aldrei geta sloppið við þessa fyrstu merkingu vegna þess að tengsl þeirra verða innsigluð með ástúðlegu faðmi undir flugeldum Santa Rosalia: Tommaso felur

hug under the fireworks of Santa Rosalia: Tommaso entrusts Pippo with the life of his two eldest children, Benedetto Buscetta (Gabriele Cicirello) and Antonio Buscetta (Paride Cicirello), also located in a central spot in the composition. But who then will be *the traitor* in this story? The father (Tommaso) who abandons his offspring in Italy and then betrays those who annihilate his colleagues and family to justice? Or the apparent friend (Pippo), who murders Benedetto literally *with his own hands*?

Pippo lífi tveggja elstu barna sinna, Benedetto Buscetta (Gabriele Cicirello) og Antonio Buscetta (Paride Cicirello), einnig staðsettur á miðjum stað í tónsmíðunum. En hver verður þá svikari í þessari sögu? Faðirinn (Tommaso) sem yfirgefur afkvæmi sín á Ítalíu og svíkur þá þá sem tortíma vinnufélögum sínum og fjölskyldu fyrir réttlæti? Eða hinn augljósi vinur (Pippo), sem myrðir Benedetto bókstaflega með eigin höndum?

2. The Screens (CM)

2. Skjáirnir (CM)

Bellocchio's rectangular frame is reformulated in a panoptic form in the video surveillance room belonging to the prison where the Mafia members betrayed by Tommaso are locked in. Multiple screens that individualise singular personalities and, at the same time, in the same frame, in a single *image of images*, gather various members of the earlier criminal family portrait. Pippo, of course, is again located in the centre and we have two perspectives: the close-up of his face (above) and the overhead shot of his cell (below). Among the different

Rétthyrndur rammi Bellocchio er endurræddur í panoptic formi í vídeóeftirlitssalnum sem tilheyrir fangelsinu þar sem Mafia meðlimir sviknir af Tommaso eru lokaðir inni. Margvíslegir skjáir sem gera einstaka persónuleika einstaka og á sama tíma, í sama ramma, í einum mynd af myndum, safnaðu ýmsum meðlimum fyrri glæpasamfélagsins. Pippo er að sjálfsögðu aftur staðsettur í miðjunni og við höfum tvö sjónarmið: nærmynd andlits hans (hér að ofan) og loftmynd af klefi hans (hér að neðan). Meðal mismunandi skjáa sem senda í

screens that transmit *live* what is going on inside the prison, three stand out: they are broadcasting an external event, the State funeral of Giovanni Falcone (Fausto Russo Alesi), the key lawyer in the State's Maxi Trial brought against the Cosa Nostra. This media event is closely linked to the criminals trapped in the same shot, thus exemplifying two of the dialectical resources with which *The Traitor* works: the occasional integration of archival images that punctuate the fictional events; and the proliferation of scenes in which the characters follow on TV the news that impact their lives (there are even TV sets in the cells of the imprisoned Mafiosi!). The fabrication of a *political tale* in Italy as elaborated by the mass media – in response to which Bellocchio offers, in several of his historical films, alternative *re-presentations* of famous people – is more evident in the following shot of another control room: the television studio were Tommaso is interviewed.

2b. The Dreams (AM)

The dreams that punctuate the film – an essential element of Bellocchio's method since the mid 1980s – are a crucial variation on the surveillance and media screens. As externalised images, dream-visions of various sorts (memories, reveries, hallucinations), they belong to the realm of the *imaginary*, and this imaginary is

beinni það sem er að gerast inni í fangelsinu, standa þrír fram: þeir senda út utanaðkomandi atburði, útför ríkisins af Giovanni Falcone (Fausto Russo Alesi), lykillögmanni í Maxi réttarhaldi ríkisins höfðað gegn Cosa Nostra. Þessi fjölmiðlaviðburður er nátengdur glæpamönnunum sem eru föstir í sama skoti og lýsir þannig tveimur af mállýskum auðlindum sem svikarinn vinnur við: stöku samþættingu skjalasafns sem greinar um skáldaða atburði; og útbreiðsla senna þar sem persónurnar fylgja í sjónvarpinu fréttirnar sem hafa áhrif á líf þeirra (það eru meira að segja sjónvarpstæki í frumum hinnar fangelsuðu Mafiosi!). Útbúning pólitískrar sögu á Ítalíu eins og hún var útfærð af fjöldamiðlunum – sem svar við því sem Bellocchio býður upp á, í nokkrum sögulegum myndum sínum, aðrar endurtekningar á frægu fólki – er meira áberandi í eftirfarandi mynd af öðru stjórnherbergi: sjónvarpsstofa þar sem Tommaso er í viðtali.

2b. Draumarnir (AM)

Draumarnir sem greina frá myndinni – ómissandi þáttur í aðferð Bellocchio síðan um miðjan níunda áratuginn – eru áríðandi afbrigði á eftirlits– og fjölmiðlasjám. Sem ytri myndir, draumsýn af ýmsu tagi (minningar, lotningar, ofskynjanir), tilheyra þeir ríki hins ímyndaða og þessi ímyndaði er alltaf sameiginlegur og félagslegur, aldrei eingöngu

always collective and social, never merely individual. Even the openly metaphorical, Eisensteinian inserts of a tiger (prowling inside its cage) and of rats ("deserting a sinking ship", as the saying goes) have an oneiric force. Trying to sleep on the plane, Tommaso sees his now dead sons spectrally passing along the aisle and out through the back curtain: a banal invisibility that, nonetheless, sparks a Shakespearean level of guilt in him. Later, an even more terrifying apparition worthy of a *giallo* – as Tommaso lies down in his relatively comfortable and secure but still soulless holding pen – shows his entire family crowding around his open coffin, as if pressing him into the circle of death with which he is so deeply associated. Tommaso, as we are told in the final, written-on-screen detail, died in bed in April 2000, in his sleep, as he always wanted. But how could this sleep ever be peaceful? In Bellocchio, sleep is forever haunted by the ghosts of personal and political, moral and ethical accountability.

einstaklingur. Jafnvel hin myndhverfu, eisensteinska innskot tígrisdýrs (stangir innan í búri þess) og rottum („fara í eyði frá skipi sem sökkva", eins og orðatiltækið segir) hafa loftslagsafl. Tommaso reynir að sofa í flugvélinni og sér nú dauða syni sína ganga fram eftir göngunni og út um aftur gardínan: banal ósýnileiki sem engu að síður kveikir Shakespearean sektarkennd í honum. Seinna sýnir enn ógnvekjandi sjón sem verðug er að fá – eins og Tommaso liggur í tiltölulega þægilegum og öruggum en samt sálarlausum pennanum – sýnir öll fjölskylda hans að fjölmenna um opna líkkistu sína, eins og að ýta honum inn í dauðahringinn sem hann með er svo djúpt tengd. Eins og sagt er frá Tommaso í lokaorritinu, skrifað á skjánum, dó í rúminu í apríl 2000, í svefni, eins og hann vildi alltaf. En hvernig gat svefninn verið friðsæll? Í Bellocchio er svefninn reistur að eilífu af draugum persónulegs og pólitísks, siðferðilegs og siðferðilegs ábyrgðar.

3. The Causes & The Effects (AM)

The Traitor is a tightly organised and hyper-structured film, like the corrupt network it depicts: each moment, each incident or detail in it has an immediate correspondence or repercussion and then, further away in time and space, a wider resonance. As a deliberately hollowed-out version of a classic gangster film, it invests the most basic plot mechanics of the genre with an eerie fatalism. This process is also fundamentally cinematic, since what is at stake in the life of a gangster – and even more so, a traitor – is literally sound and image: making a noise, and/or being seen, are what will get you killed in an instant; nobody who goes public, who steps out of the silent shadows as Falcone does, will last long. The entire film, in both its form and content, is built on this dynamic principle of image and sound. Image: Tommaso, in the courtroom, is always attempting (without much success) to shield his eyes, covering his vision in dark glasses, averting his gaze from those who want to kill him, walling his whole body in glass protection. Sound: when Tommaso makes love to his wife, Cristina (Maria Fernanda

3. Orsakir og áhrif (AM)

Svikarinn er þétt skipulögð og ofskipulagð kvikmynd, eins og spillta netið sem hún lýsir: hvert augnablik, hvert atvik eða smáatriði í henni hefur strax samsvörun eða eftirköst og þá, lengra í tíma og rúmi, víðari ómun. Sem vísvitandi holuð útfærsla á klassískri glæpakvikmynd, fjárfestir hún grundvallaratriðaveldi tegundarinnar með óheiðarlegri banasál. Þetta ferli er líka í grundvallaratriðum kvikmyndataka, þar sem það sem er í húfi í lífi glæpamanns – og jafnvel meira svikara – er bókstaflega hljóð og ímynd: að láta hávaða og / eða sjást, er það sem mun drepa þig í augnablik; enginn sem fer opinberlega, sem stígur út úr hljóðu skugganum eins og Falcone gerir, mun endast lengi. Öll kvikmyndin, bæði í formi og innihaldi, er byggð á þessari kraftmiklu meginreglu myndar og hljóðs. Mynd: Tommaso, í réttarsalnum, er alltaf að reyna (án mikils árangurs) að verja augun, hylja sýn sína í dökkum gleraugum og afstýra augum hans frá þeim sem vilja að drepa hann og veggja allan líkama sinn í glervörn. Hljóð: Þegar Tommaso elskar eiginkonu sína, Cristina (Maria Fernanda Cândido), leggur hann hönd yfir munn hennar til að kvæða grátbeiðni hennar og leiðbeinir henni að vera hljóðlát. Brátt munum við sjá annað Cosa Nostra par myrt (eins og í tilfærslu drauma) nakin

Cândido), he places a hand over her mouth to stifle her cries of pleasure, and instructs her to be quiet. Soon, we will see a different Cosa Nostra couple murdered (as if in a dream-displacement) naked in their beds, during sex. Even a family's most innocent outbursts – like cheering while watching a soccer match on TV – seem to immediately bring an answering tone of doom: the mysterious phone call addressed to Tommaso. For sounds not only betray presence, but also announce menace: the Sicilian folk song that sends the Buscetta family fleeing a New Hampshire restaurant is *verified*, six years later in Palermo, enigmatically and sinisterly, by Pippo singing it to Tommaso in court.

3b. The Gesture (CM)

The gesture of Tommaso to Cristina not only demonstrates the film's unstoppable sonic tension, but also the possessive character of its protagonist. We know he is able to make his enemies submit – but that is also true of his women, whether lovers, prostitutes or wives. When he is arrested at his home in Brazil, Tommaso vehemently orders Cristina to shut up in front of the police. When he remembers the past in the company of his Sicilian friend Totuccio Contorno (Luigi Lo Cascio), he evokes a time when voluptuous women *fell into their arms* – even while he was

í rúmum sínum, á meðan kynlíf stendur yfir. Jafnvel saklausustu útbrot fjölskyldunnar – eins og að heilla þegar verið er að horfa á fótboltaleik í sjónvarpinu – virðast strax koma með svörunardóma: hið dularfulla símtal sem beint er til Tommaso. Fyrir hljóð svíkja ekki aðeins nærveru, heldur tilkynna þau líka ógn: Sikileyska þjóðlagið sem sendir Buscetta fjölskylduna á flótta frá veitingastað í New Hampshire er staðfest, sex árum síðar í Palermo, á dásamlegan og óheiðarlegan hátt með því að Pippo syngur það fyrir Tommaso fyrir dómi.

3b. Bendingin (CM)

Látbragð Tommaso við Cristina sýnir ekki aðeins óstöðvandi hljóðspennu myndarinnar, heldur einnig yfirráða persónu söguhetjunnar. Við vitum að hann er fær um að láta óvini sína leggja fram – en það á einnig við um konur hans, hvort sem þær eru elskendur, vændiskonur eða konur. Þegar hann er handtekinn heima hjá sér í Brasilíu fyrirskipar Tommaso ákaft Cristina að halda kjafti fyrir framan lögregluna. Þegar hann man eftir fortíðinni í félagi Sikileyjarvinkonu sinnar, Totuccio Contorno (Luigi Lo Cascio), vekur hann upp tíma þegar miskunnarlausar konur féllu í fangið – jafnvel meðan hann sat í fangelsi. Minning persónunnar um þennan sigraraáfanga í hugsjóninni Cosa Nostra kemur fram á skjánum í mælsku flashback, sem táknar hylinn á milli nútíðar (þar sem

imprisoned. The character's memory of that *conqueror* phase in an idealised Cosa Nostra emerges on screen in an eloquent flashback, which represents the abysmal jump between the present (in which Tommaso dyes his hair coquettishly before a mirror to camouflage his ageing) and the past (a prison in Palermo where the inmates must leave the shared dormitory so that Tommaso can be intimate with a young woman *at his service*). However, this flashback quickly adopts a sick, morbid tone – as if the character cannot escape these ghosts that haunt him, even when he recalls his *happy days*. In the conjured scene, Tommaso observes that one of the elderly prisoners remains in the cell, so he approaches the man's bed and discovers that he has died in his sleep. Discreetly, Tommaso covers the inmate's inert body with the sheet, before returning to his bed where he fucks the prostitute he has previously invited to undress. Eros and Thanatos are inseparable in his memory.

Tommaso litar hár sitt koklega fyrir spegil til að felast öldrun hans) og fortíðarinnar (fangelsi í Palermo þar sem vistmennirnir verða að yfirgefa sameiginlega heimavistina svo að Tommaso geti verið náinn með unga konu í þjónustu sinni). Hins vegar samþykkir þessi bakslag fljótt veikan, sjúklegan tón – eins og persónan geti ekki sloppið við þessa drauga sem ásækja hann, jafnvel þegar hann rifjar upp hamingjusama daga sína. Á töfrandi vettvangi tekur Tommaso fram að einn af öldruðu föngunum sé áfram í klefanum, svo hann nálgist rúm mannsins og uppgötvar að hann hafi dáið í svefni. Í kyrrþey hylur Tommaso óvirkan líkama föngunnar með lakinu áður en hann snýr aftur í rúm sitt þar sem hann helvítir vændiskonuna sem hann hefur áður boðið að afklæðast. Eros og Thanatos eru óaðskiljanlegir í minni hans.

4. The Karaoke (CM)

The disquieting Sicilian melody sung by both the musician in an American restaurant and by Pippo

4. Karaoke (CM)

Sálræn sikileyska lag sem sungin er bæði af tónlistarmanninum á amerískum veitingastað og

is not the only song we hear twice in *The Traitor*: the emblematic bolero "Historia de un amor" ("Story of a Love") appears in two mirroring scenes that are in dialogue with each other. First, in the celebration staged by Bellocchio of the 68th birthday of Tommaso who, in front of family and friends, sings it precariously and emotionally, in a state of drunkenness. Then, in the sequence before the final credits, where murky archival video footage of that same birthday party is revived, with the real Buscetta suddenly on stage. If we focus on the first of these musical performances, we can see how Bellocchio works with one of the most stimulating (audio)visual motifs of contemporary cinema: karaoke scenes. *The Traitor*'s scene does not take place strictly in a bar of this type: the melody is not completely pre-recorded (there's a keyboardist playing live) and there's no monitor on which the song lyrics scroll. All the same, we are absorbing a privileged moment, comparable in its form to those that emerge in works as diverse as *Lost in Translation* (Sofia Coppola, 2003), *Only God Forgives* (Nicolas Winding Refn, 2013), *HHH – A Portrait of Hou Hsiao-Hsien* (Olivier Assayas, 1999), *My Best Friend's Wedding* (P.J. Hogan, 1997), *Oasis* (Lee Chang-dong, 2002), or the final

af Pippo er ekki eina lagið sem við heyrum tvisvar í The Traitor: hinn friðsæli bolero „Historia de un amor" („Saga Um Ást")birtist í tveimur speglunarmyndum sem eru í samræðum sín á milli. Í fyrsta lagi í hátíðarhöldunum sem Bellocchio á 68 ára afmælisdegi Tommaso setti upp, sem fyrir framan fjölskyldu og vini syngur það varasamt og tilfinningalega, í ölvunarástandi. Síðan, í röðinni fyrir lokaprófið, þar sem djörf skjalasafn af sömu samkvæmisafmælinu er endurvakið, með hina raunverulegu Buscetta skyndilega á sviðinu. Ef við einbeitum okkur að fyrstu þessara söngleikja, getum við séð hvernig Bellocchio vinnur með einu örvandi (hljóð) myndefni í kvikmyndahúsum samtímans: Karaoke senum. Svið svikara fer ekki fram strangt á bar af þessari gerð: lagið er ekki alveg tekið upp (það er hljómborðsleikari sem leikur í beinni útsendingu og það er enginn skjár sem lagatextar fletta. Allt það sama, við erum að taka á okkur forréttinda stund, sambærileg í sinni mynd og þau sem koma fram í verkum eins fjölbreytt og *Týnt í þýðingu* (Sofia Coppola, 2003), *Aðeins Guð fyrirgefur* (Nicolas Winding Refn, 2013), HHH – *mynd af Hou Hsiao-Hsien* (Olivier Assayas, 1999), Brúðkaup besta vinkonu minnar (PJ Hogan, 1997), *Vin* (Lee Chang-dong, 2002), eða lokaþátturinn í fjórða leikhluta

episode of the fourth season of *Better Call Saul* (Vince Gilligan and Peter Gould, 2015–).

It is well known that karaoke scenes can lead to moments of plot inflection, where characters free themselves from their fears, show us their weaknesses, transform themselves into different people, and even bring us near the level of the transcendental. In the case of Favino's interpretation, there is a noticeable evolution that Bellocchio demonstrates in a series of shots capturing the reactions of the spectators: as the performance progresses, we pass from initial cheerful smiles to solemn expressions. The melancholic tale of this bolero – which Carlos Eleta Almarán composed in the 1950s following the death of his brother's wife – plus the changing expression in Favino's perspiring face, with a contained emotion revealed in his saddened eyes, ends up giving the scene an unmistakeable bitterness. This bitterness can be attributed to the character's lament over the passing of time, but also to the insurmountable remoteness of his native Italy, and a life overshadowed by the weight of death. It is not surprising that, in this same party, Tommaso eventually confesses that he is seriously ill, while watching from the distance the guests' cheerful "musical chairs" game in which he can no longer participate. The final video images give a surplus value

Betra hringdu í Sál (Vince Gilligan og Peter Gould , 2015–).

Það er vel þekkt að karaoke-senur geta leitt til augnabliks beygingar á söguþræði, þar sem persónur losa sig við ótta sinn, sýna okkur veikleika sína, umbreyta sjálfum sér í mismunandi fólk og jafnvel koma okkur nálægt stigi yfirskilvitanna. Þegar um er að ræða túlkun Favino er það merkjanleg þróun sem Bellocchio sýnir fram á í röð mynda sem fanga viðbrögð áhorfendanna: þegar frammistaða líður, förum við frá fyrstu glaðlegu brosi til hátíðlegra tjáninga. The depurð saga af þessum bolero – sem Carlos Eleta Almarán samdi á sjötta áratugnum eftir andlát eiginkonu bróður síns – plús breytingartjáninguna í svita andliti Favino, með innilokuðum tilfinningum sem opinberast í dapurlegum augum hans, endar með því að gefa sögunni ótvíræða beiskju. Þessa biturð má rekja til harmakveðju persónunnar um liðna tíma, en einnig til óyfirstíganlegrar fjarlægðar heimalands síns á Ítalíu og lífs sem skyggja á þyngd dauðans. Það kemur ekki á óvart að Tommaso í þessari sömu veislu játar að lokum að hann sé alvarlega veikur meðan hann fylgist úr fjarlægð með hressum „tónlistarstólum" leik gesta þar sem hann getur ekki lengur tekið þátt. Síðustu myndbandsupplýsingarnar gefa myndinni umframgildi þar sem

to the scene, since they allow us to determine the similarities and differences between Bellocchio's Buscetta and the real Buscetta on the basis of their singing performances. After all, karaoke is the art of simulation, and this game of appearances finally defines what *The Traitor* is fundamentally addressing – since Pierfrancesco Favino *simulates* a historical character still very present in the imaginary of his country; and, in turn, the Italian director pursues the elusive identity of a Tommaso who is variously gangster, hero, traitor, exile and puppet of the State. Thus, an inscrutable lifetime of *simulations*, set to the rhythm of a bolero.

4b. The Cigarettes (AM)

The cigarettes form another important motif in the film, another pattern of comparisons bridging many levels. During the trial, Bellocchio places a quote from Michel Butor into the mouth of an erudite mafioso behind bars: "The gaze is the expression of reality". Butor's theory is, in fact, very close to Bellocchio's method as a filmmaker; as the writer said: "We never look at a face twice in the same way … we question it differently". So it goes with the cigarettes. The intimate (and somewhat aggressive) ritual of a shared puff is established early, when Tommaso, on their verandah in Brazil, takes Cristina's cigarette. Between Tommaso and

þær leyfa okkur að ákvarða líkt og muninn á Bellcchio's Buscetta og hinni raunverulegu Buscetta á grundvelli söngsýninga þeirra. Þegar öllu er á botninn hvolft er karaoke list eftirlíkingar og þessi útlitsleikur skilgreinir að lokum það sem svikarinn fjallar í grundvallaratriðum um – þar sem Pierfrancesco Favino hermir eftir sögulegum persónu sem enn er mjög til staðar í ímyndaðri landi sínu; og aftur á móti eltir ítalski leikstjórinn fimmti sjálfsmynd Tommaso sem er að ýmsu leyti glæpamaður, hetja, svikari, útlegð og brúðuleikur ríkisins. Þannig er órannsakanlegur líftími eftirlíkinga stilltur á hrynjandi bolero.

4b. Sígaretturnar (AM)

Sígaretturnar mynda annað mikilvægt mótíf í myndinni, annað samanburðarmynstur sem brúar mörg stig. Meðan á réttarhöldunum stóð leggur Bellocchio tilvitnun í Michel Butor í munn erudite mafioso á bak við lás og slá: „Augnaráðið er tjáning veruleikans". Kenning Butor er í raun mjög nálægt aðferð Bellocchio sem kvikmyndagerðarmanns; eins og rithöfundurinn sagði: „Við lítum aldrei tvisvar á andlit á sama hátt… við efumst um það á annan hátt". Svo er það með sígaretturnar. Hinn náinn (og nokkuð árásargjarn) trúarlega hluti sameiginlegs lundar er stofnað snemma, þegar Tommaso, á verönd þeirra í Brasilíu, tekur sígarettu Cristina. Milli Tommaso og

Falcone, it is a major dealbreaker in establishing their rapport: Tommaso tells Falcone later that he would never have accepted a smoke from him if the pack had not already been open ... Cigarettes (like bicycles) sometimes function in the film to *make strange* certain events and situations: the mafiosi imprisoned in their cages during the trial smoke furiously (cigars or cigarettes, it becomes a legal tussle!). In one of the most striking historical footnotes presented, it is argued that importing heroin spelt the end of the old Cosa Nostra; if they had stuck with cigarettes, it all would have stayed fine! And a cigarette, lovingly smoked and discarded, also figures in the final *move* made by both the film, and by myself in this writing-game of simulations...

Falcone er það mikill samningur við að koma á rapport þeirra: Tommaso segir Falcone seinna að hann hefði aldrei samþykkt reyk frá honum ef pakkinn hefði ekki þegar verið opinn ... Sígarettur (eins og reiðhjól) virka stundum í myndinni til að búa til undarlegir ákveðnir atburðir og aðstæður: mafíósarnir sem eru fangelsaðir í búrum sínum meðan á réttarhöldunum stóð reykja reiður (vindlar eða sígarettur, það verður löglegur tussle!). Í einni af sláandi sögulegu neðanmálsgreinum, sem settar eru fram, er því haldið fram að innflutningur á heróíni hafi stafað lok gömlu Cosa Nostra; ef þeir hefðu fest sig í sígarettum hefði þetta allt haldist í lagi! Og sígarettu, elskulega reykt og fargað, einnig tölur í lokaferðinni sem gerð var af myndinni og af sjálfum mér í þessum skrif-leik uppgerð ...

5. The End (AM)

Film narratives depend on spectators both remembering and forgetting things. We remember in order to identify (plots, faces, names, important information), to keep track of the unfolding story. We forget in order that we might, with a jolt of surprise or delight,

5. Lokið (AM)

Frásagnir af kvikmyndum eru háðar því að áhorfendur muna og gleyma hlutunum. Við munum til þess að þekkja (plott, andlit, nöfn, mikilvægar upplýsingar), til að fylgjast með framvindusögunni. Við gleymum til þess að við getum komist að smáatriðum

rediscover a detail in all its ultimately revealed significance. Naturally, this game of simultaneously showing and concealing things (through underplaying or understatement), so that they can eventually be uncovered, is a measure of a filmmaker's storytelling skill: it is an art of willful *misdirection*. In a stunning game inside *The Traitor*, this misdirection comes in the form of a bold sleight-of-hand, a true magician's trick worthy of Orson Welles. At 50 minutes into the film, Tommaso begins, with theatrical deliberation, to tell a story that Bellocchio visualises in flashback. It is the story of how Tommaso, as a young man, was given a designated hit: however, this other man, sensing his fate, clutched his newly baptised baby to his chest, knowing this would avert the assassin's bullet. Then – jumping through the years – Tommaso tells us how this target never left home without his son by his side. "Then the son got married" … but, right there, Tommaso digresses in order to amplify a general point to his interlocutor, Falcone: in those days, the Cosa Nostra code meant no killing of children, women or judges. Falcone begins arguing with him about this assumption of morality and ethics. And the film pursues this point, instantly going in a new direction.

How quickly we forget – taken up in the film's energetic, mosaic flow – that we have missed the punchline

með öllu á óvart eða gleði í öllu því sem að lokum leiddi í ljós mikilvægi þess. Auðvitað er þessi leikur um að sýna og leyna hlutum samtímis (með undirspili eða vanmat), svo að þeir geti loksins verið afhjúpaður, mælikvarði á frásagnarhæfileika kvikmyndagerðarmannsins: Það er list af vísvitandi rangfærslu. Í töfrandi leik inni í The Traitor, kemur þessi ranga leið í formi djarfrar handahófskenndar, sannkallað töframaður sem er verðugur Orson Welles. Þegar 50 mínútur eru eftir af myndinni byrjar Tommaso með leikrænni umhugsun að segja sögu sem Bellocchio sýnir í flashback. Það er sagan af því hvernig Tommaso, sem ungur maður, fékk sérstakt högg: En þessi annar maður, sem skynjaði örlög sín, hélt nýskírðu barni sínu fast við bringuna og vissi að þetta myndi koma í veg fyrir kúlu morðingjans. Síðan – stökk í gegnum árin – segir Tommaso okkur hvernig þetta skotmark fór aldrei að heiman án sonar síns við hlið hans. „Síðan giftist sonurinn"… en rétt hjá, segir hann Tommaso af sér til að auka almennan punkt við samtalsmann sinn, Falcone: í þá daga þýddi Cosa Nostra reglurnar ekkert morð á börnum, konum eða dómurum. Falcone byrjar að rífast við hann um þessa forsendu um siðferði og siðferði. Og myndin eltir þetta

of Tommaso's story! It was simply pushed aside, just in the way that windy monologues are often interrupted in real life by impatient listeners, never reaching their conclusion. Until – a full 90 minutes of screen-time later! – Bellocchio takes us, via a transitional comparison of two moons in the night sky, to exactly that untold conclusion, now given without a narrating voice – Tommaso may be remembering or dreaming it, but he is no longer *in control* of it; Bellocchio has well and truly taken the driver's wheel. A wedding party is ending; the father embraces his son in a fond farewell; a dog lazily sleeps at the entrance of this ample courtyard. In the present – allowing a crucial ellipse in the flashback – Cristina gently removes the rifle from Tommaso's hand (he, too, now divested of his protection) and covers his sleeping body with a blanket. Back to the past: guests leave in their cars down the road behind the dog; the proud father relaxes, alone, pulls up a chair, gazes up at the moon, smokes and discards a cigarette. Then, as he stands, there is something in his eyes, his bearing, his gaze, that possibly signals that he knows exactly what is coming. Tommaso, as if magically, arrives from the darkness – Bellocchio giving us now an ageless character unconstrained by strict historical chronology, this could be happening in any year – and carries out his initial command. So much about *The*

stig og fer strax í nýja átt.

Hversu fljótt gleymum við – tekin upp í orkumiklu, mósaíkflæði myndarinnar – að við höfum misst af holrinu í sögu Tommaso! Því var einfaldlega ýtt til hliðar, bara með þeim hætti að vindasamir monologes eru oft rofin í raunveruleikanum af óþreyjufullum hlustendum, en komast aldrei að niðurstöðu sinni. Þar til – heilar 90 mínútur af skjátíma seinna! – Bellocchio tekur okkur, í bráðabirgðatölum samanburðar tveggja tungla á næturhimninum, að nákvæmlega þeirri ósögulegu niðurstöðu, sem nú er gefin án frásagnarröddar – Tommaso man kannski eftir því eða dreymir það, en hann hefur ekki lengur stjórn á því; Bellocchio hefur tekið og örugglega tekið ökumannshjólið. Brúðkaupsveislu er að ljúka; faðirinn faðmar son sinn í kærri kveðju; hundur sefur leti við innganginn í þessum ríflega garði. Í núinu – leyfa afgerandi sporbaug í endurspiluninni – fjarlægir Cristina riffilinn varlega úr hendi Tommaso (hann er líka búinn að losa sig við verndina) og hylur sofandi líkama sinn með teppi. Aftur til fortíðar: gestir fara í bílum sínum niður götuna á bak við hundinn; stoltur faðirinn slakar á, einn, dregur upp stól, horfir upp á tunglið, reykir og fleygir sígarettu. Þegar hann stendur, þá er eitthvað í augum

Traitor's deepest themes is implied here: the ambiguity of honour, the obedient (almost robotic) carrying out of orders (like another "simple soldier" in *The Irishman* [Martin Scorsese, 2019]), the question of what changes and what does not change with time ... As Tommaso exits, the film holds on this final, archway frame (my chosen screenshot) that recalls the opening verse of Bob Dylan's "One Too Many Mornings" (1964):

Down the street the dogs are barkin' /
And the day is a-gettin' dark./
As the night comes in a-fallin' /
The dogs'll lose their bark. /
An' the silent night will shatter /
From the sounds inside my mind. /
Yes, I'm one too many mornings /
And a thousand miles behind.

© Adrian Martin & Carles Matamoros, Dec. 2021 / English translation © Cristina Álvarez López & Adrian Martin, Dec.

hans, bera hans, augnaráð, sem hugsanlega gefur til kynna að hann viti nákvæmlega hvað kemur. Tommaso kemur, eins og töfrandi, úr myrkrinu – Bellocchio gefur okkur nú ótímabæra persónu sem er ekki hömluð af ströngri sögulegri tímaröð, þetta gæti verið að gerast á hverju ári – og framkvæmir upphafsstjórn hans. Svo mikið um dýpstu þemu svikarans er gefið í skyn hér: tvíræðni heiðurs, hinn hlýðni (næstum vélfærafræði) sem framkvæmir fyrirmæli (eins og annar „einfaldur hermaður" í Írinu [Martin Scorsese, 2019]), spurningin um hvað breytist og hvað breytist ekki með tímanum... Sem Tommaso hættir, kvikmyndin heldur í þennan loka, bogarammann (valinn skjámynd mín) sem minnir á upphafsvers Bob Dylan's „*Einn of margir morgnar*" (1964):

Neðar á götunni barkin hundarnir /
Og dagurinn er dimmur.
Þegar nóttin kemur í fall–'/
Hundarnir týna gelta. /
En 'hin þögla nótt mun mölva /
Frá hljóðunum í huga mínum. /
Já, ég er einn of margir morgnar /
Og þúsund mílur á eftir. Q

© Michael Lohr, Dec. 2021